Scar Tissue

SCAR TISSUE

A Brady Coyne Novel

WILLIAM G. TAPPLY

St. Martin's Minotaur
New York

www.minotaurbooks.com

Library of Congress Cataloging-in-Publication Data

Tapply, William G.
    Scar tissue / William G. Tapply.— 1st ed.
        p.   cm.
    ISBN 0-312-26679-0
    1. Coyne, Brady (Fictitious character)—Fiction.   2. Traffic accident
investigation—Fiction.   3. Boston (Mass.)—Fiction.   I. Title.

PS3570.A568 S28 2000
813'.54—dc21
                                                          00-040229

First Edition: October 2000

10 9 8 7 6 5 4 3 2 1

For Blake and Ben

ACKNOWLEDGMENTS

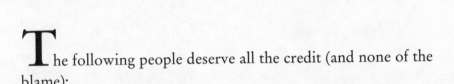

The following people deserve all the credit (and none of the blame):

Ken Quat, for his lawyerly expertise, willingly and freely given, and for his continuing friendship and support; Dr. David Johnson, for the medical lore that informed early drafts of this story (most of which ended up on the cutting-room floor); Rick Boyer, still my training wheels after all these years, for telling me the truth; Vicki Stiefel, for her wise critical readings and level-headed support, for keeping my machines running, and for her love; Mike, my son, for his amazing work on our Web site and for his all-round computer expertise; Melissa and Sarah, my daughters, for their absolute conviction that their dad is the world's best writer; Jed Mattes and Fred Morris, my loyal agents, for keeping me going; and Keith Kahla, my editor, for insisting that I make this a better book and for showing me the way.

Thank you all.

SCAR TISSUE

ONE

February 2. Groundhog Day, my favorite holiday of the year. The pagans called it Imbolog and celebrated it, well, religiously. They drank barrels of mead, defiled virgins, and sacrificed inedible animals such as goats to the gods whom they depended on to keep the seasons turning.

February 2, as the pagans, those expert astronomers, had figured out, is a cross-quarter day, a key celestial moment precisely halfway between the winter solstice and the vernal equinox. I usually celebrated this important holiday more quietly, but no less thankfully, than the pagans. I just loved knowing that another New England winter was officially half gone and that spring was practically around the corner.

Imbolog fell on a Friday this year. Our annual January thaw had actually arrived sometime the previous night—a couple of days late—and outside my office window the Boston cityscape was a blurry black-and-white photograph. Thick gray clouds hung so low in the sky that they obscured the top floors of the Pru and the John Hancock Building. Raindrops pattered in the puddles on the brick plaza, and a layer of fog hovered over the dirty piles of old snow along the edges of the sidewalks.

1

I hoped it was also raining and thawing in Punxsutawney, Pennsylvania, because if it was, Phil-the-groundhog would not be spooked by his own shadow when he poked his head out of his hole. He would venture boldly where no groundhog had gone before, in search of grass to eat and Phyllis-the-groundhog to impregnate, guaranteeing, according to the ancient legend, that spring would arrive in early February rather than late March.

I'd managed to squander nearly half of this Imbolog Friday drinking coffee instead of mead, smoking cigarettes instead of sacrificing goats, gazing out the window, daydreaming about an early start to the trout season, remembering all the virgins I'd neglected to defile in my youth, and avoiding the pile of paperwork that Julie had stacked on my desk . . . when she buzzed me.

I swiveled around, putting my back to the hopeful scene outside, and picked up the phone.

"Did I wish you a joyous Groundhog Day?" I said.

"You certainly did," she said. "I've got—"

"Did I properly explain the pagan origins of this important celebration?"

"Yes, Brady." Julie sighed dramatically. "You lecture me about Groundhog Day every year. In vast detail. Now, shush. I've got Jacob Gold on line two and he says it's urgent."

"What's urgent?" I said. "I'm pretty busy here, you know, watching the snow melt and the rain patter in the puddles and thinking about virgins and trout."

"Brady," said Julie, "cut it out and listen to me. Mr. Gold sounds extremely distraught. Please talk to him."

"Distraught, huh?" Julie tended to exaggerate. "Yeah, okay. Got it." I poked the blinking button on the console and said, "Jake? What's up?"

"Sharon insisted I call you." Jake cleared his throat. "I told her—I said, there's no reason to drag Brady into this. This is our own . . . our tragedy. But . . ."

"What's going on, Jake? Where are you?"

2

"We're home twiddling our damn thumbs. It's Brian. There's been an . . . an accident."

Sharon and Jake Gold had been my clients almost as long as I'd been practicing law. Brian, their only child, was going on sixteen years old now, a sophomore in high school. I'd known him since he was a baby, seen him grow into a young man.

I remembered when my sons had been teenagers and the low-grade apprehension I lived with constantly, worrying about all the bad things that could happen to kids, dreading the phone call in the night and that awful word that Jake had just uttered: *accident.*

Billy and Joey were in their early twenties now, but that dread had never diminished. I was slowly coming to grips with the likelihood that it never would.

"What happened, Jake?" I said gently.

"Automobile accident," he said. I heard him blow out a shuddering breath. "He was with his girlfriend. She was driving. They—the car went off the road and into the river. It was around nine last night. By the time they pulled the car out of the water, little Jenny . . . she was DOA."

I didn't want to ask the obvious question, but finally, after Jake seemed disinclined to speak, I said, "Jake, what about Brian?"

He was silent for a moment. Then I heard him sigh. "Brian— they started diving for him—for his body—at sunup. Apparently the passenger door came open when the car, um, hit the water, and they figure he got thrown out or got sucked out by the currents. You know the river there below the dam. Turbulent, deep, churning currents. Downstream, where it slows down, is iced over." Jake cleared his throat. "They quit diving about an hour ago. Sharon and I were there the whole time, watching them look for our boy's body. It was hard, Brady. Watching, I mean. Hoping they'd find him. Hoping they wouldn't." He hesitated. "Anyway, they haven't yet. Found him. His body."

"So what happens next?"

"They're going to bring a boat to break up the ice down-stream, see if he . . . They figure Brian's under the ice somewhere."

"Jake, listen—"

"Sharon wanted me to call you. I'm sorry to bother you. There's nothing you can do. We don't need a lawyer."

"How about a friend?"

Jake laughed softly. "Yeah, I guess we could use a friend about now."

"I'm on my way."

It took me nearly an hour to drive from my parking garage in Copley Square to the old mill town of Reddington, southwest of the city just beyond Route 128, and it was nearly two in the afternoon when I got there. Normally, it was about a half-hour trip to Reddington, but because of the fog and the puddles, they had the 40 mph speed-limit signs lit on the Mass Pike. The ten-wheelers were ignoring it, and when they passed me, great gouts of rain and slush showered my car. Even with my windshield wipers on high speed, I had panicky moments of blindness.

The Groundhog Day rainstorm had moved in just about the time the sun should have come up. The previous night, I remembered, had been starlit and chilly when I checked it out from my balcony overlooking the harbor. Brian's accident could not have been caused by poor driving conditions.

Jake and Sharon lived in a pleasant middle-class suburban neighborhood on a meandering country road that had been carved out of the Reddington woods about twenty-five years earlier during the real-estate boom. All the houses were architectural variations on the same old-timey New England theme. There were colonials, full-dormer Capes, bungalows, and some homes, like the Golds', were imitations of traditional New England farmhouses with wraparound front porches and adorable little fake cupolas on top of the garages.

4

I pulled into the driveway. A basketball hoop was mounted on the garage. I remembered a summer afternoon eight or nine years earlier playing HORSE with Brian and Jake in the driveway. Brian was so little he could barely heave the ball up to the hoop. Sharon had sat on the front steps watching and laughing and applauding Brian's efforts. I'd tried fancy hook shots and long three-pointers, showing off for her like a teenager.

Jake must have been watching for me, because when I got out of my car, he was waiting for me on the front porch. I climbed the steps, started to shake his hand, then gave him a hug. He held on to me for a long moment, and when he pulled back, I saw dampness in his eyes.

Jake had a long, gloomy face and bushy gray hair. He was a stooped, lanky, heronlike man somewhere in his late fifties. He was the chairman of the humanities department at Reddington Community College, and on this Groundhog Day he was wearing his professor outfit—scuffed leather boots, wrinkled Dockers, green-and-black checked flannel shirt, and brown corduroy jacket with leather elbow patches.

"Well, old friend," he said, "thanks for coming." He put his arm across my shoulder and we went inside.

Sharon was sitting on the sofa in the living room. She was wearing snug-fitting blue jeans and a bulky sweatshirt and sneakers. She was small and dark and cute, and she could've passed for a teenager herself.

She looked up at me and blinked. She tried a smile, which didn't work, then stood up and came over to where I was standing. "Oh, God, Brady, thank you for coming," she whispered, and she wrapped her arms around my waist. She squeezed me hard and burrowed her face into my chest. The top of her head barely came up to my chin. I held her while she cried on my shirt.

After a minute, I gripped Sharon's shoulders and gently pushed her away from me. "Any news?" I said.

She shook her head. She had high, prominent cheekbones, a long narrow nose, and a generous mouth. Her enormous brown

5

eyes swam with tears. Sharon Gold was about twenty years younger than Jake. He'd married one of his students.

"Ed was here," she said. "He promised us they'd . . . they'd keep looking."

"Ed?"

"Ed Sprague," said Jake. "He's our chief of police. He was Brian's soccer coach. He's been great."

"Do you want some coffee or something?" said Sharon.

"Coffee would be good," I said.

She smiled quickly and went out to the kitchen.

"Feel like a smoke?" said Jake.

"Sure."

"We've got to go outside," Jake said. "Sharon has put her foot down. Says my pipe smoke stinks up the whole house."

We went outside and stood on the front porch. I lit a cigarette, and Jake fished out his pipe and tobacco pouch.

I've always suspected that pipe smokers are not really committed to smoking the way we cigarette addicts are. Most of the pipe smokers I know love to collect pipes. They're very particular about how they break in a new meerschaum, and they hang around tobacco stores pinching and sniffing and tasting exotic Turkish blends. Cleaning and filling a pipe seems to be a ritual for them, a way to postpone saying or doing something, and Jake was taking his time. He was digging a straight-stemmed, big-bowled briar around in his leather pouch, packing and tamping in the tobacco with his forefinger. It looked as if he were having a sensual experience, burrowing around in his tobacco pouch.

Finally he got it filled, clamped it between his teeth, brought a Zippo out of his pocket, and fired it up. He blew out a big cloud of smoke. I noticed that he inhaled.

"What can you tell me?" I said.

He sighed. "They were heading north on River Road," he said. "It happened about nine last night, they think. They went off the road right where it cuts close to the river just down from the dam. Ed says it was the only place on the whole road where they would've gone into the water. It's about a fifteen-foot drop, almost straight down. Maybe they were going a little too fast, couldn't make the turn. Maybe a deer or something ran in front of them, or a car came at them with its high beams on." He shrugged. "The truth is, they have no idea what happened. It was just a damn random, senseless accident." He took a deep breath, blew it out. "None of this feels real, Brady. I'm sorry. I shouldn't have dragged you out here."

"Cut it out," I said. I flipped my cigarette butt out into the snow. "Tell me about the girl. The driver."

"Jenny?" Jake pulled out his Zippo and got his dead pipe lit again. "Nice girl. Smart, pretty. Couple years older than Brian. Sharon never liked that. Figured, I don't know, that she'd lead him astray or something. Older woman, huh?" Jake snorted a quick laugh. "Hell, she was barely seventeen. Looked about twelve." He shook his head. "Tom and Emily—her parents—they're friends of ours. I guess everybody in this little one-horse town are friends. So, they spent the night at the hospital with their dead little girl, and we spent the night on the river-bank waiting for them to dredge up our dead little boy, and . . ." Jake shook his head.

"Have you talked with them since—?"

He nodded. "They called this morning. We exchanged con-dolences. It was pretty tense. I think they're feeling guilty. Jenny was driving. Nice people. They're devastated. Sharon and I, we can relate to that."

"Jake," I said, "how do you know Brian was in that car?"

He cocked his head and looked at me as if I were one of his Brit lit students who'd asked a stupid question. "If he wasn't in that car," he said, "he'd be here with us. Where else would he be?"

I nodded. It was a stupid question.

"They were always together," Jake said after a minute. "Jenny came by, picked him up in her car around seven-thirty.

7

They were to be back by ten. That was Sharon's rule. Ten on
school nights, midnight on weekends. Sharon's always been big
on rules."

"Where were they going?"

He flapped his hands. "Where do teenagers go in cars?"

"I mean, where does River Road take them?"

"I don't know, Brady," he said quietly. "It doesn't really
matter, does it?"

"No, I guess it doesn't."

Jake was silent. "I used to have a rule," he said after a minute,
"back after my divorce, when the world was full of willing
women. My rule was: Never sleep with a woman who can't
remember exactly where she was and what she was doing when
she heard Kennedy got shot."

I did some quick math. I figured Sharon had been in diapers
in 1963. "It's been a little rough, huh?"

He shrugged. "She's blaming this on me."

"Ah, come on, Jake."

"No, I mean it. She thinks this is my fault, what happened
to Brian."

"What'd she say?"

"Say? She doesn't have to say anything. It's her look, her
body language, the way she turns away from me every time I
look in her direction. I know what she's thinking. She thinks
I've been too soft on him, that Brian knows she and I don't
agree on how to discipline him, that he plays us off against each
other, that he thinks he can get away with anything because I'll
defend him. As if he did something wrong, being in that car
last night, for Christ's sake, and that if I'd been a sterner parent
it wouldn't have happened. And she thinks I'm that way because I need to compensate for the fact that I've . . . I've tended
to ignore him." Jake glanced at me, then gazed up at the sooty
sky. "Which, God help me, I guess I have. I was forty-four
years old when Brian was born. Sharon was—what?—twenty-
three? She doted on him when he was a baby. Made me feel
like I was the grandfather. Let me hold him now and then, but

8

she always watched and criticized how I did it. It was Sharon who got up with him at night, nursed him, changed his diapers, dressed and undressed him, gave him his bath. Actually, that was okay by me. I never was big on babies. Figured when he was older he'd become a person and we'd be pals, and in the meantime his mother could do the dirty work." He shrugged. "Next thing I know, he's a teenager, and we hardly ever played catch or shot hoops or went fishing together. Hell, you did as much of that stuff with my son as I did."

"Jake, you can't—"

He shook his head. "I know the truth, Brady. Oh, I think we liked each other, Brian and I. I went to his soccer games. He was a terrific athlete. I liked watching him play. But he was always his mother's son, no doubt about it. And since Ed came by last night, said there's been an accident, told us Brian was in the river somewhere, all I've been thinking about is that I never did get to know my boy, never did take him fishing, and now, God help me, it's too late."

I put my hand on his shoulder. "It sounds like it's you, not Sharon. It's you, blaming yourself."

"Projecting, huh?" He shrugged. "Yeah, maybe I am."

"I'm sorry, man. It's got to hurt like hell."

"Oh," he said softly, "you can't imagine."

There didn't seem to be anything else to say. We stood there on the porch for a while, smoking and watching the sky break up. Finally, Jake rapped his pipe against the rail, put it to his mouth, blew through it a couple of times, then jammed it into his jacket pocket. "We better go back in," he said. "Sharon'll have the coffee ready."

9

Two

───────◆───────

W hen we got inside, we found Sharon on the sofa, slouched down on her spine. She'd slipped off her sneakers. She was wearing white cotton socks, and her feet were propped up on the coffee table beside a carafe and three coffee mugs. Her eyes were closed, and she had her hands folded over her stomach. Her chest rose and fell slowly. Her face looked soft and peaceful and young. In her tight Levi's and loose-fitting gray sweatshirt, she could've been Brian's teenage sister, not his mother.

Jake leaned to me and whispered, "Look at her. Isn't she fantastic?"

I nodded. "Remembering when Kennedy was shot isn't everything."

He went to her, bent down, and touched her shoulder. "Why don't you go upstairs and lie down for a while," he said.

Her eyes blinked open, then darted from Jake to me. "Sorry," she mumbled. "I just closed my eyes for a minute. Rude."

I smiled. "Don't be silly. Go have a nap."

She rubbed her temples with her fingertips. "I don't want to sleep. I'm afraid I'll dream. I'm afraid when I wake up . . ." Her eyes brimmed, and she cried.

Jake put his arm around her and helped her up. She didn't resist. He led her over to the staircase. "Be right back," he said to me.

I sat on the sofa and poured myself a mug of coffee, and a few minutes later Jake came back down. He took the chair across from me. "She's a wreck," he said.

"How about you?"

He nodded. "Sure. Me, too. We've been up all night."

"So, why don't you go lie down?"

"I couldn't sleep," he said. "It's a fucking nightmare, Brady. It's like I'm watching this happen to somebody else, you know?" He poured himself some coffee. "I really appreciate your coming out. Sharon does, too."

"I wish there was something I could do."

"You can find Brian for us." He shook his head and laughed ironically. "Sorry." He blew out a breath. "Just being here for us, that's a help. It really is. I needed someone to talk to. Sharon thinks you're God. It's like, if Brady's around, everything's got to be okay."

"I can't make this okay, Jake."

"I know. I wish you could."

We sipped our coffee in silence. Jake slouched forward in the chair—his head bowed down and his forearms on his knees cradling his mug in both hands—taking an occasional, absentminded sip. After a while, he looked up at me. "It's Friday night, for God's sake. I bet you've got a date."

I smiled. "I think I do."

"Evie?"

I nodded.

"There's no sense hanging around," he said.

"I don't mind."

"We'll be all right," he said. "If anything happens, I'll let you know. You go ahead. Sorry to drag you out here for nothing."

"Not for nothing," I said. I drained my coffee mug, put it

onto the table, and stood up. "Say good-bye to Sharon for me. I expect to be close to home all weekend. You've got my number. Please keep me posted."

He nodded. "Sure."

Outside, the rain had stopped. The clouds were skidding across the sky, and here and there patches of blue showed through. The temperature had dropped about ten degrees, and it was feeling like winter again. I hoped Phil had enjoyed a shadowless day down there in Punxsutawney and had tracked down a sexy young groundhog. Maybe he was already shacked up with her, deep under the ground where, if the sun peeked out before evening came, he wouldn't see it.

The freshening breeze sliced through my topcoat. I figured the wet roads would freeze once the sun went down. It would be a good night for automobile accidents.

The police aren't always forthcoming with the families of victims, I knew, so I decided to drop in at the Reddington police station before I headed home. I took the two-lane north-to-south road from Jake's house. I passed apple orchards, horse farms, stubbly cornfields, and conservation land.

Reddington had been settled by farmers sometime in the 1700s. They raised corn and squashes and apples in the fertile valley of the Reddington River. Then in the early days of the American industrial revolution, the village transformed itself into a mill town. They built a dam across the river and used its power to run their machines. Gunpowder had been the main product.

Today, Reddington is a Mass Pike commuter town, remarkably devoid of commerce. There's a hospital, three or four churches, one elementary school, a 7–12 high school. A couple of bookstores and restaurants and convenience stores are clustered around the community college in the northwest corner of town, and there's one strip mall for the supermarket, the bank, the dry cleaner, the take-out pizza joint, the video rental, the pharmacy, and the camera store. I passed a garage and a gas station and a couple of farm stands, now closed for the season, on my way from the Golds' house to the village green, where the police station shared space with the town offices in the big barnlike old New England town hall.

I parked out back and went in.

A uniformed officer sat behind a glassed-in booth like a ticket-seller at a movie theater. She was thirtyish, I guessed, with clear, fair skin, an angular face, and straight blond-streaked brown hair in a no-nonsense short cut that showed her ears. A plaque on the left breast pocket of her uniform shirt read V. WHYTE. When I cleared my throat, she looked up at me and smiled. She had enormous gray-green eyes and a fetching little gap between her front teeth.

"Can I help you, sir?" she said. Her voice came at me through a round perforated metal plate set into the bottom of the glass.

I bent down to speak into it. "I'm here to see Chief Sprague."

"Is he expecting you?"

"No. It's about the accident last night."

She narrowed her eyes. "You from the media or something?"

"No. I'm the Golds' lawyer." I fumbled a business card out of my wallet and held it against the glass.

She squinted at it, then said, "Hang on a minute."

She picked up a telephone, spoke softly into it, then looked up at me and said, "Okay. The chief's with somebody, but he said for you to wait."

The door to the left of her booth buzzed, and I opened it and went into an empty waiting room. It was small and sparsely furnished—ten or a dozen plastic chairs, a couple of end tables strewn with magazines and newspapers, a pay phone on the wall beside the door, and a coffee urn on a scarred wooden table in the corner.

A cluster of framed black-and-white photographs hung on the inside wall. I wandered over to look at them. The police bowling team, half a dozen head-and-shoulder shots of police officers, and several team photos showing the same middle-aged

14

man surrounded by boys and girls in shorts and soccer jerseys. Jake had said that Chief Sprague coached Brian's soccer team.

I peered at the photos and found Brian in each of them. Brian Gold had always been small for his age. He knelt in the front row in each photo, the way they always arranged it—tall kids in back, short ones kneeling in front. It didn't look as if Brian had aged or grown from one photo to the next. He looked eight years old in the oldest photo, and in the most recent one, he still looked about eight.

Hell, they all looked young. They all *were* young. It took me back to when my boys, Billy and Joey, were that age, back to a time when I lived in suburban bliss with my ex-wife, Gloria, and watched my kids play Saturday-morning co-ed soccer.

Not that blissful, actually.

Brian Gold looked younger even than the other kids on Chief Sprague's soccer team. Brian was a cute boy—the word *handsome* didn't work, but *pretty* wasn't right, either. He had his mother's black hair and big, dark eyes and delicate, almost-but-not-quite feminine features, but he was long-legged, and you could see how he might grow into Jake's gangly body.

Now he was somewhere in the Reddington River, under the ice. Brian Gold would not grow into any body whatsoever.

"Somebody helping you?"

I turned. A police officer was standing behind me. He was in his mid-thirties, I guessed, a big redheaded guy with a friendly Huck Finn face.

"I'm all set," I said. "Just waiting to talk to your chief."

"Anything I can do?" said the officer. "The chief's pretty busy. It might be a while."

"That accident, huh?" I said.

He nodded. His nameplate read L. MCCAFFREY. He pointed at one of the soccer pictures. "That's Jenny Rolando, there, and that's Brian Gold."

Jenny had flashing dark eyes and blond hair pulled back in a ponytail. She had a terrific smile. She was standing directly

15

behind Brian in the most recent photo. She was one of the tall ones. When I squinted at the picture, I could see that her hand rested on Brian's shoulder.

"I knew Brian," I told McCaffrey. "I'm the family lawyer."

"Lawyer, huh?"

I shrugged. "Friend. Today, I'm their friend."

"Boy," he said. "Something like this, they can use all the friends they've got." He shook his head. "I was first on the scene."

"Last night? The accident?"

He nodded. "Helpless damn feeling, knowing those two kids were down there—"

At that moment, V. Whyte, the female cop from the ticket-seller's booth, came in. She was taller and lankier than she'd looked sitting behind the bulletproof glass. "Beware of the coffee," she said to me. She ignored McCaffrey. "I'll check on the chief for you."

"Thank you," I said.

She went through a door in the back of the waiting room.

I turned to McCaffrey. "That accident," I said. "You didn't see—?"

He held up his hand. "I'm not supposed to talk about it. You'll have to talk to my boss."

I shrugged. "I understand."

"Well," said McCaffrey. "If you're all set, I got work to do." He held up the thick manila folder he'd been carrying. "Paperwork, you know?"

I smiled. "I know it well."

He went out through the same door the female officer had used. I poured myself a cup of coffee and sat in one of the plastic chairs. It was spectacularly uncomfortable, so I stood up and sipped my coffee, which was spectacular, too, if you liked crankcase grease.

I put the coffee cup back on the table and wandered over to the window. Darkness had begun to seep in over the Reddington village green. Yellow lights glowed from the windows of

16

the colonial houses across the way. Soon Groundhog Day would be over.

I tried sitting again. The chairback stopped right where my shoulderblades began. It was molded in a way that forced me to hunch my shoulders.

V. Whyte came back. She had changed out of her uniform into a pair of Levi's, a red sweater, and a hip-length black leather jacket. "The chief knows you're here," she said. "He'll be with you. It might be a while."

I thanked her again, which earned me an over-the-shoulder smile as she walked out.

I stood up, went to the pay phone, fished some quarters from my pocket, and called Evie Banyon's office at Emerson Hospital in Concord, where Evie was the assistant to the administrator.

When she answered, I said, "Happy Imbolog."

"Brady!" she said, and I don't think the delight I heard in her voice was wishful thinking on my part. "I was just thinking about you."

"Anything you can say out loud?"

"Goodness, no. What's Imbolog?"

"Groundhog Day, honey," I said. "A joyous pagan holiday. The orgy begins at sundown."

"It does?"

"It does this year. It requires a barrel of mead, a sacrificial goat, and at least one virgin."

"Nuts," she said. "I'm fresh out of virgins."

"I just wanted you to know that I don't know how long I'll be here."

"Where are you?"

"I'm out here in Reddington."

"Reddington," she repeated. "Shining the light of truth and justice into every corner of the land, are we?"

"That's me," I said. "Have briefcase, will litigate."

"Something's wrong," she said. "I can hear it in your voice."

"Yeah," I said. "I'm extremely bummed, actually. I'm not

17

sure I'll be very good company tonight. Maybe we should—"
At that moment two men emerged from the corridor. "Gotta
go, honey," I said to Evie. "I'll call you when I get home,
okay?"

"You're the boss," she said.

"Yeah, right."

One of the men was Chief Sprague. I recognized him from
the soccer pictures. He was about my height, maybe twenty
pounds heavier, late thirties, early forties. Light brown hair in
a military razor cut, rimless glasses, round, open face, thick
neck, big shoulders. He was wearing his uniform—pale blue
shirt, dark blue necktie, trousers that matched the tie, spit-
shined shoes. The tie was pulled loose at his throat, and his
shirtsleeves were rolled halfway up his forearms.

I recognized the man with him, too. It was August Nash, the
district attorney. Nash was a small, fiftyish guy with thinning
gray hair, bifocals, and a mouthful of man-made teeth, a relic
of his career as a shifty little left-winger for his college hockey
team. He was one of those Boston guys who never left town—
Central Catholic High, criminal justice major at Northeastern,
Boston College Law School. I'd opposed Gus Nash a few times
when he was an ADA, and I knew him to be smart, scrupulous,
and a helluva tough prosecutor. There were rumors that the
state Democratic party was trying to convince Gus to run for
attorney general in the fall election. If he did, I guessed I'd
probably vote for him.

Nash and Sprague had their heads tilted toward each other,
and they were talking intently as they crossed the waiting room.

Gus Nash saw me and smiled. "Hey, Brady. What's a slick
city lawyer doing in a little hick town like Reddington?" He
turned to Sprague. "Ed, do you know this scoundrel?"

The chief shook his head and held out his hand to me. "Ed
Sprague," he said. "You're waiting to see me, right?"

I shook his hand. "Right. And don't worry. I'm not all that
slick."

"That tragedy over on River Road, huh?"

I nodded.

He shook his head. "Two wonderful young people. Just a shame." He turned to Nash. "We should probably talk some more, huh, Mr. Nash?"

"Yes," said Nash. "I'll call you." He clapped my shoulder. "Brady, good to see you again. It's been too long. How's about I buy you a drink sometime."

"Why not?" I said. "I rarely pass up a free drink."

After Nash left, Sprague turned to me and said, "Let's go to my office." He waved toward the coffee urn. "Coffee?"

I shook my head. "Tried it."

He smiled. "Yeah. Sorry."

I followed him down the short corridor. Along the right wall were several closed doors. One was labeled MEN and one WOMEN. The others had small square windows of glass sandwiched around wire mesh. Conference rooms, I guessed. Or interrogation rooms, if they ever actually hauled in criminal suspects worth interrogating in sleepy little Reddington.

On the left was a big open room, the cops' bullpen. I guessed it had been a couple of parlors in the original Victorian layout, but now the wall separating them had been removed. There were six or eight metal-topped desks piled with manila folders, in- and out-boxes, computers and telephones, and the walls were lined with gray chest-high steel file cabinets and copiers and fax machines and wastebaskets. Officer McCaffrey, the big redheaded cop, was sitting at one of the desks. He was hunched forward with his elbows on his desktop and his chin in his hands, staring at his computer monitor.

Sprague had the end office, which was in the back corner of the building. It might once have been a downstairs bedroom. Waist-high maple wainscoting was topped with a mural-like wallpaper depicting a Revolutionary War scene. Tall double-wide windows on two walls looked out over the Reddington village green, and a big square oak desk sat in the corner between them. One inside wall was dominated by a fieldstone fireplace, which was set with birch logs waiting to be fired up.

19

"Nice office," I said.

Sprague shrugged. "I practically live here. Might as well try to make it homey."

Above the mantelpiece hung a print of pintail ducks bursting into panicky flight from a salt marsh on a wintry dawn. I jerked my head at it. "Do you hunt?" I said.

He smiled and shook his head. "I like birds."

The fireplace was flanked by built-in bookcases. They held worn leather-bound volumes—Dickens and Trollope, Hawthorne and Melville, Whitman and Eliot, Plato and Aristotle, Dante and Machiavelli, Cicero and Aquinas, Darwin and Adam Smith.

I slid out his copy of *Moby Dick* and thumbed through it. "I've been trying to read this for years," I said.

"I plowed through it in college," he said. "Took me an entire weekend. It was hard going. I keep thinking I should try it again, see if I can figure out what all the fuss is about."

A dozen or so framed photos hung on another wall. They all showed Ed Sprague shaking hands with somebody. I recognized Bill Weld, Ted Kennedy, Rick Pitino, Nomar Garciaparra.

If it weren't for the photos, I could've been in the office of a college professor.

The floor was covered with the same industrial-beige wall-to-wall carpeting as the corridor outside. Along one wall stood a faded upholstered sofa. Facing the desk were two wooden armchairs. Sprague waved at them, and we each took one.

He leaned back, crossed his arms over his chest, and said, "So you know our DA, huh?"

I nodded. "I've opposed him a few times."

"He's a good prosecutor."

"Yes," I said. "A worthy adversary."

Sprague smiled. "So how can I help you, Mr. Coyne?"

"I've just come from visiting with Jake and Sharon Gold. You knew Brian?"

"Sure. I know everyone in Reddington. It's a small town."

"You coached Brian's soccer team, huh?"

Sprague shrugged. "I'm not married myself. I like kids."

"The accident last night . . ."

"Bad one," he said with a quick shake of his head. "Real bad. I was there all night and all morning." He stared out the window. "It makes you want to cry. For those kids, for their parents, for all of us. Just another goddamn senseless thing, Mr. Coyne. Teenagers, automobiles, alcohol. I visit the schools every spring around prom time, preaching the same old sermon. I go to driver's ed classes with my statistics and slide shows and horror stories. Reddington's a small town. There were less than a hundred kids in last year's graduating class. But you know what?" He peered at me through his schoolteacher glasses.

I nodded.

"Hardly a year goes by," he said, "that we don't have something like last night. If not here, in one of the nearby towns. If I had my way, we'd change the legal driving age to eighteen, and we'd lock up any grownup who lets kids into their booze cabinet. It's worse than guns, if you ask me. It's killing our kids."

"Jake didn't mention that the kids had been drinking."

"They're always drinking," he said.

"But do you—?"

"No," he said. "No evidence of it. Maybe they weren't. What difference would it make?" Sprague stole a glance at his wristwatch.

"I know you're busy," I said. "But I have a few questions for you, if you don't mind."

He looked up at me. "Why? You contemplating a lawsuit?"

I wasn't, but the lawyer in me kicked in before I could tell him the truth. So I shrugged and smiled in a way that was intended to tell him: *Sure. Of course I'm contemplating a lawsuit. I'm a lawyer, aren't I? But I have way too much class to come right out and say it.*

21

He smiled and nodded, and I guessed he saw through me. "How can I help?"

"How do you account for the accident?" I said. "Aside from the possibility of booze, I mean."

"High speed, narrow road, inexperienced driver? Who knows? Nobody saw it. The reconstruction guys'll probably be able to make some sense of it."

"The girl—"

"Jenny," he said. "Jenny was her name. A sweet kid. She drowned, strapped in there behind the wheel. Tom and Emily— her parents—they're in shock, as you can imagine."

"What about Brian?"

He flapped his hands. "The car went through the guardrail and rolled over. It's a steep bank, all rocky riprap. Landed up-side down in about ten feet of water. Hitting those rocks must've sprung the door. Looks like Brian wasn't wearing his seat belt. Probably got thrown out and hit the water uncon-scious. Or maybe he was dead already. The state cops had their scuba team here before sunrise, but no luck."

"So what happens next?"

"They're going to get some boats here to break up the ice downstream." He pressed his lips together. "We'll find him, Mr. Coyne."

"Something's bothering me here," I said.

He arched his eyebrows.

"Why is everybody so sure Brian was in that car?"

Sprague shrugged. "Where else would he be? Both sets of parents said they left together. Friday-night date."

"Any chance he might've survived?"

Sprague looked at me. "So where is he, then?"

I nodded. "I guess if he wasn't in that car, he'd be home with his parents."

"Obviously." He hesitated. "Look. Everybody's praying that Brian's okay. But it makes no sense. It's just wishful thinking. For one thing, his athletic bag was in the backseat."

"Brian's?"

Sprague nodded. "It had a couple changes of clothes and two hundred dollars in it. Jenny had a duffel in there, too. Also packed with clothes."

"As if—?"

"As if they were going off for the weekend or something. I don't know, and their parents didn't say anything about it." He smiled. "Kids, you know?"

I remembered my two sons. I knew.

"Anyway," he said, "unfortunately, there's not much doubt that Brian was in that car."

"I guess so," I said. I took out a business card and handed it to him. "I'm really not interested in a lawsuit, Chief. I'm just a friend of the family, trying to help out, do whatever I can do to comfort them. They're not going to start healing until Brian's body is found. I hope you'll keep me posted. And if anything comes up, any witnesses, any new information about what happened, let me know, okay?"

"Sure," he said. He tucked my card into his shirt pocket. "Please, when you see Jake and Sharon, tell them that my prayers are with them, will you?"

I nodded and stood up, and Sprague did, too. He walked me out through the waiting room, and we shook hands by the door. Then I went out to the parking lot.

I paused to light a cigarette. All the clouds had been blown out of the sky. A blush of pink bled into the purple sky over the western horizon, and directly overhead a few stars had winked on. The wind rattled the bare limbs of the big oak trees that surrounded the green.

I climbed into my car and headed for home. I drove more slowly and alertly than I usually do. I was thinking about Brian Gold's accident, how a deer could jump in front of me at any minute, how a carful of drunken teenagers could come at me from around the bend, how I might not notice a patch of black ice until it was too late—how you never know what might happen in the next instant of your life.

23

THREE

I thought about Jake and Sharon all the way back to Boston. When I pulled into my slot in the basement parking garage of my apartment building on Lewis Wharf, I felt as if I'd swallowed a shot put. Jake had said it: I couldn't imagine what they were going through. By comparison, Jenny Rolando's parents were lucky. At least they knew their daughter was dead. For them it was all over, and they could start putting the pieces back together.

I took the elevator to the sixth floor, unlocked the door to my empty bachelor's apartment, and went in. I dropped my briefcase beside the door, and I was fumbling for the light switch when I noticed an odd, faintly fruity scent—cantaloupe, or maybe it was apricot. Then I heard the soft tinkle of harpsichord music and saw a dim orange light dancing on the walls of the hallway.

Evie.

I hung up my topcoat in the closet and went into the living room.

Evie must've had fifty candles going. They were scattered around the edges of the room, on the floor, on end tables, on

25

bookshelves, and lined up along the bottom of the glass sliders that looked out over the harbor. There were tall skinny candles in Chianti bottles, short fat ones in their own glass containers, little squat ones clustered on saucers. There were orange candles and plum-colored candles, raspberry, strawberry, and lemon-and-lime candles, and their fruity scents mingled, and they lit the room in a soft, flickering orange glow.

It was Bach. The harpsichord. A Brandenburg concerto playing softly from the big speakers in the corners of the room.

I felt fingers on the back of my neck. "Happy Groundhog Day," Evie whispered. She hugged me from behind. Her arms slid around my chest, and one of them wormed its way inside my shirt. Her breath brushed my ear and her soft breasts pressed against my back. "I wasn't sure how the pagans did it," she murmured. "The music, especially. Bach doesn't sound all that pagan."

I turned around and stepped back to look at her. In the candlelight, her hair was the color of maple syrup. It was wavy and thick and loose, and it fell halfway down her back. She was barefoot and wearing a sheer ankle-length white gown—some silky diaphanous material with short, puffy sleeves and a squared-off low neck. It hugged her bust, waist, and hips, then flowed like a waterfall around her long legs. In the backlit candle-glow, I could see that she was naked underneath it.

I smiled at her. "The sacrificial virgin."

"We can surely pretend," she said. She came to me and put her arms around my neck.

I kissed her hair, then held her shoulders and pushed her gently away.

She frowned. "What's the matter?"

"I'm sorry, honey," I said. I waved my hand around the room. "This is great. I just . . ." I felt my eyes start to burn, and I turned away from Evie, went across the room to the floor-to-ceiling sliding doors, and pressed my forehead against the cold glass.

Evie stood behind me. "What's wrong, Brady?"

26

I shook my head. I thought if I tried to speak, the tears would break free.

"Maybe I should go," she said.

"No," I mumbled. "Give me a minute."

She touched my shoulder, hesitated, then put her arms around me from behind and laid her cheek against my back. "Do you want to talk about it?"

I cleared my throat. "I want to call my boys. Do you mind?"

"Of course not."

I went into the kitchen, sat at the table, and pecked out Joey's number. My younger son was a sophomore at Stanford. I looked at my watch. Seven-thirty. That made it four-thirty out there, where the grass was green year-round and flowers bloomed on Groundhog Day.

After four or five rings, the recorded voice of one of Joey's roommates said: "Frankie, Win, Joe, and Chuck aren't here. Leave a message if you want."

I waited for the beep, hesitated, then hung up. My message would've been, "I love you, son." But Joey already knew that.

What I wanted was to hear his voice, know he was okay. He didn't need a message from me. Kids don't worry about their parents the way we worry about them.

Billy, two time zones away in Idaho, wasn't home, either, but at least it was his voice on the answering machine.

I went back into the living room. Evie was huddled in the corner of the sofa. She'd wrapped my ratty old bathrobe around herself. She'd turned off the stereo and doused the candles and turned on a couple of lights.

I sat beside her. "I'm sorry, honey," I said. "This—" I waved my hand around the room "—it was clever and fun. Any other day but today . . ."

She shrugged. "It was a stupid idea."

I leaned over and kissed her mouth. "It was an inspired idea," I said.

She peered solemnly into my eyes. "Do you want to tell me about it now?"

I nodded. "Yes, I do."

And I did. I told her about my call from Jake, about Sharon, about my talk with Chief Sprague, about what had happened to Brian, about the constriction in my chest and the awful thoughts that refused to stop ricocheting around in my head.

"I'm sorry your boys weren't home," she said when I was done. "You'd feel better if you talked to them."

"Talking to you helps," I said.

She nodded as if she didn't believe me.

"I wouldn't mind just being held for a while," I said.

"I wouldn't mind that, either," she said.

We both drifted off to sleep tangled in the sheets and each other, and by the time we got around to cooking dinner it was nearly nine o'clock. Evie pulled on a pair of my baggy old sweatpants and an Asheville Tourists T-shirt that I'd picked up several years ago when Doc Adams and I went trout fishing in the mountain streams of western Carolina.

We were a little awkward with each other. I'd meant it, about just being held, and we had not made love. I'd dozed and dreamed about my sons.

Evie had brought lamb chops, which she said was the closest thing Bread & Circus had to goat, and a fifth of applejack. The package store had claimed it was all out of mead.

In the kitchen, I rubbed rosemary and crushed garlic into the chops and coated my big cast-iron skillet with peanut oil to sear them. Evie scrubbed a dozen baby red potatoes and set them to boiling. While we waited to get the timing right, we tore up some spring greens in a big wooden bowl for our salad. We sipped applejack on the rocks with a twist of lemon as we worked, and we put on a Stevie Ray Vaughan CD, and it was homey and familiar there in my kitchen, preparing a Friday-night dinner with Evie.

I'd met Evie Banyon about five months earlier. She'd hinted vaguely that she'd recently extricated herself from a bad relationship. I'd never pushed for details. She'd tell me what she wanted to tell me when the time was right.

A year and a half ago, I'd lost Alex. That had been a good relationship, and I'd been nursing my guilt and misgivings. Evie had made it clear that she'd like to hear my story, but I told her there wasn't much of a story, and she seemed content to leave it at that.

Neither of us was really looking for an entangling alliance, but we had fun and respected each other's secrets, and as those things seem to go when they're not going badly, after a couple of months she started sleeping over on an occasional Friday or Saturday night, which gradually evolved into a more-or-less regular weekend routine.

There were a lot of things we still didn't know about each other. I liked the not knowing, and I liked gathering the bits and pieces as they emerged. Evie kept surprising me, and so far, at least, none of the surprises disappointed me.

When our Imbolog repast was ready, we relit the candles, put the Bach back on the stereo, and took our feast to the table in front of the sliding glass doors. While we ate, we watched the tugs and barges and ferries, all showing their night lights, crawl around on the harbor below us. Planes, with their flashing lights, swooped over Logan in their landing patterns, and a steady stream of headlights paraded across the Tobin Bridge.

Evie and I didn't say very much. That was another thing I liked about her. She understood silence and didn't take it personally.

After we cleaned up, we took another glass of applejack into the living room. "Maybe I should go home," Evie said after a few minutes.

"I'm not much fun tonight, I know," I said. "But I hope you'll stay."

She smiled. "Okay. You talked me into it."

Evie was gone when I woke up on Saturday morning. She'd gathered up her candles and taken them with her, and she'd left a note on the kitchen table. All it said was: "Call me if you want." She signed it with a few Xs and Os and a big capital E.

I looked at the note, trying to read between the lines. She hadn't said, "Please call me" or "See you tonight?" There were a lot of things she hadn't said.

After we'd eaten dinner I'd tried calling Joey and Billy again, but they still weren't home. When Evie and I finally went to bed, I hadn't felt like making love. She said she understood, but I'd sensed the hurt.

I couldn't get Jake and Sharon out of my mind.

A high-pressure front had moved in behind the Imbolog rainstorm, and the Saturday-morning sky was high and blue and cloudless. Little whitecaps rolled across the blue water six stories below my apartment, and the sun shone pale and yellow and without warmth. When I stepped onto my balcony with my coffee, a frigid breeze drove me right back inside. It felt awfully damn wintry to me.

Punxsutawney Phil got his weather forecasts right about half the time, the same as the television meteorologists. This time, it looked like he'd gotten it wrong.

It was about ten in the morning. I called Jake's number in Reddington. It rang five times before the answering machine clicked on. "Hi," came Sharon's cheerful voice. "Sharon, Brian, and Jake aren't here right now, but we do want to talk with you, so please leave your number and we'll get right back to you."

I did not leave a message. I wondered where they were, what they'd heard, how they were doing.

I spent the morning trying to deal with the stuff that Julie had sent home with me for my weekend homework, but my mind kept flipping back to Reddington. I called the Golds' house several times and got the answering machine each time.

I tried Joey and Billy a little after noontime. Just as I figured, in their time zones they were both asleep, and I woke them up. Neither of them seemed to mind. I told them I just wanted to say hello and restrained myself from saying what was really on my mind: I wanted to know they were okay.

After talking with my boys, I was able to concentrate on my paperwork a little better. But Jake and Sharon still lurked in the corners of my mind, and they were not answering their telephone.

Finally, around two in the afternoon, I said the hell with it.

Traffic was light on the Mass Pike, and it took about half an hour to get to Reddington. A black-and-white Ford Explorer with a light bar on the roof and the Reddington Police logo on the door panels was parked in the Golds' driveway, so I pulled up on the side of the street. The Explorer's motor was running and somebody was sitting behind the wheel.

I'd just started to get out of my car when the front door opened and Jake and Chief Sprague came out. Jake was in shirt-sleeves. The Chief wore a bomber jacket and blue jeans and leather boots. The two of them paused on the front porch. Jake looked down at his feet, and Sprague gripped his hand with both of his and spoke to him for a long moment.

Jake nodded. Sprague leaned close to him and said something else, and Jake looked up and shrugged. Then he saw me. He lifted his hand and waved.

Sprague came down the walkway, and I met him halfway.

"Mr. Coyne," he said. "Hello, again." He held out his hand.

I shook it. "Anything new?"

He shook his head. "Afraid not."

"Brian?"

"No. I'm sorry." He jerked his head back at the house. "Jake and Sharon aren't doing very well. Maybe you can cheer them up."

"I don't see how."

"No," said Sprague, "I don't, either."

He got into the passenger side of the cruiser. The driver, I

31

noticed, was McCaffrey, the redheaded cop I'd met at the station. I waved to him, and he raised his hand. Then he backed out the driveway, and they drove away.

I went up onto the porch, where Jake was waiting for me with his arms folded across his chest.

I gave him a hug. "No news, huh?"

"No. Nothing."

"I've been trying to call you."

"Sorry," he said. "We finally turned the ringers off the phones. All night they were calling. Friends, well-meaning, I guess, but we didn't feel like talking to anybody. I would've called you. I kept waiting, hoping I'd have something to tell you."

"It's okay, Jake," I said. "Maybe this is a bad time. . . ."

"No," he said. "Sharon would like to see you, I know." He tried to smile. "Me, too, of course. But she's . . ." He shook his head. "She's not dealing with this at all. She's trying to convince herself that Brian's alive, and I'm worried that if they don't find him—his body—pretty soon, she'll . . ." He waved his hand. "I don't know what she'll do, Brady. The doctor came by yesterday after you left, gave her some medication. But she refuses to take it. Says she wants to be awake and alert when Brian comes home. I keep trying to tell her he's not going to come home. It's like a knife in my gut. Saying it, seeing the anger and pain in her eyes. She hates me when I say that to her. But what'm I supposed to do?"

"I don't know, Jake. I wish I did."

"Well," he said, "her mother's coming to stay with us. That'll help. Come on in."

Sharon was wearing what appeared to be the same jeans and sweatshirt she'd worn the day before. She huddled in an armchair next to the fireplace with her feet pulled up under her. Her face was blotched and swollen. In that big chair, she looked like a child.

She gave me a wan smile. "Hello, Brady."

I went over and kissed her cheek. "How're you doing?"

32

"The waiting is hard. I miss my boy."

"I know," I said.

"Want some coffee?" said Jake. "A drink?"

"Bring me a glass of wine," said Sharon.

"Coffee's fine," I said.

Jake went out to the kitchen.

"The Rolandos were here this morning," said Sharon. "Tom and Emily. I felt so bad. They were very kind. It had to've been awfully hard for them, coming to see us. We all cried together."

"And Chief Sprague was here," I said. "I just met him outside."

"Ed's such a good man." Sharon rubbed her eyes. "He's trying to make me understand that Brian's dead. Part of me knows that. But part of me thinks, no, he'll be back. Jake thinks I'm crazy, but I'm not. It's weird, but you know, when Tom and Emily were here, I was jealous of them. At least they know. How much easier it has to be, knowing, not wondering and hoping." She touched my arm. "I'm just about all cried out, Brady. I'm just waiting for this to be over with. Now my mother's coming, and she's gonna drive me nuts, I know. It was Jake's idea. I think he just wants to foist me off on somebody else."

"That's not it at all," said Jake, who had come back into the room. "When I called her, she insisted on coming." He handed Sharon a glass of white wine, and he gave me a mug of coffee. He patted Sharon's arm. "She wants to be with you."

Jake had poured himself a beer, and the three of us sat in the gloom-filled living room sipping our drinks and not saying much. I felt uncomfortable and out of place. There was no way I could share their grief or make them feel better.

I'd talked to my two boys today, and that was the difference between us.

I stayed for about an hour, and when I got up to leave, both Jake and Sharon thanked me for coming. But it sounded mechanical, and as I left, I realized there was nothing I could do to help them.

33

It occurred to me that if I wanted to analyze it, I might discover that my real reason for visiting them was to make myself feel better. I decided that I wouldn't return unless they asked me to, or until something changed.

Four

I picked up River Road a mile or so past the Reddington village green and headed north. At first the narrow country road played tag with the winding river, touching it here, bending away from it there, following it upstream. The river was fifty or sixty yards wide in most parts, and it was sheeted over with snow-covered ice from bank to bank. If you didn't know it was a river, you could mistake it for a winter field.

As I neared the dam, I saw that a channel had been opened in the middle of the river where the state police scuba rescue team had extended their search for Brian's body. Big slabs of broken ice lined both sides of the open water. They'd apparently given up about a mile down from the dam.

Brian and Jenny had crashed through the snowbank and the guardrail and smashed into the water directly across the river from the old Reddington powder mill. It was one of those typical nineteenth-century New England brick factory buildings—five stories high, a hundred yards long, built right on the water's edge. Someone had optimistically begun to renovate it for office suites in the economic boom of the eighties. But the boom busted before they finished, and now the old factory's flat back wall loomed up over the river, and its dark empty windows gazed forlornly across the water to the place where Jenny and Brian had died.

For about a hundred yards downstream from the dam the riverbank was riprapped with big jagged hunks of blasted granite. Here, River Road was just two lanes wide, bounded by a steep hillside on the left and the river on the right. It curved slightly, then followed tight to the riverbank, with a narrow frozen sand shoulder barely wide enough for a car to pull off. You'd have to be driving awfully fast not to negotiate that soft curve.

It wasn't hard to spot the place where Jenny Rolando's car had gone in. A car's width of guardrail and old plowed snow was torn away.

A black Chevrolet pickup truck was pulled against the guardrail just past the site of the accident. I pulled in behind it and walked back.

The swollen river poured over the top of the dam into a heavy tumult of water funneling between the rocky riprapped banks. Here it was twenty-five or thirty yards across. The dam itself was about ten feet high, and at its base where the water crashed down onto itself, a faint mist rose into the wintry air.

The water was dark and swift and cold-looking, and the powerful currents and eddies swirled and scraped across the riverbed. It was easy to see how they could suck a person down and smash and tumble him against the rocky bottom until he lost all sense of direction. The river widened below where the riprap ended. There the now-frozen water flattened out into the placid, shallow, meandering river that typified the Reddington all the way down to Rhode Island, where it merged with a couple of other rivers before it emptied into the sea.

Chief Sprague had said it: If Jenny and Brian had gone off the road anywhere else along the river, they'd probably have survived.

Two figures were sitting on the big squarish hunks of granite along the top of the riverbank where the guardrail was broken away. Their backs were to me, and as I approached them I saw that they were tossing white flowers into the water. They were young women. Teenagers. Friends of Jenny and Brian, I guessed, come here to remember and to mourn.

I didn't want to interrupt them. I stood there quietly for a minute and thought about Brian. When my thoughts flipped to Billy and Joey, my own sons, I let out a long breath and turned back for my car.

"Hey, mister."

I stopped and looked back.

One of the girls had stood up, and she was shielding her eyes with her hand and squinting into the afternoon sun at me. She wore a red parka and baggy blue jeans and Bean boots.

I lifted my hand. "Hi."

She approached me. She had a bunch of daisies in one hand. "Who're you?" she said. "You're not from Reddington."

"The Golds are friends of mine," I said.

She was a chunky girl with hair so black that I figured it was dyed. She stood in front of me and frowned. "You're not one of those gawkers?"

"I'm not gawking," I said.

"There have been a lot of gawkers. You should've been here when they were diving for Brian. There was a mob, all of them hoping to see a body. Some of them had cameras, for God's sake. Sick."

I nodded.

"So why're you here?" she said.

I shrugged. "Same reason you are, I guess."

"We're remembering Jenny," she said. "She was our friend. Flowers on the water."

"Brian wasn't your friend?"

She frowned, and her eyes darted away from mine for an instant. Then she nodded quickly. "Of course he was. Brian, too. Flowers for both of our friends." She held her bunch of daisies to me. "You want to toss in a flower?"

I plucked two daisies from her hand. "Thank you," I said. "I'd like to do that."

I followed her to the edge of the river, closed my eyes for a moment to focus my thoughts on Brian, then tossed one of the daisies into the water. Then I tried to think about Jenny Rolando. I remembered her photo on the wall in the police station, and the image of that young girl strapped behind the wheel of an upside-down car with water pouring in was vivid in my mind. I tossed the other daisy onto the swirling currents.

The girl touched my arm. "I'm Sandy," she said.

"I'm Brady Coyne. I knew Brian when he was a baby." I arched my eyebrows at Sandy and jerked my head in the other girl's direction. She had continued to sit there on the rock with her back to me. She wore a grayish quilted ankle-length coat and a black knit watch cap. Her head was bowed and she was hugging herself.

"That's Mikki," said Sandy. "She's pretty broken up."

"I guess everybody is," I said. "Brian's parents are devastated. The fact that they can't find his body..."

Sandy's eyes flickered, and she turned quickly and tossed a daisy onto the water. She glanced at me, then went and crouched beside Mikki. She whispered to her for a moment, then helped Mikki stand up and led her over to where I was standing. "This is Mikki," said Sandy. To Mikki she said, "This is Mr. Coyne. He's a friend of Brian."

Mikki was a tiny Asian girl. She looked like a papoose huddled in her ankle-length coat. She had smooth olive skin and dark eyes and long ebony hair. She held out her hand to me. "Hello," she said softly.

I took her hand. "Hello, Mikki." I looked from one girl to the other. "What do you think happened here?"

Mikki stared at me for a moment. Then her eyes brimmed. She shook her head, turned, and went back to sit on the rocks.

"I'm sorry," I said to Sandy. "I've upset her."

"She's already upset," said Sandy. "You're not exactly help-ing."

"How about you?" I said. "What do you think happened?"

She shrugged. "What do you mean? What kind of question is that? Their car went into the water, and—and they died. What are you, anyway? Some kind of cop?"

"No," I said. "I'm actually a lawyer. The Golds have been my clients and friends for years."

"So you gonna sue somebody? That why you're snooping around?"

"No. I'm not here as a lawyer, and I'm not snooping. I'm here as a friend. I'm sad about what happened just the way you are."

"I doubt that," said Sandy.

"Hey," I said. "Lawyers have feelings, too, you know."

She smiled for the first time. "Yeah, right." She squinted at me. "So why *are* you here?"

"I was visiting Brian's parents. They're out of their minds with grief, and they will be forever until their boy's body is found."

Sandy shook her head. "That's pretty awful."

"Do you have any idea where Brian and Jenny were going the other night?" I said.

She flapped her hands. "Just out, I guess. They were together all the time."

"Did you know that they'd packed some clothes?"

"I heard that, yes."

"Then what—?"

"How should I know?" she said quickly. "Look, mister. You've got no right to come here and bother us and—and in-terrogate us." Tears welled up in her eyes. "Why don't you just leave us alone?"

I nodded. "I'm sorry." I took out my wallet and fished out two of my business cards. "Here," I said. "Give one to Mikki. If you hear anything or think of anything, I'd appreciate it if you'd give me a call."

"Like what? What could we tell you?"

"I don't know," I said. "Take them anyway. Maybe you'll think of something."

She shrugged, took the cards, glanced at them, then stuffed them into her pocket.

I held out my hand to her. "I'm sorry I bothered you," I said.

She started to reach for my hand, and then her eyes darted past me.

I turned. A black-and-white police Explorer had pulled in behind my car, and Chief Sprague and Officer McCaffrey had gotten out. Sprague looked in my direction with his hand shielding his eyes. Then he turned and said something to McCaffrey, who shrugged and got back into the cruiser.

Sprague waved and came toward us. When he got to where we were standing, he said, "Well, Mr. Coyne. I see you've met my friends."

"Yes," I said. "We tossed daisies into the river."

He smiled quickly at me, then turned to Sandy. "You okay, kiddo?"

She shook her head, then went to him and hugged him. He patted her shoulder. Then Mikki came over, and they had a three-way hug, with their arms across each other's shoulders and their heads close together.

I turned and started for my car.

"Mr. Coyne," called Sprague. "Hang on."

I stopped. Sprague spoke earnestly to the two girls for a minute. Then Sandy held out her bunch of daisies to him. Sprague plucked out two of them, tossed them into the water one at a time, then stood there with his head bowed.

After a minute, he turned, gave each of the girls another hug, and came to where I was standing. He was shaking his head. "It's going to take a long time for this town to heal," he said.

"It'll be forever for Jake and Sharon," I said, "unless they find Brian's body."

"Man, you got that right." He waved at the river. "They dove all through this deep water here, and they broke the ice and searched for almost a mile down below before they quit. I'm going to do everything I can to get them to come back. Mr. Nash, our DA, he's pulling some strings. Brian's body is stuck somewhere under the ice down there, and the idea of not finding him until the river breaks up in the spring is just intolerable."

"So the state police have given up the search?" I said.

"Mr. Nash and I are working on it," he said. "But you know the staties. They've got their priorities, and little Reddington isn't one of them."

We started back to our vehicles. "What did the kids have to say?" he asked.

I shook my head. "Nothing. They're sad. They seem like good kids."

"They are," said Sprague. "Jenny and Brian were, too. I believe in kids, Mr. Coyne. I believe that all kids start out as good kids. A big part of my job is keeping them that way."

"That's admirable," I said.

"Admirable?" He shook his head. "It's just common sense." He cocked his head at me. "Oh. You were being sarcastic, huh?"

"Not at all," I said. We stopped at Sprague's cruiser. Inside, Officer McCaffrey was talking on the radio. "Yesterday," I said to Sprague, "you told me the kids had packed some clothes, as if they were planning to shack up for a few days."

"I didn't say they were planning to shack up."

"Right. Anyway, I was wondering what their parents said about that."

"About their shacking up?"

"About their bringing clothes with them."

"I didn't tell them about that."

"Why not?"

He shrugged. "Why? To give them something else to think about?"

41

"Yeah," I said. "Good point. It wouldn't bring those kids back to life."

"No," he said. "It wouldn't." He reached for my hand and gripped it. "Good to see you again."

"You, too," I said. "And if—"

"Right. If anything happens, I'll let you know. I've got your card."

My encounter with Sandy kept nagging at me as I drove the back roads home to Boston through the gathering twilight. I had the feeling she knew something. For one thing, she knew that Brian and Jenny had taken clothes with them. According to Chief Sprague, only the police knew that. They hadn't even told the parents.

If Sandy knew that, maybe she knew *why* Brian and Jenny had taken clothes with them.

Well, as Sprague had said, what difference would it make?

I couldn't come up with a good answer to that.

FIVE

———✦———

I got back to my apartment around five o'clock. The first thing I did was pour a couple of fingers of Rebel Yell over some ice cubes, take the portable phone into the living room, and call Evie.

"You still mad at me?" I said when she answered.

"Me? I'm not mad."

"I thought you were mad at me."

"I don't get mad. You should know that. Why should I be mad?"

"Upset, then," I said. "I got the feeling you were unhappy with me."

"You were sad and I couldn't do anything to make you feel better," she said. "That upset me, sure."

"Upset that you couldn't make me feel better?"

"No, dummy. I know I'm not Supergirl. I was sad that you were sad, that's all. Are you still sad?"

"I'm not exactly giddy," I said, "but I'm better. I talked to Billy and Joey this morning. That evened out my keel a little."

"I'm glad, Brady. That's nice."

I hesitated. "Um, feel like coming over?"

She laughed softly. "Tempt me."

"Grandmother Coyne's old-fashioned fish chowder."

"Good enough. Give me an hour."

I made the fish chowder while I waited for Evie to arrive. She'd said an hour. I figured it would be two hours, minimum.

In the microwave I thawed a quart of fish stock I'd made and frozen back in the fall, dumped it into a big pot and added a three-pound slab of fresh haddock cut into two-inch chunks, slivered onions and diced salt pork sauteed in butter, cubed potatoes, canned evaporated milk, salt, freshly ground pepper, and a dash of cayenne.

It was bubbling on the stove and I was reading the current issue of *American Angler* in the living room when I heard Evie's key scratching in the door. I glanced at my watch. She'd made it in an hour and three-quarters.

She tossed her jacket on the sofa. She was wearing tight black jeans, a tight black sweater, black leather calf-high boots. Her auburn hair looked almost red against all that black.

I whistled, and she put one hand on her hip and the other behind her head and thrust out her chest. Then she grinned and gave me a goofy, cross-eyed look.

She tilted up her face and sniffed. "Smells good."

"It needs to simmer for another hour or so," I said. "That's a hint."

She came over to where I was sitting, put her hands on my shoulders, bent to me, and kissed me lightly on the mouth. I reached up with both hands, held her face there, and kissed her properly.

She pushed her forehead against mine and blinked her eyes. Our faces were so close that our eyelashes brushed. "So," she said. "Do we just want to be held tonight?"

"Being held," I said, "would be mere prologue."

We made love, napped for an hour or so, showered together, wolfed down the chowder with pilot crackers and a chilled sau-

44

vignon blanc, played a game of Trivial Pursuit, and sipped Rebel Yell while we watched a fifties movie called *The Man with the Atomic Brain* on my old black-and-white TV. Around midnight, we pulled on sweatshirts and went out on my little balcony to sniff the wintry ocean air and check the sky.

Then we went to bed and made love again.

Then we slept.

If I had any dreams, I forgot them before I woke up.

A perfect Saturday night.

It was snowing the next morning. Hello, there, Punxsutawney Phil.

We had English muffins with marmalade and orange juice and coffee on the living room floor, passed sections of the *Sunday Globe* back and forth, and heated the leftover chowder for lunch. We agreed that it tasted better reheated. Gave the flavors a chance to mingle.

The snow changed over to rain sometime in the middle of the morning, but by early afternoon it had changed back to snow, so Evie decided to head back to her condo in Concord before the roads got icy.

My apartment felt suddenly empty after Evie left. I realized I'd barely thought about Jake and Sharon Gold while she'd been there with me.

Julie had already left the office the following Tuesday afternoon, and I was rinsing out the coffeepot when the phone rang.

It was Gus Nash, the DA I'd run into at the Reddington Police Station.

"Glad I caught you, Counselor," he said.

"Lucky you," I said. "I was just shutting down the office for the day."

"How about that drink we talked about?"

"Sure," I said. "When?"

45

"What's wrong with right now?"

"Okay. I could use a drink. You buying?"

"I said I would," he said, "and I'm a man of my word."

"The entire Commonwealth knows that, Gus, assuming they believe what you've been telling them."

His booming laugh caused me to jerk the phone away from my ear. When I put it back, he was saying, ". . . Copley Plaza in half an hour?"

"What's the agenda?"

"No agenda, Brady. Meet me in the bar."

The Copley bar featured muffled, conspiratorial voices, dim lighting, and dark woodwork, and when I walked in a few minutes after six on that grimy Tuesday evening in February, it was half empty. I looked around, and Gus Nash waved at me from a table in the corner.

I draped my topcoat over the back of the chair and sat down across from him. He was cupping a half-empty glass of dark beer in both hands.

A waiter appeared almost instantly. I ordered a bourbon old-fashioned on the rocks, and when the waiter left, I lit a cigarette, leaned back, and let out a long breath. "So what's up, Gus?"

"Up?" He shrugged. "Nothing's up. It's been a while since you and I had a drink, I was in the neighborhood . . ." He peered at me. "You look like shit, you know that?"

I waved my hand. "That tragedy in Reddington. I'm identifying big-time with the parents. I've got a couple boys of my own, you know. It's been kind of a reality check for me. Reality sucks."

He reached across the table and gripped my arm. His eyes behind his glasses were intelligent and sympathetic. "Anything I can do?"

I smiled. "Find Brian Gold's body."

He nodded. "We're working on it."

The waiter brought my drink and asked Gus if he wanted another. He shook his head.

When the waiter left, I said, "So let's talk about you. Rumor has it you're running for AG."

He smiled. "You should know better than to listen to rumors."

"It's not true?"

He shrugged. "I'll tell you the truth. I wouldn't mind being attorney general. And, yes, there is some talk about it. But I'm not running for anything. I guess if they end up asking me to run, I'd probably do it."

"So this—" I waved my hand around, indicating the Copley bar "—has nothing to do with politics?"

He grinned. "And what could a candidate possibly gain from buying *you* a drink?"

I looked at him for a moment, then smiled. "Valid point," I said. "Sorry. I'm just in a crappy mood."

He waved his hand. "Ah, don't worry about it." He sipped his beer, then wiped his upper lip on the back of his forefinger. "That accident," he said. "Damn shame. Terrible thing."

I nodded.

"Devastating for that little community," he said after a minute. "Ed—Ed Sprague, the police chief—he's very upset. Takes that sort of thing personally. Reddington's got a lot of healing to do."

"And he's anxious to get on with it," I said. "The healing, I mean."

Gus nodded. "Well, yes. Naturally. Small-town police chief, that's part of his job."

"I ran into him a couple times over the weekend," I said. "He probably thinks I'm a nosy pain in the ass."

"Yeah, probably. Hell, you *are* a pain in the ass. Ask anybody." He smiled quickly. "Sprague understands. I told him he should be cooperative with you."

"He's been fine. Seems like a good guy. I just feel bad for

Jake and Sharon." I peered up at Nash. "I met a couple of kids when I was out there on Saturday. I'd've sworn they knew something."

"Like what?"

I shrugged. "I don't know. They clammed up when Sprague arrived."

"Clammed up? They had secrets to tell you?"

"I don't know," I said. "Maybe."

He grinned. "I know you, Coyne. You think there's some mystery to be solved in Reddington, right?"

"Unanswered questions, that's all. Brian Gold's body hasn't been found. How'd that car go off the road? Where were those kids headed? What was on their minds?"

"I'm still negotiating with the state cops," said Nash. "Hopefully we'll get a boat and some divers back out there, find the boy's body."

"Yeah," I said, "that would be a start."

Nash smiled. "You're a terrific lawyer, Brady. You take good care of your clients. You go after the facts. You're dogged. No one pulls any surprises on you. You—"

"Come off it, Gus," I said. "Why're you buying me a drink? What do you want?"

"I don't want anything," he said. "I'm buying you a drink because we're old friends and because I was in the neighborhood."

"Did Sprague put you up to this?"

"No one puts me up to anything, Brady. You should know that." He leaned across the table toward me. "Ed's an old friend. He's a good man. He's one of those cops who takes things hard. Damn few of them around. But he doesn't tell me what to do."

"I riled him, though, huh?"

"Yes." He smiled. "In fact, you did, a little. Ed's easily riled. He's very protective of his community."

"Snoopy Boston lawyer, poking around his peaceful little

48

town, annoying the local kids, stirring thing up." I nodded. "Hard to blame him for getting riled."

Nash shrugged.

"And you'd rather I didn't rile him anymore."

He spread his hands. "You'll do what you've got to do anyway, Brady."

"I'm really not contemplating a lawsuit, if that's what's bothering Sprague. I'd just like to know what happened, that's all."

"I'll tell him that," Nash said. "I'm sure it will ease his mind."

I finished my drink, then stood up. "You did say this was on you, right?"

"Of course."

I slipped into my topcoat. Nash stood up, and we shook hands.

"Thanks," I said.

He waved his hand. "You can buy next time."

"I mean for not talking politics," I said.

"Oh, that's way down the road," he said. "Believe me, I don't even think about that."

"Because if you had," I said, "I would've told all my friends not to vote for you."

He smiled and clapped my shoulder. "All three of them, huh?"

SIX

Gus Nash called me a couple of days later. He'd pulled every string he could think of, but the state police underwater search team wasn't going back to Reddington. Gus said he was sorry, and I believed him.

When I called Jake, he told me Chief Sprague had already been there. Sprague had apologized, but Jake claimed he'd already resigned himself to the fact that they'd never find Brian's body. He said Sharon was doing as well as could be expected, whatever that meant. Her mother was staying with them, keeping Sharon busy, dragging her off to the mall every day, doing the cooking and vacuuming, insisting that both of them eat. Jake sounded grateful.

He'd been putting in his time at the community college, trying to restore some rhythm to his life. Looking out over a classroom of young faces, he said, sent an arrow into his soul. He was waiting for it to get better.

There was nothing I could do, he told me, and I figured that seeing me would just remind them of Brian and crack open whatever fragile shell might be growing over Jake's and Sharon's hearts.

So I stayed away from Reddington, and I didn't call the Golds, and they didn't call me.

Sometime in the middle of the following Tuesday morning, Julie scratched at my door. I called, "Enter, if ye dare," as I always do, and she came in bearing coffee.

"Let's take a break," she said.

I don't argue with Julie. We took the coffee over to my conference area.

"I bet you don't know what tomorrow is," she said.

"Ha!" I said. "It's Wednesday. Gotcha."

She rolled her eyes. "I didn't think so."

"What am I missing here?"

"You got plans with Evie tomorrow?" she said.

"Of course not. Not unless they've decided to stick an extra Saturday in between Tuesday and Wednesday. I see Evie only on weekends. You know that."

"You're sending her flowers, at least, right?"

"Flowers?"

She rolled her eyes and shook her head. "I'll take care of it. You want the card to say *love* or *lots of love* or *I love you*, or is there some private mushy thing you two say to each other?"

I gazed out my window for a minute before I turned to her and said, "Aha."

"The light dawns."

"Valentine's Day, right?"

"You like Groundhog Day," she said. "Women like Valentine's Day."

"Thank you just the same," I said. "I will take care of everything."

And I did. After we finished our coffee and Julie went back to her desk, I called the florist and told them to deliver a dozen long-stemmed pink roses to Evie's desk on Wednesday.

The card I dictated said:

52

Violets are blue
Roses are red
I can't get you
Out of my head.
Or bed.
Nor do I want to.

I also told them to deliver a mixed bouquet to Julie's desk, and be sure there was one of those big red balloon hearts with it. Julie loved balloons.

Her card read:

Violets are blue
Roses are red
Without you
I'd be dead.

Having flowers delivered to their offices, I knew, was inspired. Women like to display flowers on their desks so that all visitors, strangers and acquaintances alike, will know that they are beloved.

Besides preventing my personal life from falling into complete disarray, Julie works harder than I do, and she's much smarter than I am when it comes to doing business. Julie, for example, believes in keeping full and complete records of billable hours. Telephone time is eminently billable. A three-minute phone conversation is billed as ten minutes, the minimum segment as specified in the standard agreement she designed for me and insists that my clients sign. Travel time is likewise billable. So, of course, is research time. I'm supposed to bill my clients for having drinks while I consult or negotiate with other lawyers, and Julie gets furious if I'm sloppy about keeping track of my court time, including all the hours I inevitably spend sitting around courthouse lobbies waiting my turn. Every ten-minute increment of my workday, in fact, must be accounted for, and since Julie knows I'm careless about my time, she has devised a variety of ways to keep track of it herself. Julie knows when I go to the bathroom and when I leaf through fly-fishing catalogs and when I make weekend plans with Evie.

Julie believes in being aggressive, going after business, getting there first. If she had her way, I'm convinced she'd have me chasing ambulances.

The early bird gets the worm. That's her motto.

I remind her that it's the *second* mouse that gets the cheese.

If Julie's merely meticulous about record-keeping, she's downright Machiavellian when it comes to creating what she calls "the proper impression" for clients and other lawyers. She chose all the furnishings and appointments for our suite of offices and arranged them to create the illusion that I am a smart, powerful, wealthy, and in-demand Boston attorney.

She believes that if a lawyer can see a client who has neglected to make an appointment, it conveys the impression of actually needing clients, and any lawyer who actually needs clients cannot be smart, powerful, wealthy, or in demand.

The fact is, I am smart enough, and I have no interest in accruing any more power or wealth than I already have. I have as many clients as I want, which is considerably fewer than I could handle if I really wanted to work hard. The demand for my services is greater than my supply of enthusiasm for performing them. I'll trade billable hours for a day of trout fishing any time.

When I try to explain this basic economic equation to Julie, she rolls her eyes and shakes her head.

So when she buzzed me on Thursday afternoon to announce that Jake Gold was there and wanted to see me, I was suspicious. "How long have you kept him waiting?"

"He just arrived. I explained that you're busy."

I knew she was talking for Jake's benefit. Julie's desk is right there in the reception area.

"I'm not busy at all," I said. "I was just daydreaming about fly-fishing on Martha's Vineyard next September with J. W. Jackson, in fact. We're planning to enter the Derby this year, you know."

"You're almost done, then," she said.

"Julie, for Christ's sake, there's no need for this charade. You know what Jake's been through. Bring him in here."

"Excellent," she said—a bit frostily, I thought.

A moment later she scratched on my door, and when I called "Enter," she pushed it open and held it for Jake.

I got up from behind my desk and went around to shake hands with him. "How're you doing, Jake?" I said, though I could see how he was doing. His face was pinched and there were dark circles under his eyes. Jake was in his late fifties. Today he looked about eighty.

"I'm all right," he said.

"Coffee, gentlemen?" said Julie.

Jake shook his head.

"No, thank you," I told her.

She gave Jake her pretty Irish smile, stuck out her tongue at me, and pulled the door shut behind her.

I took Jake's elbow and steered him to the informal conference area in the corner of my office, which Julie had arranged with an oxblood leather sofa, a pair of matching leather armchairs, a glass-topped coffee table carefully strewn with copies of *Field & Stream* and the *Yale Law Review*, framed Audubon bird prints on the wall, and a view of Copley Square out the big double window. Jake sat on the sofa. I took one of the chairs across from him.

He had a large manila envelope tucked into his armpit. He put it on the coffee table, then looked at me. "Well," he said, "we're split."

"Huh? Split?"

"Sharon and I. We decided we needed some time apart."

"God, Jake. I'm sorry."

He shrugged.

55

"It's temporary, I hope," I said.

He bowed his head and clasped his hands between his knees. "I don't honestly know, Brady. It's just . . . she can't stand the sight of me, and I can't bear it anymore. It's all mixed up with Brian, of course." He forearms were braced on his thighs, and he was talking down at the floor. His voice was soft and mournful. "We're—neither of us is doing very well with it, and instead of consoling each other, we seem to be reminding each other about it. She blames me, and I guess I blame myself, so every time we see each other, it's a reminder. Of him. Brian. Of what happened. Of . . . of how it used to be." He shook his head. "It seems like a long time ago."

"How does Sharon feel about this . . . your splitting?"

"Her mother's with her. She probably doesn't even notice I'm gone."

"Haven't you talked with her about it?"

"Talked?" He smiled. "I bet we haven't exchanged ten words since . . . since the accident."

"That was only two weeks ago," I said. "It's going to take time, Jake."

He nodded. "Oh, sure. But I think we need to spend that time apart from each other. I just can't stand the way she refuses to look at me."

"Well," I said, "maybe a little time away from each other wouldn't be such a bad thing."

"No," he said, "but the best thing . . ." He shook his head and let the thought die.

"So what're you going to do?" I said after a minute.

"I told the college I was taking a bereavement leave for the rest of the term. I don't think they liked it, but fuck them. I can't teach right now. I see a young person, all bright-eyed and . . . and alive, and I want to cry. Beyond that, I don't know."

I reached over and tapped his knee. "Do you want to talk about it?"

He shook his head. "Not really."

56

"Because if you do," I said, "I'm happy to listen. Or I can help you find somebody."

"No. There's really nothing to talk about." He looked up at me. "Unless you know somebody whose boy went into a river and never came out."

"Think about it, Jake. My friend Doc Adams can hook you up with a good—"

"I don't want a shrink, Brady. Thank you, anyway."

"Well, if you change your mind . . ."

"Sure," he said. He picked up the manila envelope he'd put on the coffee table between us. "Actually," he said, "the reason I came here was to ask you if you'd mind holding on to this for me."

"What is it?"

He waved his hand. "Oh, just some documents. Some stuff I—well, that I don't want Sharon to get ahold of." He handed the envelope to me. "I just want to know it's in a safe place."

It felt as if it held a dozen or so sheets of paper. It had been sealed with cellophane tape. "You want me to keep this for you?" I said.

He nodded. "Until I get settled somewhere. Or move back home."

I shrugged. "I'll stick it in my safe. You can fetch it whenever you want."

"Good. Thanks." He stood up. "Well, that's it. I just wanted you to know what was happening. I won't keep you any longer."

He started for the door. I went along with him. "I hope you'll keep in touch," I said.

"Oh, sure. Of course."

"I want to know how you're making out."

He nodded.

"It'll take a while, Jake," I said. "This has to be awfully painful for both of you."

"You can't imagine," he said.

After Jake left, I took his envelope to my wall safe. Julie and I had cleverly hidden it under a big framed black-and-white photograph of Billy and Joey, sitting side by side in a rowboat on a Maine lake. The photo was taken when the boys were seven and five. Gloria, their mother and my ex-wife, who became a professional photographer after our divorce, had given me the framed photo that Christmas.

Even back then, about fifteen years ago, you could see the intensity in the eyes of Joey, who turned out to be a scholar, and the devil in Billy's grin. Billy's main ambition was to guide fly-fishermen in the summer, ski every mountain in Idaho in the winter, and screw all the girls west of the Mississippi year-round. As far as I could tell, he'd already achieved his goals and should be ready to retire, but he was still working hard at it.

Joey was a dean's list sophomore at Stanford. I kept urging him to abandon his law-school plan, but he'd always had enough sense to be skeptical of my advice.

I didn't see either of them enough anymore.

I rarely used the safe and probably wouldn't have bothered having it installed if Julie hadn't insisted that a lawyer should have a safe in his office. The only thing I normally kept in it was the secondhand Smith & Wesson .38 revolver that Doc Adams had talked me into buying many years ago. I'd shot it with Doc a few times at his club until he was satisfied that I could handle it. He told me to keep it loaded with the hammer on an empty chamber and to put it in a safe place. I took him literally.

I ran through the combination—Billy's and Joey's birthdays—and the heavy door swung silently open. I reached inside, fingered the reassuring blued steel of the S&W, then slid Jake's envelope in beside it. Whatever it was, it was safe with me.

SEVEN

Jake Gold called the office a little after noontime the following Tuesday. "We gotta talk," he said.

"Sure," I said. "What's up?"

"Not on the phone."

"Sounds mysterious, Jake."

"Mysterious is hardly the word for it." Jake sounded as if he was out of breath.

"So, give me a hint."

"I'll tell you all about it when I see you. This is gonna blow your mind."

"How's this afternoon? I'm free anytime after three."

He hesitated. "Better make it tomorrow," he said. "I got a couple loose ends to clear up first."

I checked my appointment calendar. "One o'clock okay? Meet me here. We'll have lunch."

"Perfect," he said. "I'll see you then."

The next day, Wednesday, one o'clock came and went, and by two-thirty my stomach was growling and Jake still hadn't showed up. I went out to the reception area and asked Julie if he'd called to cancel or postpone our appointment.

She shook her head.

"That's not like Jake," I said.

Julie nodded. "Meanwhile, I'm hungry."

"Me, too. Whose turn?"

"Yours."

So I went out to the deli and picked up a tuna on toasted wheat for Julie, a corned beef and Swiss cheese on pumpernickel for me, two bags of potato chips, and two Pepsi Colas. Each sandwich came with a giant kosher dill pickle.

I got back to the office a little after three. Jake still hadn't showed up, nor had he called. Julie turned on the answering machine, and we ate our sandwiches off waxed paper on the coffee table in my office.

After we finished, I lit a cigarette and said, "Jake had something important to tell me. He said it would blow my mind."

"If you're worried about him," Julie said, "you should call him."

"He's not living at home. I don't know how to reach him."

She grinned. "We got that caller ID, remember?"

"Oh, right. So you could keep track of all my calls, make sure I didn't overlook anything billable."

"I logged the phone number he called from yesterday."

"You're amazing."

"I know," she said.

She went out to her desk and was back a minute later with a phone number written on a scrap of paper. I took it over to my desk and dialed it.

"King's," answered a man's heavily accented voice.

"I'd like to speak to Jake Gold," I said, wondering who or what the hell King's was.

"Who zat?"

"Mr. Gold." I spelled it for him.

"Okay. Hang on." He put me on hold, then came back on the line a minute later. "No Gold, sorry."

"What is this place?" I said.

"Wha' place?"

60

I took in a long breath and let it out slowly. "King's. What's King's?"

"Motel, man. Wha'd you think?"

"And there's no Jake Gold staying there?"

"I tol you, no."

"What about yesterday? He might've checked out last night or this morning."

"You want me to look?"

"Please."

"Sure, man. No sweat." He put me on hold again. This time he was gone for close to five minutes. Then he said, "Sorry, man. Nobody name Gold."

"Could someone not staying there have used your phone?"

"Not this one. Maybe in one of the rooms, huh?"

"Do you keep a record of calls made from the rooms?"

"Oh, sure. Gotta charge 'em. Outgoing calls, they come through the switchboard here."

"Then I want you to check your records and tell me about a phone call that was made around twelve-fifteen yesterday afternoon." I gave him my office number. "Do that for me, okay?"

"Listen, man—"

"It's a police matter," I said. "I appreciate your cooperation."

"Like I got nuthin' else to do," he grumbled. But he put me on hold again. When he came back on, he said, "Yeah. Unit Ten."

"Who's staying in Unit Ten?"

"Mr. Silver."

Real clever, Jake. "John Silver, right?" I said.

"Yeah, tha's him."

"Suppose you ring Mr. Silver's room for me, okay?"

"You got it, man."

I let it ring a dozen times. Jake didn't answer, nor did my friend at the switchboard pick up, so I disconnected and hit the redial button.

"King's."

"No answer from Mr. Silver," I said. "He is still registered there, isn't he?"

"Oh, yeah. Paid by the week. You get good deal for a week."

"Where are you located?"

"Route Nine."

"Where on Route Nine?"

"Framingham, man. Practically next to Ken's, you know?"

"Ken's Steak House?"

"You got it."

"Listen," I said, "do you know who Mr.—um—Mr. Silver is?"

"Oh, sure. Tall old guy, funny hair. I check him in. I see him come and go."

"Did you see him come or go today?"

"No, man. I been here since eight. Din see him all day. But he don' have to check with me, you know."

"Okay, listen," I said. "I want you to give him a message for me, okay? It's very important. I want him to get it just as soon as he comes in. The message is this: Call Brady Coyne immediately." I spelled my name and recited both my office and home phone numbers.

"Wait a minute," mumbled the guy. "How you spell *immediately*?"

I told him and repeated the two phone numbers.

"Okay," he said.

"It's very important," I said.

"Gotcha, man. Police business, huh?"

"Exactly."

Jake didn't call that afternoon, nor did he call me at home that evening or at the office on Thursday. It worried me. It was out of character for Jake to blow off an appointment, especially one he'd set up himself. He would've called if he couldn't make it. And if he couldn't call ahead of time, he'd call later.

And why register under a phony name?

This is going to blow your mind, he'd said.

I called King's Motel after Julie left for the day. A woman with no accent answered this time. I asked her to ring Jake's room. Ten rings, no answer. I disconnected, then called her back. She told me Mr. Silver had not checked out. I asked her if she'd mind going to Unit Ten and knocking on his door. She said she couldn't leave the desk. When I told her it was a police matter, she decided maybe she could do it after all.

She came back on the line five minutes later. "Mr. Silver's got his Do Not Disturb sign on the door," she said. "I knocked, but he didn't answer."

"Could you use your key, go in?"

"Sure," she said. "And get fired."

"I left a note for him yesterday," I said. "Would you mind checking his room slot, see if he picked it up? It's from Brady Coyne. That's me."

"Okay." A minute later she said, "Nope. Your message is still here."

I thanked the woman and hung up.

Where the hell was Jake?

The question nagged me the whole time it took me to walk across the city to my apartment on the waterfront, and it nagged me while I changed out of my lawyer suit into my flannel shirt and jeans, and it nagged me while I sipped my glass of Rebel Yell and ice in my living room.

The more I thought about it, the more it worried me.

Jake had been through a lot. He'd lost Brian, he'd stopped working, he'd left his wife. Any one of those things was a certifiable reason for profound depression.

He'd hardly sounded depressed when he called me on the phone to make the appointment he'd broken. When I talked to him, in fact, he'd sounded manic.

It was an easy decision. I went down to the parking garage, got into my car, and headed for Route Nine in Framingham.

It took nearly three-quarters of an hour to get there. Route Nine in Framingham is a divided highway lined with commerce: restaurants and night clubs, carpet warehouses and computer stores, giant shopping malls with twenty-acre parking lots. Every hundred yards or so a light stops traffic to make it easy for shoppers to enter and leave the places where they want to spend their money, and to hell with anybody who just wants to keep going.

Fluffy snowflakes the size of pennies whirled in my headlights, and a big neon sign with blinking bulbs heralding KING'S MOTEL appeared out of the blur. Under it, a smaller lighted sign read VACANCY. I got into the right-hand lane, thanked the green arrow on the traffic light, pulled into the parking area, and found a slot by the end of the building directly in front of Unit Ten.

King's Motel was a big oblong building with a white-brick facade, an overhanging roof, and an outside corridor running the length of the second floor. Ten units up, ten units down, front and back. Forty units in all. A tiny in-ground pool, now empty, sat directly beside the highway.

Back in the seventies (when I guessed it was built), King's Motel probably had been considered elegant. Now it looked like it had stopped trying.

I went directly to Unit Ten. A dim yellow bulb glowed beside the door, and the DO NOT DISTURB sign still hung on the doorknob.

I knocked on the door. When there was no answer from inside, I knocked louder and called, "Hey, Jake. It's Brady. Open up."

He did not open up.

I tried the knob, but it was locked.

I spotted the neon-red OFFICE sign in a window down at the other end. I walked down there, opened the door, and went in.

A middle-aged woman with honey-colored skin and high cheekbones was talking on the phone behind a chest-high counter. She glanced at me, turned her back and whispered something into the phone, then hung up.

She put her elbows on the counter and smiled. "Want a room?"

"No," I said. "I talked to you a couple hours ago. I want you to let me into Unit Ten."

"I'm sorry," she said. "I told you—"

"You said you were worried about getting fired," I said. "I appreciate that, and I don't mean to threaten you. But if you don't let me into that room, you will regret it, I promise."

She rolled her eyes. "And that's not a threat?"

I shrugged. "Okay, it's a threat."

"Did you say you were a cop?"

"No. I said it was police business. I'm a lawyer."

"Can I ask you why you've got to get into that room?"

"Because I'm worried that your guest—my friend and client—might've killed himself in there."

She laughed quickly. Then she narrowed her eyes. "You're serious."

"Yes," I said. "I am."

She nodded. "Okay. Let's go."

She took a key off a hook, slipped on a jacket, and I followed her back to Unit Ten.

She hesitated at the door, then knocked softly. "Sir?" she called.

When there was no answer, she shrugged and used her key to unlock the door. She pushed it open for me. "Go ahead," she said. "I'm not going in there."

I stood in the open doorway and looked inside. A muted television flickered at the foot of the bed. All the lights were turned off. It took my eyes a moment to adjust to the dimness.

Then I saw the silhouette of a human figure slumped in the upholstered chair against the wall on the other side of the bed. I stepped inside the doorway, and that's when I caught the foul, sweet smell of death.

"Jesus," I mumbled.

I backed out and pulled the door closed.

The woman touched my arm. "What ... ?"

"You wait here," I told her. "Be sure nobody goes in there. I'm going to use your phone."

I went back to the motel office and called state police headquarters, which happened to be located just a few miles down Route Nine from King's Motel.

When the dispatcher, or receptionist, or whoever it was answered, I told him I had to speak to Lieutenant Horowitz.

"Lieutenant Horowitz is homicide," he said.

"I know that," I said. "That's why I want him. Tell him it's Brady Coyne."

A minute later Horowitz came on the line. "This better be good, Coyne," he said. "I was just about to go home."

"It's not good," I said. "We've got a dead body down the street here in King's Motel."

"Well, fuck," he said. "Okay. We're on our way. Don't touch anything."

I started to say, "I know that." But he'd already hung up.

EIGHT

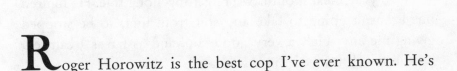

Roger Horowitz is the best cop I've ever known. He's honest, smart, tough, and relentless.

He's also the grouchiest, most cynical, rudest son of a bitch in captivity.

Horowitz has the disconcerting habit of grinning when a normal person would frown. His grin is cynical—evil, almost. It's the grin of a man who's seen everything. Nothing will ever surprise or shock Roger Horowitz again. To him, everything is a senseless, dirty joke.

When Horowitz grins, he reminds me of Jack Nicholson.

His plainclothes detective sedan with the portable blue flasher blinking on the roof pulled up in front of the King's Motel office fifteen minutes later. I was waiting outside the office. When Horowitz slid out of the passenger door, he was already wearing that evil, mirthless grin.

"Where's the body?" he said.

I pointed. "Unit Ten. The clerk's outside the door. She's got a key."

Marcia Benetti, Horowitz's attractive young partner, climbed out from behind the wheel and came over. She gave me a quick smile, then said, "What've we got?" to Horowitz.

"Dead body in Unit Ten, he says. You baby-sit our witness here. I'll go check it out."

Benetti and I went into the motel office. There was just one chair in the room, one of those cheap plastic ones that are not designed for comfort. Neither of us took it.

She leaned back against the counter. She was wearing a blue ski parka and black pants. Her badge hung on a cord around her neck. She looked at me and smiled. "It's been a while, Mr. Coyne."

I nodded. "You must've set a record. You've been his partner, what, over a year, now?"

"Two years next month. We're getting along fine. He figured out I wasn't going to take any shit from him, so he stopped giving me any. He's a very good cop, and as far as I can tell, he still hasn't noticed I'm a woman."

"He's the best," I said, "if you can take his personality."

She shrugged. "He's all business. Suits me." She crossed her arms and rubbed them with her hands. "So you want to talk about it?"

I flapped my hands. "I'll just have to tell him all over again."

Benetti shrugged.

A minute later, the cop radio she wore on her belt squawked. She listened for a minute, said, "Got it," and stuck it back into its sheath.

"He's called in the troops," she told me. "He wants you to sit tight."

"Did he say—?"

She shook her head. "That's it, Mr. Coyne. I've got to go fetch the desk clerk. Stay here, please. I'll be right back."

When she left I lit a cigarette and sat in the plastic chair. If you didn't lean back, it was okay.

Benetti returned a minute later with the desk clerk. I stood up and offered the woman the chair. She shrugged and sat down.

68

"Now what?" she said to Benetti.

"Now we wait."

A few minutes passed, and then a couple of vehicles with flashing lights pulled into the lot and stopped down at the end.

About a half hour later, Horowitz opened the office door. He pointed his finger at me. "Okay," he said. "Let's go."

I followed him down the walkway under the overhang to Unit Ten. The door was open and lights blazed inside.

Horowitz paused in the doorway. "Don't touch anything, Coyne," he said over his shoulder. "You know the drill." Then he took a pair of latex gloves from his pocket, snapped them onto his hands, and stepped inside.

I stopped at the doorway. They'd turned on the air conditioner. It was going full blast, so that the inside of the room felt almost as cold as the outdoors. It didn't quite disguise the odor that still hung in the room, a combination of unflushed toilet and sour milk.

The wallpaper was yellowish, and a big print of a seascape was screwed to the wall over the queen-size bed against the far wall. A telephone and lamp stood on the bedside table. The big TV at the foot of the bed was still flickering silently. There was a closet with no doors, and no clothes hanging in it. To the left was an open doorway into a bathroom.

A young Asian man with two cameras around his neck was leaning against the wall, and a gray-haired man was squatting in front of the chair by the wall beyond the bed. He was wearing a tweed jacket and latex gloves.

The body was sprawled in the chair. His legs were stretched out in front of him and his arms dangled down over the sides of the chair. He wore chino pants and a plaid shirt and brown socks, no shoes. His chin was slumped down on his chest so that I couldn't see his face. His hair was light brown and cut short, so that his scalp showed through.

He looked thoroughly dead.

It wasn't Jake.

Horowitz spoke to the gray-haired man, who stood up and

stepped away from the body. Then he turned to me and grinned. "Know him?"

"It's not who I thought it would be."

"This ain't John Silver?"

"John Silver isn't his name. Jake Gold's his name. Except it's not Jake."

"You don't recognize him?"

"I think I do," I said. "I've got to see his face."

He handed me a pair of latex gloves. "Put these on and come over here," said Horowitz.

I snapped on the gloves, and when I moved closer to the body, I saw that his chest was splotched with blood. Not a lot of blood. Two separate stains on the plaid shirt, each about the size of a silver dollar, one high on the left side just under his collarbone and the other lower, dead center, just above the solar plexus. I knelt in front of him so I could see his face.

His eyes were staring down into his lap through his glasses, which had slipped down toward the tip of his nose. His mouth was open wide, as if he'd been stopped in the middle of a yawn. There was a black hole just under his left cheekbone, right at the corner of his nose. A little blood had dribbled out of it and dried there on the side of his face.

I looked up at Horowitz. "Yeah, I know him."

He nodded and grinned.

"His name is Sprague," I said. "Ed Sprague. He's the police chief in Reddington."

Horowitz turned to the gray-haired man, who I assumed was the medical examiner. They held a brief mumbled conversation, and then Horowitz puffed out his cheeks, blew out a quick breath, and started out the door. "Let's go, Coyne," he said. "We gotta talk."

I followed him back to the motel office. Marcia Benetti was leaning back against the wall with her arms folded. The desk clerk was perched uncomfortably on the edge of the chair, staring at the floor.

Horowitz opened the door and said, "Hey, Marcia, get outta

here and bring her with you. We'll talk to her later. I need this
room."

Benetti shrugged, then nodded at the woman. As the two of
them left the office, Benetti glanced at me over her shoulder
and rolled her eyes.

Horowitz took the only chair in the room. He slouched back
with his arms folded across his chest. "Tell me about John Silver. What'd you say his name was?"

"It's Gold," I said. "Jake Gold. He's head of the humanities
department at Reddington Community College. Sprague was
the police chief in Reddington. Jake's my client, you know, so
I can't . . ."

"Yeah," said Horowitz. "Fuckin' lawyers." He shrugged. "So
tell me what you can."

I told him how Jake's son had died in an automobile accident
about three weeks ago, how they hadn't been able to recover
his body from the river, how Jake had told me he felt he had
to get away from his wife for a while, how he'd struck me as
depressed and manic, and how King's Motel was apparently
where he'd ended up. I told him that Jake had called from his
room here for an appointment, that he said he had something
to tell me that would blow my mind, that he'd failed to keep
the appointment, and that I'd tried to call him but hadn't suc-
ceeded.

"Which is why there was a message from you in his mail
slot."

I nodded. "He never returned my call."

"So you came here looking for him."

I nodded.

"What's Gold's beef with the police chief?"

"Far as I know, he didn't have a beef. He held Sprague in
high esteem. You think Jake killed him?"

Horowitz grinned. "What do you think?"

I shrugged. "I guess it looks that way."

"Did the professor own a gun?"

"I don't know. What kind of gun was it?"

71

"Small caliber. Twenty-two, probably."

"So how do you reconstruct it?" I said.

"Shooter's sitting on the bed holding his gun on the vic, who's sitting in the chair. Shoots him three times. First one probably in the face, next two in the chest. Cleans up after himself, hangs the Do Not Disturb sign on the door, takes everything that ain't nailed down, and leaves. No clothes in the closets, no toothbrush in the bathroom, no wallet in the dead guy's pocket. No matchbooks with phone numbers written inside, no highball glasses with prints on 'em, no crumpled-up notes in the wastebasket. Mr. Silver's car is gone from the lot."

"Jake's a college professor," I said.

"So?"

"So," I said, "if he did have a beef with Sprague, and if he did end up killing him, Jake's smart enough, I think, not to do it in his own motel room."

"Smart enough to take the room under a phony name, pay cash, and smart enough to clean up afterwards, though, huh?"

I shook my head. "I don't know what to think, Roger."

"His son just died, you said?"

"Yes."

"What was his frame of mind?"

"What do you think?"

"Angry," said Horowitz. "Fired up."

"Not really," I said. "Like I told you, he was devastated, depressed."

"You said manic, too."

I nodded. "He had something to tell me. He was excited about it."

"He didn't give you a hint what was on his mind?"

"No."

"Who was he mad at?"

"Just himself," I said. "He was blaming himself. It was an automobile accident."

Horowitz looked up at the ceiling. "Suppose it wasn't."

"What do you mean?"

"Suppose it wasn't an accident. Or suppose the professor got it in his head that it wasn't."

"You think Jake decided it was Sprague's fault that those kids went off the road into the river and died?"

"Tragedies get people worked up," said Horowitz. "They latch on to some crazy idea and end up doing things they never did before."

"Mild-mannered professors turn into killers," I said.

"Sure," he said. "Seen it plenty of times."

"Do they turn into clever killers who remember to pick up after themselves?"

"Absolutely," he said.

I didn't say anything.

"Well, okay," said Horowitz after a minute, "if it wasn't your client, who, then?"

I shrugged. "From everything I could tell, Sprague was well liked by everyone out there in Reddington. He coached the kids' soccer teams, went into the schools, knew everybody. I've seen him with kids. Teenagers, Brian's friends. He was good with them. It was obvious they respected him. Hell, everybody seemed to like the guy, including Jake."

Horowitz blew out a quick, impatient breath. "I don't trust people like that," he said.

"No," I said. "Me, neither, actually."

"Guys like that generally turn out to be phonies."

"That's been my experience," I said. "Although Sprague didn't seem like a phony to me."

"When people figure 'em out, all of a sudden they've got enemies."

I nodded.

"Looks like that's what happened here, huh?"

"Somebody didn't like him," I said. "That's obvious."

"So who besides Professor Gold would kill him?"

"Maybe you should talk to Gus Nash."

Horowitz frowned. "What about Nash?"

I shrugged. "He and Sprague were friends." I told Horowitz

about seeing Sprague and Nash together at the police station the day after the accident and how a few days later Nash had bought me a drink. "I had the feeling neither of them wanted me snooping around," I said.

"Why not?"

"I don't know," I said. "I figured Sprague was just watching over his people, trying to help them heal after their tragedy. I got the impression he liked to be in control, didn't like the idea of some Boston lawyer sticking his nose into things."

"Hard to blame anybody for that," said Horowitz.

"You should talk to the day man," I said. "He's the one I spoke with on the phone yesterday. He checked Jake in. He might've seen something."

"We're looking for him as we speak."

"So when—?"

"The ME says he thinks it happened about forty-eight hours ago. Tuesday night sometime. When was that appointment you had with Gold?"

"Yesterday afternoon. He called me Tuesday."

Horowitz scratched his eyebrow. "Okay. He called you Tuesday, said he had something to talk to you about. Something that would blow your mind. Wanted to—how did you say it?—tie up some loose ends first. So you set up the meeting for yesterday. Wednesday. Except he didn't show up. Got his loose end tied up, all right. Then he disappeared himself." Horowitz shrugged. "The deed was done right there in Unit Ten." He let out a long breath, then pushed himself to his feet. "Well," he said, "you ain't much help, as usual."

"What about Jake?" I said.

"We'll find him." He arched his eyebrows at me.

I shook my head. "I don't know where he is or what his connection is to this."

"Would you tell me if you did?"

"Not without his okay. He's my client."

"Looks like he's your killer," he said. "You catch up with

74

him, you better bring him in." He sighed and pushed himself up from the chair. "Well," he said, "let's get outta here."

He opened the door and steered me outside. It was still snowing, and both of us turtled down into the turned-up collars of our topcoats. Several more official vehicles had pulled up in front. Their lights were flashing and their radios were squawking, and a cluster of gawkers had gathered on the sidewalk. Stop-and-go traffic was squishing slowly over the wet pavement of Route 9.

"Gonna be a long fuckin' night," mumbled Horowitz.

"What happens now?"

"Now we go looking for Professor Gold. You hear from him, you be sure to tell him I'd like to have a chat with him, okay?"

"Hey," I said. "I'm an officer of the court."

Horowitz grinned. "Don't you forget it, either."

NINE

Around noontime the next day—Friday—Sharon Gold called. "Brady," she said, "what in hell is going on?"

Her voice sounded hoarse and brittle, as if she'd been crying—or screaming—or maybe both—and might do so again at any moment.

"Sharon, listen—"

"Those two police officers just left," she said. "The one with that evil smile, and the pretty one, and they're asking these questions about Jake, and they won't tell me anything, and . . . and I just don't think I can do this anymore, Brady, I really don't. . . ." Her voice trailed away.

"Is your mother still with you?"

"She left a couple days ago. It was bad enough when Jake was here. After he left, I had too much on my mind. I couldn't stand her—her phony cheerfulness anymore. She was driving me nuts. I told her to go home. Told her I needed to be alone for a while."

"Let's have lunch," I said.

She was quiet for a moment. Then she said, "Lunch?" as if she weren't sure what the word meant.

"Sure. Name a place out there in your neck of the woods. I'll meet you. We'll have a nice lunch. We can talk."

"Today? Now?"

"Why not? It's lunchtime. I can be there in less than an hour."

She cleared her throat. "Well, okay. That would be nice. I'd like that."

Sharon told me how to find a place in Reddington near the campus where Jake taught. It was called Drago's. She said it was a bit pricey for the students, so it shouldn't be too crowded, and they even had a smoking section. I told her it sounded perfect. First one to get there would grab a table.

I walked in a few minutes before one. The place hummed with the muffled clink of dinnerware and the murmur of voices. Soft piano music came from hidden speakers. Chopin, it sounded like. Half a dozen men in business suits sat at a bar along the right-hand wall watching stock prices trail across the bottom of the muted TV. The dining section was separated from the bar by a front-to-back head-high partition. Leather-cushioned booths lined the inside walls. A row of tables along the windows overlooked a meadow that rolled away to a wooded hillside. There were white tablecloths and bunches of fresh flowers in little bud vases on each table.

A dark-eyed young hostess standing behind a podium smiled at me. I told her I was meeting Sharon Gold and gave her my name. She checked a list, smiled again, and led me to a booth toward the rear.

Sharon was sitting there twirling a glass of white wine around on the tablecloth. She looked up when I slid in across from her. She was wearing a pale green blouse with a thin gold chain around her throat. She'd tried some makeup tricks, but her eyes looked red and swollen and bruised, as if she'd spent more time crying than sleeping lately.

I told the hostess I wanted some coffee, then reached across the table and took both of Sharon's hands in mine. "Are you okay?" I said.

"Me?" She laughed quickly. "Well, let's see. My boy is dead, in the river somewhere, my husband has disappeared, my friend, our chief of police, he's apparently been murdered, and these detectives are asking me questions that make no sense whatsoever. Should I count any of that? Because if none of that counts, then, oh sure, I'm terrific."

I squeezed her hands. "I'm sorry," I said. "Stupid question. I'm a bumbler from way back."

She tried to smile. "That's okay. Thank you for caring. I really—"

She looked up, and a college-age waitress wearing a white blouse and a short black skirt slid a cup of coffee in front of me. "Would you folks like to order?" she said.

Sharon asked for a Caesar salad and another glass of wine. I ordered a cheeseburger, rare, and asked her to keep my coffee cup topped off.

When the waitress left, Sharon said, "Have you talked with Jake?"

I nodded. "He dropped by a few days ago, told me you guys had decided to split for a while, and—"

"He told you *what*?"

"You were separating."

"And did he happen to mention why were we separating?"

"Well, actually he said you, um, you two weren't getting along, had stopped talking to each other, and he felt you were blaming him for what happened to Brian, though he realized he might've been projecting, but either way . . ." I shrugged.

"Why would he tell you something like that?"

"It's not true?"

"He said we weren't getting along? Weren't talking?"

I nodded.

"That's . . ." She looked at me, smiled quickly, and shook her head. "I know I've been a total wreck. I was angry and bewildered and I wasn't much good to Jake. He was hurting as much as I was, I knew that, but I just didn't want to talk to him. I didn't want to talk to anybody, really, but especially not Jake.

79

Brian was so much like him, you know? Always had that same sad, frightened look in his eyes. But Jake and I, we were okay, I thought. Considering the circumstances, I mean. He tried to be sweet. I know he was feeling guilty. So was I. What parent wouldn't? But once in a while he'd hold me and try to talk to me. He kept insisting how we had to accept what had happened, that we had to get on with our lives. He was trying to help me get better. Maybe I wasn't always as receptive or appreciative as I should've been, and I don't think my mother being there made it any easier, but when he left I didn't understand it. It made no sense. It sure wasn't my idea."

"That's not exactly the way Jake explained it," I said gently.

"What?" she said. "You think I'm lying?"

"Different perceptions, probably. Why else would he leave like that?"

Sharon rolled her eyes. "Because he was planning to rent a motel room on Route Nine and assassinate our chief of police. Makes good sense to me."

I smiled. "Have you heard from him since he left?"

She shook her head. "Not a word."

"He didn't tell you where he was going?"

"He didn't tell me anything, Brady." She took a deep breath. "Whatever day it was. Sunday or Monday? Sunday, it was. . . . It's all such a blur lately. . . . Sunday morning we were sitting in the living room after breakfast. Mother had gone to church. Tried to get me to go with her, but I wasn't up to it. Somehow, religion . . ." She waved her hand. "Anyway, Jake started talking about Brian. He's good that way. He forces me to think about him even when I don't want to, keeps trying to make me talk about him, remember him. I knew what he was trying to do. He wanted me to accept it. That Brian was . . . is gone." She stared down at the tablecloth.

I nodded. "I understand."

She sipped her wine. "I think that's good," she said after a minute. "The way Jake forces me to think about Brian. It makes me sad—angry, sometimes, I guess, too. But it helps. Anyway, maybe I wasn't so receptive, and after a while he wandered upstairs. He did that a lot. Jake would go up to Brian's room and just sit there on his bed. Me, I can't stand to go in there. Too much of Brian in that room. It hurts too much. I keep his door shut. Don't want to be tempted to peek inside. But Jake spent a lot of time in Brian's room. The difference between us, I guess. Jake's a confronter. I'm more of an avoider. I know he was feeling that he hadn't been a very good father. They didn't do much of that father-son stuff, but he really wasn't a bad father. He loved Brian, and Brian knew it. Anyway, that morning he was up there for a long time. I got a little concerned, so I went up. Jake had left the door open, so I peeked in. He was lying back on Brian's bed with his hands under his head, just staring up at the ceiling. So I went back downstairs, and after a while, he came down. He had an overnight bag in his hand, and he told me he had to go somewhere, he'd be gone for a few days, he might not be able to call me, but he didn't want me to worry. He loved me, he said, and he'd be back. That was Sunday. I haven't heard from him since then. I didn't know what he was up to, but he told me not to worry, so I tried not to." She gave her head a little shake. "Then this morning when those two detectives showed up and—"

"Horowitz?" I said.

"Yes. And the female officer. I didn't get her name, but she was very sweet. They rang my bell, and when they showed me their badges, my first thought was Brian. Then they asked if I knew where Jake was, and I thought: Oh, no. Oh, God, no. Not Jake, too. I asked them what was wrong, and that man with the evil smile, he said nothing was wrong, they just wanted to ask me a few questions. As if they went around randomly asking questions when nothing was wrong. But they wouldn't tell me anything, Brady. They just wanted to find Jake. That's all they asked me about. And I told them the truth. That I had no idea where he was, that he'd left around noontime on Sunday, didn't tell me where he was going, and I hadn't seen or talked to him since then. That Horowitz man kept smiling like he didn't believe me, repeating the same questions over and over again, where's Jake, did he own a gun—a *gun*, for God's sake—and I kept asking him if Jake was all right, and all he'd do is smile. After a while he asked if I had a photo of Jake I could give them, which I did, and then they thanked me and left, and I know goddamn well something's wrong. . . ." And then the tears brimmed over and spilled down her cheeks. "I don't know if I can do this," she mumbled.

"*Does* Jake own a gun?" I said.

She shook her head. "Of course not. He hates guns. Jesus. Do *you* think he shot Ed, too?"

"I don't know," I said.

Sharon patted her face with her napkin, and a minute later our waitress arrived. She glanced at Sharon, then at me, frowned quickly, and put our plates in front of us. She gave Sharon a fresh glass of wine and replaced my empty coffee cup with a full one. "Can I get you something else?" she said.

Sharon shook her head.

"No," I said. "We're fine, thank you."

I doused my burger with catsup. Sharon picked up her fork, poked around in her salad, then put the fork down, picked up her wineglass, and took a sip.

"Sharon," I said, "I know Lieutenant Horowitz. If something had happened to Jake, he'd tell you."

"He would?"

"Yes."

"Would *you*?"

I nodded. "Of course I would."

"Okay," she said. "So has anything happened to Jake?"

"I . . . don't know. Not that I know of."

"*But?* I'm hearing a *but* in your voice."

"Sharon, look. Maybe it's better—"

"Tell me," she said.

"What did you hear about your police chief?"

She took another sip of wine, put it down, then dabbed at

her mouth with her napkin. "One of my neighbors called me this morning. Said she'd heard it on the news. Ed got murdered somewhere in Framingham. That's all I know. I guess that should be a huge shock. But after what's happened, I don't feel like I can even react to it." She bit her lip. "Wait a minute," she said. "You don't really think—?"

"Chief Sprague's body was found in a motel room on Route Nine," I said. "It's the room Jake was renting. He was using a false name. John Silver."

"A false name?"

I nodded.

She stared at me. "What about Jake?"

I shrugged. "He wasn't there. Neither was his car."

"So that policeman this morning with all his questions about guns, he actually thinks that Jake—?"

"Jake's the obvious suspect, Sharon. Horowitz wants to find him and talk with him. I guess he was hoping you could tell him where he is."

"Well," she said, "I don't know."

"You're sure?"

She held my eyes and nodded. "I would *not* lie to you, Brady."

"Of course you wouldn't. Do you have any idea why Jake would leave suddenly like that and go rent a room in a motel on Route Nine?"

"No. I've been trying not to let my imagination get the best of me. I don't think I want to know. I can't think of a good reason. A lot of bad reasons, but no good ones. I guess he just needed to be alone for a while. Away from me."

"He called me on Tuesday," I said. "He sounded excited, as if he'd learned something. He wanted to meet with me. We made an appointment for the next day, but he didn't show up."

"What could he have learned?" she said.

"I don't know. I was hoping you might have an idea."

"Well," she said, "I don't. Not a clue."

83

"It might be important."

"I know. But as far as I know, the only person Jake might've wanted to kill was himself."

"How did Jake and Sprague get along?"

"Get along? Like would Jake want to shoot him?" She laughed quickly. "They got along great. Jake liked Ed. Respected what he did. He coached Brian's soccer team. He was a good coach. The kids had fun playing for him. Ed really cared about kids. Jake appreciated that."

"That morning," I said. "Sunday. The day he left. Was anything different?"

"Different?"

"Did he mention Sprague?"

She shook her head.

"Did Jake say or do anything unusual? Anything that might explain why—?"

"Why he left?" She shrugged. "Not really. He went upstairs, and when he came back down he had a suitcase. Said he was leaving, and he left."

"Did he seem angry?"

"No. Sad, distracted, maybe. Depressed, I guess. We both were. But no, not angry."

"He stayed in Brian's room longer than he usually did, you said."

She shrugged. "It seemed like it."

"And you saw him lying on the bed."

"So?"

"I don't know."

"Before he went upstairs, did you have any sense that something was different?"

"No."

"Something bothering him? Other than . . ." I waved my hand.

She shook her head.

"So something happened upstairs."

"What could happen?"

84

"I don't know. Something to make him decide to leave."

"I assume he just got the idea he wanted to leave, that's all. He thought of it, and he lay down on the bed to think about it some more, and then he decided to do it."

"Sure," I said. "Maybe he'd been thinking about it for a while."

"Maybe," she said. "But if he had been, I didn't have a clue. I still don't. Not a clue."

While we were talking I finished my burger and Sharon emptied her wineglass. She hadn't touched her salad. The waitress appeared and asked us if we were finished. Sharon waved the back of her hand for the waitress to take away her salad and asked for another glass of wine. I asked for more coffee.

"I'm drinking too much," Sharon said after the waitress left.

"Is it helping?"

"Yes."

The waitress brought Sharon's wine and my coffee, and we lapsed into a silence that was not uncomfortable. I drank my coffee and smoked a couple of cigarettes, and Sharon sipped her wine. She kept touching the condensation on the outside of the glass, staring down into it, and I watched her, thinking how young and pretty she looked, too damn young to have to endure the sudden death of her only child and the strange disappearance of her husband, who was now a murder suspect.

When we slid out of the booth to leave, she grabbed my arm. "Geez," she said. "I maybe shouldn't've had that last glass of wine."

I helped her into her jacket, and she held on to my arm as we walked out.

"I'll drive you home," I said.

"I'm okay."

"Humor me, okay?"

She looked up at me and nodded. "What am I thinking? I'm not okay. Actually, I'm a little drunk. You're right."

"You must have a neighbor who'll bring you back for your car later."

85

"Sure. I've got lots of friends."

I unlocked the door to my car for her and held her elbow while she got in. Then I went around to the driver's side and slid in behind the wheel.

Sharon huddled against the door with her chin down on her chest. "I don't know if I can do this anymore," she mumbled.

"It's going to be okay," I said.

She turned her face away and looked out the side window. "You think so?"

"Yes," I lied. "I'm sure of it."

It took about ten minutes to drive from the restaurant to Sharon's house. I pulled into the driveway, turned off the ignition, and went around to open the door for her. She reached out her arm, and I took it to help her out. She leaned against me. "Don't let go," she said. "I'm feeling kinda woozy."

I helped her up the sidewalk and into the house. She went into the living room, dropped her jacket on the floor, and flopped onto the sofa. She closed her eyes and sighed deeply.

"I better make some coffee," I said.

"Good idea."

I went into the kitchen and got a pot brewing. Then I went back into the living room. "It'll be ready in a few minutes," I said.

Sharon nodded. She was lying on her back with her arm across her forehead. Her eyes were closed.

"Would you mind if I went up to Brian's room?" I said.

She waved her hand, then let it fall. "Go ahead."

"I'll be right back," I said.

Brian's bedroom was at the end of a short hallway. I opened the door and stood there in the doorway, overwhelmed for a moment by the realization that the boy who had slept virtually every night of his life in this room would never come back.

It had a sloping ceiling with two large windows looking out onto the backyard. A desk with a laptop computer and a printer, a chest of drawers, a wall-size bookcase, a twin bed, a bedside table, and a stereo system on a table against one wall. A collection of CDs was stacked under it. A big steamer trunk sat at the foot of the bed.

I knew what teenage boys' bedrooms looked like, and Brian's would've fooled me. No Jockey shorts or athletic socks lying on the floor, no torn posters of Twisted Sister or Michael Jordan or the Patriots cheerleaders on the walls, no baseball gloves or basketballs or skis or hockey sticks strewn around. Brian's room was neat and uncluttered, almost sterile.

In fact, the only indication that the room had been lived in was the pillow on the bed, which had a head-shaped dent in the middle of it. The head had been Jake's.

I opened the closet. Pairs of shoes, boots, and sneakers were lined up on the floor. Shirts and jackets and pants hung precisely on hangers—jackets on the right, shirts in the middle, pants on the left. Sweaters and sweatshirts, neatly folded, were stacked on the shelf.

I didn't know what I was looking for.

The chest of drawers held boxer shorts and socks and handkerchiefs and T-shirts. There were pencils and paper clips and rubber bands in the single desk drawer.

Brian's CD collection featured artists like Smashing Pumpkins, Rage Against the Machine, Jewel, and Janet Jackson, although there were a few by the Beatles and the Rolling Stones and Fleetwood Mac, too.

I studied the books in the bookcase. A completely eclectic collection—paperback mysteries and Westerns and sci-fi, some Hemingway and J. D. Salinger and Stephen King, a set of World Book encyclopedias, an atlas, a dictionary.

What had Jake seen that sent him off?

The steamer trunk at the foot of the bed was secured with a combination lock. When I knelt down to look at it, I saw that the rivets holding the latch were missing. I flipped the latch with my finger and the whole thing—lock and latch—lifted away.

Jake, I thought. Jake had jimmied it open.

If a boy had any secrets—and every boy has secrets—a locked trunk would be a logical place in which to keep them.

I imagined how it had been for Jake. Every time he came into Brian's room he saw this trunk, wondered what private stuff his son had kept locked in it, what the contents of this trunk might tell him about his dead boy, and he had to force himself to resist the temptation to pry it open.

He'd think about that trunk and the secrets it might reveal. It would haunt him. His son was dead. They hadn't known each other very well. At least that's how Jake saw it. And it was driving him crazy.

Finally he couldn't resist. He'd popped the rivets, forced it open, and lifted the lid. And when he did, he found something that caused him to pack a bag and move to a motel on Route Nine in Framingham, and that, in turn, had resulted in the execution of the local chief of police. Maybe at Jake's hand.

Far-fetched, Coyne.

Maybe not.

I lifted the lid of the trunk.

Blankets.

On top was a patchwork quilt. I took it out and put it on the floor. Under it was a brown Army blanket. I took it out, too. Another blanket, this one blue, and under it a crocheted afghan.

That was all.

I stared into the empty trunk, sat back on my heels, then looked in again. The bottom was a solid sheet of plywood. I tapped it with my knuckle. It made a hollow sound. I estimated the depth of the trunk from the inside, then looked at it from the outside. It looked like there was a space of three or four inches between that sheet of plywood and the bottom of the trunk.

I fished out my Buck pocket knife, slid the blade along the edge of the false bottom, and pried it up. It was quarter-inch plywood, and it wasn't nailed down. I got a finger under it and took it out.

Then I saw what Jake had seen.

At first I thought it was just a couple of handfuls of torn green-and-white paper. I scooped some up in my palm and looked closer.

It was money. Bills. United States currency. They'd been torn into scraps the size of postage stamps. Mostly tens and twenties.

It was impossible to tell how much ripped-up money was in the secret compartment at the bottom of Brian Gold's trunk. A few hundred, anyway.

What did it mean?

Jake had found this currency confetti and had asked the same question.

His answer had sent him to King's Motel in Framingham.

I shook my head. I was overreacting.

I put the money scraps back, then the plywood, then the blankets. Then I closed the lid the way I had found it and went back downstairs.

Sharon had rolled onto her side with her face pressed against the back of the sofa. She had kicked off her shoes and drawn her knees up to her chest. Her skirt had ridden up high on her slender legs. Her cheek rested on her hands and she was snoring quietly. She looked peaceful and vulnerable and young.

An afghan similar to the one in Brian's trunk was folded over the back of the sofa. I spread it over Sharon and tucked it around her.

The aroma of fresh-brewed coffee lured me to the kitchen. I poured myself a mugful and sat at the table.

Little gangs of titmice and chickadees and nuthatches were taking polite turns plucking sunflower seeds from the bird feeder that hung over the back deck. I watched them eat while the shadows lengthened in the Golds' backyard, and I sipped my coffee and waited for Sharon to wake up.

TEN

When I first came downstairs from Brian's room, I was eager to ask Sharon about the ripped-up money I'd found in the trunk. But the more I thought about it, the less I wanted to mention it to her. She'd insist on knowing what I suspected, how it explained Brian's accident, what it had to do with Jake's sudden departure, how it could be connected to Ed Sprague's murder.

I had no answers for her. It would only upset her and she'd start imagining terrible scenarios. She didn't need that.

I decided not to leave Sharon alone while she was still sleeping. I thought it would be better if someone was there when she woke up. Afternoon naps—especially those induced from drinking too much white wine on an empty stomach—can be disorienting and depressing in the best of times. But crawling up out of some vivid nightmare late on a Friday afternoon and finding yourself alone in a dark, silent, empty house when your only child has been killed and your husband has disappeared and the police are looking for him, suspecting him of murder, and with a long lonely weekend facing you . . . I couldn't let that happen to Sharon.

I figured it would be better if I was there with a mug of coffee and a smile for her when she woke up.

I kept going into the living room to check on her. This was no fitful nap. This was deep, sound sleep. Aside from the soft burble of her slow breathing and the faint rise and fall of her chest under the afghan, she wasn't moving. I figured she hadn't been getting much sleep lately.

At quarter of five she'd been asleep for nearly two hours and was showing no signs of waking up. I used the kitchen phone to call Evie's office.

"Glad I caught you," I said when she answered.

"Why are you whispering?"

"Long story," I said. "Wanted you to know that I'm tied up here and don't know when I'll be able to make it."

"Where's here?"

"Reddington."

"Snooping, huh?"

"Sort of. Things have been happening. I'll tell you all about it when I see you."

"Okay. Thanks for calling."

"I'll come over when I'm done here."

"No," she said, "that's all right. I'm totally wiped. Long day, long week, you know?"

"Honey—"

"All I want to do is go home, soak in a bubble bath, and go to bed. You do what you've gotta do."

"I'll probably be done here in an hour or two."

"Why don't you call me tomorrow?"

"Well, okay." I hesitated. "Are you all right?"

"I'm fine."

"I mean—"

"Brady, really," she said, "I'm very busy, and I just wanna get out of here. Call me tomorrow, okay?"

"Right," I said. "Have a nice evening, then."

"I expect I will. You, too."

When I was an adolescent, I had no problem understanding

women. My friends and I firmly believed that girls' moods were entirely explained by their menstrual cycles. If a girl was grouchy or teary or otherwise unfathomable, it was because it was her "time of the month." The girls did nothing to disabuse us of this idea. They used funny euphemisms like "I got the curse," or, "I fell off the roof."

Over the years, I've gradually learned that it's far more complicated than that. Now the only thing I understand about women is that I do not, can not, and never will understand what makes them tick, and if it's hormones, that's no help whatsoever, so there's no sense in trying.

I suppose that's progress.

I sat there at Sharon's kitchen table drinking coffee and trying not to decipher Evie's mood while darkness seeped into the backyard and the birds went to bed. After a while I turned on some lights and got another pot of coffee brewing.

It was close to seven o'clock when I heard Sharon mumble from the living room. I poured a mug of coffee and brought it in to her.

She was sitting up on the sofa. The afghan was still wrapped around her.

"Hi," I said.

She rubbed her face, then stretched. "Hi, yourself," she said softly.

"Here." I handed her the coffee. "Careful. It's hot."

She took the mug and held it in both hands. "Thank you." She bent her head to it and took a sip. "What time is it?"

"About seven."

"God," she said. "I haven't slept that well since . . ."

"I guess you needed it."

"Yeah," she said. "I guess I did." She patted the sofa beside her. "Sit with me, Brady."

I sat beside her.

She sat in the corner of the sofa wrapped in her afghan with her legs tucked under her. "I dreamed that I was lying here and Brian and Jake walked in," she said. "They were coming home from soccer practice. In my dream, Jake was the coach, and he and Brian were laughing and punching each other on the shoulder, and I was feeling terribly guilty that I didn't have any dinner ready for them, and . . ." She looked at me with big glittery eyes. "And I forget the rest of it. Maybe that was it. The entire dream. But I was thinking, 'Oh, Brian's still alive after all. The accident, it didn't happen. And Jake's back, too. They're both here, and everything's fine.' It was such a—a relief, Brady. I was so happy in my dream. And just now, when I woke up, for a minute there I was *still* happy."

I just nodded. There was nothing to say.

"It was better than the other dream I've been having," she said.

"Sharon—"

"In that one, I'm standing outside some building. It's like in a city, and there's all this traffic wooshing past right behind me, and there's a big plate-glass window, and Brian's inside the building, and he's pressed against the glass, clawing at it, trying to get out, and he's got this scared look on his face and he's yelling at me, except I can't hear what he's saying through the glass. And I start screaming at him, but no words come out of my mouth. And . . . and then I wake up."

I reached for her hand and squeezed it.

"Will it ever go away?" she whispered.

"Not entirely," I said. "But you'll learn to accept it. It'll take a long time."

"It's so strange," she said. "I can't tell what's real anymore. Sometimes I feel like I'm watching myself from high up in the sky somewhere, like I'm two people, and I can study myself and analyze myself. It's like I can look around corners and over hills, see what's there waiting for me before I get there, as if I could yell down to myself, tell myself to watch out. And then that faraway me zooms down into my other self, and the two of us merge, and then it's just me again, and I'm all alone."

"It might help to talk to somebody," I said.

94

She looked up at me and smiled. "I've got somebody," she said.

"Not me," I said. "I mean a professional."

"I like talking to you. You're my dear old friend. I trust you."

"Friends are important," I said. "But for someone who's been through what you've been through, professionals are important, too."

"Sure," she said. "You're probably right." She bent her head and sipped her coffee. "I'm kind of hungry. Should've eaten my salad, I guess. Are you hungry?"

"I'm getting there."

"I could make us some soup. Canned soup, I mean. Nothing fancy. I've got split pea, lentil, black bean, chicken..." She looked up at me and shook her head. "Geez, I'm sorry. You've probably got a date or something. It's Friday night."

"No," I said. "I don't have a date. Soup sounds good."

Sharon poured some Old Grand-Dad on the rocks from one of Jake's bottles for me and a glass of wine for herself. She dumped two cans of Progresso black bean soup into a pot and set it simmering on top of the stove. Then she sat down across from me at the kitchen table.

"So what'd you think of Brian's room?" she said.

I shrugged. "Typical boy's room, I guess."

"I always thought teenagers were supposed to be slobs," she said.

"Some are. I have two boys. One was a real slob and the other was just moderately slobbish."

"I only had one boy," she said.

I nodded.

"So I'm no expert on teenagers, I guess." She put her elbows on the table and rested her chin in her palms. "What did you see up there?"

"Nothing. Just a neat room."

"Since he was a little boy, he always vacuumed and took care of his own clothes and made his bed himself. He didn't like me and Jake going in there. He wanted to take care of it himself."

"Everybody likes privacy," I said.

"So you didn't figure out why Jake went away?"

I shook my head. "Like you said, he probably just decided he had to go away for a while."

"There doesn't have to be some big dramatic reason for everything, I guess."

"No," I said. "Some things just happen."

"They sure as hell do."

When the soup was hot, Sharon ladled it into bowls. She put a loaf of crusty French bread on a plate and sat down across from me.

We ate in silence for a few minutes. Then I said, "Do you know a girl named Sandy?"

She looked up at me and frowned. "Sandy who?"

"I don't know her last name. Heavy-set girl, black hair. I met her the day after the accident. She said she was a friend of Brian's. I thought maybe he'd brought her around sometime, or she was on his soccer team or something."

"Brian didn't bring his friends around much. He had a lot of friends, but he usually went to their houses. I don't know why. I'd tell him, I'd say, 'Why don't you have some friends over? Order some pizza or something.' He'd just shrug. 'Maybe sometime,' he'd say." She frowned at me. "Why? What about Sandy?"

I waved my spoon in the air. "Oh, nothing. I talked with her a little. She seemed bright."

Sharon put her elbows on the table and leaned toward me. "You think this Sandy knows something about Jake and what happened to Ed?"

I smiled. "No, Sharon. That seems unlikely. I guess I was just making conversation."

We had finished eating and Sharon was loading the dirty dishes in the dishwasher when the phone rang. The kitchen phone sat on the counter, and she picked it up and said, "Hello?"

Jake, I thought.

Sharon glanced at me, rolled her eyes, and said, "Oh, hello, Mother."

The phone was on a long springy cord. Sharon tucked it into the crook of her neck and finished putting our dishes into the dishwasher. Then she dampened a sponge and began wiping off the counters and table. Now and then she said, "Yes, I know," and, "He's fine," and, "Of course I'll tell him," and, "I don't think so," but mostly she just listened, and I couldn't help wondering if it really wasn't Jake, and Sharon was putting on an act for my benefit.

She talked—listened, really—for about ten minutes. When she hung up, she flopped into the chair across the table from me. "My mother," she said. "Calling from Wisconsin. She drives me nuts. She will not mention Brian. She's called me every day since she left, and not once has she given any hint that she knows anything's changed. She talks about her bridge games, her friends, her stupid cat, her television shows, asks after Jake as if she didn't know he'd packed his suitcase and gone away, and she just goes on and on, and she gets upset when I don't chatter right back at her."

"I was thinking it might be good if she'd come back to stay with you again," I said.

"Oh, God," she said. "I'd end up killing her."

"It's not good that you're alone."

"Jake will be back." She looked at me. "Won't he?"

There was no sense in reminding her of the fact that Jake was the prime suspect in a murder. "I'm sure he will," I said. "But in the meantime . . ."

"I can take a phone call from my mother now and then," she said. "That's about it. Anyway, I've got plenty of friends."

97

I nodded.

"Well," she said after a minute. "How about some tea or something? Or are you in a hurry?"

"No," I said. "Tea would be nice."

She brewed a pot of Lapsang souchong, and we took it into the living room to steep. Sharon fetched two bone china cup-and-saucer sets, poured the tea, and we sat beside each other on the sofa.

There was a photo album on the coffee table. Sharon picked it up and put it on her lap. "Jake took this out a week ago," she said. "Just left it here. He never said anything, but I know he was hoping I'd pick it up, look through it. It's full of Brian. I think Jake figured it would—would help me feel better. I've been thinking it would just make me sad. What do you think?"

"I think you're already sad."

She looked up at me and nodded.

"Why don't you show it to me?" I said.

She flipped it open. Brian had been a well-photographed child. There were pictures of Sharon lying in a hospital bed holding a tiny baby on her belly. She looked about sixteen in the picture. There was Brian crawling around in diapers, Brian pulling himself upright by holding on to somebody's pantsleg, Brian on a tricycle . . .

At first, Sharon just turned the pages silently, pointing to the pictures, smiling to herself. Gradually, she began telling me about them—the occasions when they'd been taken, what she remembered about those days, what Brian was like. He'd been a smart little boy, precocious, even. He began reading when he was four, and he could do subtraction before first grade. He'd always been a good student, very conscientious, well-organized. There was a photo of Brian pushing a lawn mower that was taller than he was, and Sharon said he'd started doing chores to earn an allowance when he was about six. He'd always been interested in making money. He was funny about it, so serious and frugal.

"He saved his money?" I asked.

"Oh, lord, yes," she said. "This is the boy who made his own bed and vacuumed his room. A very organized, sensible boy. He squeezed every penny." She laughed. "Just like Jake. Not like me, that's for sure. When he started getting an allowance—it was a quarter a week, I think—Jake got him a piggy bank. But Brian said piggy banks were stupid. Real banks paid interest. He was in first grade, and he wanted to earn interest."

So why, I thought, would he rip several hundred dollars' worth of bills into shreds and hide them in the bottom of a locked steamer trunk?

I watched Brian get older as the album pages turned. Brian on a merry-go-round, Brian at the beach, Brian dressed up in his first suit, Brian and his soccer team with Ed Sprague—the same photos I'd seen on the wall at the police station. There was even a picture of seven- or eight-year-old Brian shooting hoops in the driveway with me and Jake.

By the time Sharon turned the last page and closed the album on her lap, Brian had morphed from a bald-headed, toothless, red-faced newborn on his mother's belly into a slender adolescent boy.

Sharon leaned forward and carefully placed the album on the coffee table. Then she sat back on the sofa and sighed.

"You okay?" I said to her.

She turned her head, smiled at me, and nodded. "I like thinking about him. Jake's right and my mother is wrong. I think I need to remember him." She reached over and put her hand on my arm. "Thank you," she murmured.

"Nothing to thank me for."

We sat there quietly for a few minutes, and then Sharon said, "Do you want more tea?"

I glanced at my watch. "It's late. I better get going."

I stood up, and she did too.

She followed me to the front door and helped me with my coat. Then she put her hands on my shoulders, tiptoed up, and kissed my cheek. "I'm sorry for falling asleep like that," she said. "It was incredibly rude."

"Don't apologize."

Sharon had her hand on my wrist. She gave it a squeeze. "Thanks for everything, Brady. You're a good friend."

"Please be well," I said.

She smiled. "I will. I'm tougher than you think. Don't worry about me."

"You can call me anytime."

She smiled. "I know. I will."

I opened the door and had started to step outside when she said, "If you talk to Jake, you tell him I'm still here waiting for him, okay?"

"I'll do that," I said.

I got into my car and aimed it for Boston. The back roads of Reddington were dark, and I was filled with sadness for Sharon. I remembered her dream—Brian pressed against the glass, beseeching her, and Sharon on the other side unable to do anything, unable even to speak.

It was her vision of her boy under the ice, and at night, when her defenses were down, it was haunting her.

It would haunt her for a long time.

And I thought about my own boys, how far away they were and how I missed them, how I wanted to hug them and tell them I was glad they were alive.

And I thought of Evie. When I got home I'd call her, and my mind flipped to the music she liked to put on the stereo when she was feeling romantic, Ella and Duke and Count Basie and Sarah Vaughan, and I found myself humming "How Important Can It Be" . . . and when I noticed the blue light flashing in my rearview mirror, I had no idea how long it had been there.

ELEVEN

I pulled to the side of the road, and the cruiser pulled in behind me. His high beams and the blue lights from his roof bar were flashing in my eyes.

Normally he'd sit there running my plates through the cop computer to see if my car had been stolen or if I was wanted for violating the Mann Act or sticking up a liquor store, taking his time, enjoying the power of it, making me wait with those irritating lights reflecting in my eyes, fuming and rerunning old scenarios, remembering every damn speeding ticket I'd ever gotten, how officious and patronizing a patrolman could be, some smart-ass kid fresh out of cop school, and me an honorable attorney, for Christ's sake, an officer of the court myself . . .

But this time it didn't happen that way. He didn't pause to run my plates. He climbed out of his cruiser and came to the window beside me. He tapped it with his big flashlight, and I rolled it down.

He bent to the window, and I saw that it was the tall female officer I'd met at the police station the day after Brian's accident. V. Whyte, her nameplate had said.

"Mr. Coyne," she said, "would you mind following me?"

"Did I—?"

"You didn't do anything wrong, sir. Follow me, please."

I nodded. "Sure. Okay."

She went back to her cruiser, turned off all the flashing lights, and pulled out in front of me. I followed her for about a mile down the road and then into the parking lot of a small strip mall, now closed down for the night.

She stopped in front of a bank, and I pulled in beside her. She got out of her cruiser, opened the passenger door of my car, slid in beside me, and closed the door, dousing the dome light.

"What's up, Officer?" I said.

"It's Tory," she said. "Tory Whyte. I wanted to talk with you."

"About what?"

She was staring out the front window of my car. The dim night lights from the bank exaggerated the shadows on her face. "About what's been going on around here," she said.

"Why me?"

"Yeah, good question." After a minute, she turned and looked at me. "Believe it or not," she said, "I don't know who else I can trust, and I gotta talk to somebody. You're a lawyer, right?"

"Right."

"So I can trust you."

"Oh, we lawyers are eminently trustworthy."

She laughed quickly.

"This about what happened to your chief?"

"I don't know," she said. "I was hoping you could tell me."

"How did you know I was—?"

"We've been told to keep an eye on the Golds' house."

"In case Jake comes home?"

"Yes. I saw your car, ran your plates and remembered you, that you were a lawyer. So can I talk to you?"

"Sure."

"Confidentially, I mean."

"Yes. Consider me your lawyer."

"Good." She cleared her throat. "I can't make any sense out of this. Maybe I just need to get it off my chest. That accident?"

"The two kids," I said.

"Right. I came up with a witness."

"I didn't think—"

"Right. Exactly. The official word was, there was no witness. But I found one. He didn't actually see it happen, but he was heading south on River Road, and just before he got to the place where those kids went into the river, he saw this car coming at him, going like a bat out of hell. You understand?"

"This car your witness saw, it was headed in the same direction that Brian and Jenny Rolando were headed?"

"North. Right."

"So it could've been behind them, seen it happen, and it kept going."

"Maybe. The timing was right. Certainly worth tracking down. But there's something else." She hesitated, glanced out the window, then looked back at me. "I saw the car those kids were in. I was there when they dragged it out of the water. There was a big scrape along the driver's side."

"That car had crashed on the rocks, hadn't it?"

"Yes. But this was a different kind of scrape. And there was red paint in it. The kids' car was blue."

"You're saying they got sideswiped by a red car?"

"Yes. I believe that's what happened."

"And you think the car your witness saw did it?"

"I don't know that. But it's certainly worth a follow-up, wouldn't you say?"

"I would say that, yes," I said. "And I surmise there was no follow-up."

"No, there wasn't. Sprague read my report, thanked me, said he'd take care of it, and that was it."

"Did you mention it to him again?"

"Sure. Several times. First he told me that he was on top of

103

it, whatever that meant. Then he told me it was a dead-end, and I know damn well he didn't pursue it at all."

"What about the car? The one the kids were in? What happened to it?"

"Good old Ed, helping the dead girl's parents, he got the insurance company to settle the next day. It was a total, of course. So they took it away."

"If I might say so," I said, "you don't sound exactly enamored of your late chief."

"I'm not happy that he got murdered, if that's what you mean."

"But?"

She hesitated. "But nothing. Everybody's in shock."

"So who's running the show?"

"The DA is for now. He's going to appoint someone temporarily until they can find a replacement for Ed."

"Are you in line for the job?"

"Me?" She laughed. "Hardly. Reddington isn't ready for a female chief. No, I think Luke's got his eye on it."

"Luke—?"

"McCaffrey. He's been here the longest, put up with more of Ed's shit than anybody. Luke deserves it."

"How would you feel, working for McCaffrey?"

She shrugged. "It'd be an improvement."

"I do get the sense that you weren't a great admirer of Chief Sprague."

"Yeah, well, I try to keep personal things separate," she said softly.

I cracked my window, lit a cigarette, and said nothing.

After a minute, Tory said, "Yeah, okay, we had a thing, Ed and I. Shortly after I started here in Reddington. I knew it was stupid. Christ, screwing my boss?" She snorted a quick laugh through her nose. "Anyway, he got sick of me, and that was that. Back to business, on to the next conquest. He didn't let it get in the way of the job, I'll give him that. He treated me pretty much like he treated all the other officers."

"And how *did* he treat you and all the other officers?"

"Like we were stupid and incompetent. He told us what to do, and we did it. Anybody showed a spark of initiative, started to become popular with the kids or something, they were out of there."

"He fired them?"

"He got rid of them, one way or the other. Usually just made their lives so miserable they quit. A lot of cops have come and gone here in Reddington. I've been looking for something different practically since I got here."

"What about Luke McCaffrey?"

"Oh, Luke just hunches his back and does what he's told and doesn't complain. He just bought a house in town, got a pregnant wife, big mortgage. He's kinda stuck." She cranked her window halfway down and waved at my cigarette smoke. "Anyway, all that's irrelevant. The townspeople loved Ed. I guess they should. He was like everybody's big brother. Coaching his soccer teams, putting on his parties for the teenagers. Halloween parties, Christmas parties, last-day-of-school parties, Friday-night parties in the summer. It was like open house at the chief's. Sprague's Teen Center, people called it. They thought it was great. A place for kids to go, keep out of trouble. He's got about twenty acres, nice swimming pool, woods, pond, big barn."

"He sounds like the perfect small-town police chief," I said.

"Yeah," she said, "if you didn't have to work for him. Anyway, all that, my—my personal feelings about him, that's not the point."

"The point is," I said, "you think there was another vehicle involved in that accident."

"Yes."

"Are you thinking that it wasn't an accident?"

She let out a long breath. "I don't know. But regardless of whether it was an accident or—or on purpose—you've obviously got to find the person who was driving that other vehicle. Hit-and-run, leaving the scene of a fatal accident? Jesus."

"And Sprague ignored it."

"Covered it up, if you ask me," she said.

"And now he's been murdered."

"Yes."

"And Jake Gold, the father of the boy who was in that car, is the most likely suspect."

"I guess he is. Him or some other soccer dad."

"Your chief fooled around with the soccer moms? Is that what you're saying?"

"I told you," she said. "Everybody loved him."

"And you're thinking—?"

"I don't know," she said. "The accident, and then Ed getting murdered? I can't quite make sense out of it. But it sure doesn't seem like a coincidence to me."

"Me, neither," I said. "I've got a suggestion."

"What's that?"

"You should tell this to the DA. Gus Nash. He should know this."

She shook her head.

"Why not?"

"I don't like him."

"Who, Gus?"

She nodded.

"Why not?"

She shrugged. "Just, he and Ed were friends, and a couple times when Mr. Nash was here in Reddington, I caught him kinda looking at me funny. Like he knew something, like there was some joke, you know? I always thought Ed talked about me to him. Locker-room stuff."

"I can talk to Gus Nash if you want."

"You mean about that witness?"

"Sure."

"You'd have to tell him you heard it from me, right?"

"I'd have to tell him something."

"Don't. Please."

"But—"

She reached over and touched my wrist. "Just don't. Look, I'm sorry. This was stupid. I should just forget the whole thing. Those poor kids are dead, so what difference does it make?"

"Sprague was murdered," I said.

"I know," she said. "But they'll catch Mr. Gold, and then it will all be clear, and that will be that." She opened the car door, and when the dome light flashed on, I saw that Tory Whyte had been crying. "I'm sorry I bothered you, Mr. Coyne. Please. Just forget the whole thing. Okay?"

"I promised you I wouldn't tell anybody," I said. "And I meant it. But I doubt if I'll forget it." I took out a business card and handed it to her. "Call me anytime, okay?"

She nodded and put the card into her pocket. Then she handed me a card. "My pager number's there if you need me. I'll return your call."

When I got back to my apartment, I climbed out of my office clothes and into my sweats, poured an inch of Rebel Yell over some ice cubes, and took it out onto my balcony. The moonlight reflected off the harbor and lit up the night, and a spring-like breeze was huffing in off the water. It reminded me that Punxsutawney Phil had slipped out of his hole exactly three weeks ago, and he'd seen no shadow to scare him back in. March was less than a week away.

The air smelled salty and warm and promising, but I couldn't shake the spooky, jangled feeling I'd picked up that afternoon when I walked into Brian Gold's room and found the torn-up bills hidden in the bottom of his trunk.

Coincidences, I know, occur all the time. Things happen that make no sense, that have no cause or explanation or connection. They just . . . happen. But we human beings are uncomfortable with coincidences. It's our nature to crave explanations. That's why we call ourselves *homo sapiens*. We need to know. A child's first sign of intelligence is the word *why*. For every effect, we need a cause. When the cause isn't obvious, people who

107

are too lazy or too stupid to look beyond the obvious shrug and call it "fate." The concept of fate is sort of a poor man's explanation. It presumes some kind of orderly plan, however beyond our understanding that plan might be. Fate takes various forms—gods, or demons, or the alignment of the stars and planets. For those who believe in it, fate is infinitely preferable to coincidence.

Coincidence is utterly random. It unmasks a world of chaos, a world without sense or logic, an insecure, frightful world in which anything can happen to anybody at any time. By definition, there is no explanation for a coincidence.

The human drive to understand has produced religion and art and science. It has dragged us out of caves and into the computer age. When rational analysis doesn't give us answers to that primal "Why?" question, it drives us crazy.

I'm a rationalist. I don't believe in fate or astrology—or God, for that matter. I believe in explanations. When I can't find them, I assume it's because I don't know enough, and I try to learn more.

When it stumps me, I feel jangled and spooked.

So I sat there on my balcony, sipping my Rebel Yell and smoking cigarettes and trying to understand what was going on in the quiet little town of Reddington, where until three weeks ago a big news story was the score of the high-school basketball game.

Then two young teenagers smashed through the guardrail into the river and died, the chief of police was murdered in a Framingham motel room, and an English professor at the local college, who had paid a week's rent on that room, disappeared.

The dead boy had torn up several hundred dollars and hidden the pieces in a secret compartment in the bottom of his steamer trunk.

One of the local cops was so spooked—or frightened—that she spilled her guts to a lawyer she'd barely met.

Coincidences?

I refused to believe it.

Explanation? Cause and effect?

I thought hard about it. But I had neither science nor art nor religion for it, and I came up with nothing.

It was nearly midnight when I downed what was left of the melted ice cubes in my glass. I snapped my cigarette butt off the balcony and watched it spark its way down to the water below. Then I went inside. I put the glass in the sink, turned out the lights, and went into my bedroom.

I glanced at my answering machine. No messages.

I flopped down on my bed, bunched the pillow up under my head, and picked up the telephone.

It rang five times before Evie's machine picked up. "Hi," came that throaty voice of hers that never failed to make my stomach clench. "It's Evie. I can't come to the phone right now, but your call is important to me, so please leave a message and I'll get back to you, I promise." Then came a series of beeps. Then her tape began to roll.

I held the phone against my ear for several seconds, listening to the almost subsonic static. Then I clicked the OFF button. Still in the bathtub, probably. Evie had the habit of falling asleep in the tub. Or maybe she was already in bed. She always turned off the ringer on her phone before going to sleep.

I'd call her in the morning.

TWELVE

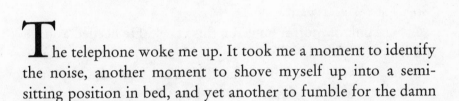

The telephone woke me up. It took me a moment to identify the noise, another moment to shove myself up into a semi-sitting position in bed, and yet another to fumble for the damn phone. The clock on my bedside table read 7:10.

No one but Evie would call me at seven on a Saturday morning.

"Hi, honey," I mumbled.

"Rise and shine, sweetheart." It was a sarcastic, masculine growl.

"Christ," I said. "Horowitz. What do you want?"

"I'm on my way over. I got coffee."

"Wait a minute—"

But he'd disconnected.

I pulled on my jeans and a sweatshirt and a pair of socks, went into the bathroom to splash water on my face, and by the time I got out to the living room, my intercom was buzzing.

I hit the button, and Horowitz thumped on my door a couple of minutes later. I opened it for him, and he brushed past me and headed for the kitchen, where he deposited two Dunkin' Donuts bags on the table.

He took two extra-large Styrofoam cups from one bag, pried off the tops, and pushed one toward me. "Black, right?"

"Right."

He ripped open the other bag. "Muffins," he said. "I got honey-bran, orange-cranberry-nut, and corn. Two of each. They're still warm."

"What a delightful surprise," I said. "This is awfully sweet."

"Fuck you," said Horowitz.

"Where's your partner?"

"I sent her home an hour ago, told her to get some sleep. You disappointed?"

"Choice between you and Marcia? Of course I'm disappointed." I put a tub of margarine, two mugs, two plates, and a stack of paper napkins on the table, then sat across from him. "So what do you want?"

A big hunk of muffin bulged in his cheek. He needed a shave and his eyes looked red and piggy. He held up a hand while he chewed and swallowed. Then he took a sip from the big Dunkin' cup. "I want Professor Gold," he said.

I poured my coffee into a mug and took a sip. "I don't know where he is."

"I been on this since Thursday night," he said. "Guy kills a cop, I get no sleep. How it always works. I need my fuckin' sleep. So what *do* you know?" He took another bite out of his muffin.

I told him about my talk with Sharon and about finding the ripped-up money in Brian's footlocker. I also told him that there might've been a witness to the accident.

"A witness, huh? Who told you that?"

"I can't tell you."

He blew out a quick, cynical laugh. "Fuckin' lawyers. Anyways, what's that got to do with anything?"

"I don't know. I also heard that Sprague might've fooled around with the soccer moms in town."

"Hmm," he mumbled. "Suppose you can't tell me where you heard that one, either."

I shook my head.

"So whaddya think, Coyne? Sprague was humping the professor's wife? That why he killed him?"

"No," I said. "I don't think anybody was humping Sharon Gold except her husband."

"I see it all the time," said Horowitz. "It's our number-one murder motive, hands down. Sex and jealousy. She's a good-lookin' woman. I been checking up on the victim. Sprague was the kind of guy women like, the way I hear it. One of those sensitive type of guys, you know? Bachelor, nice place out there in the woods . . ."

I shrugged. "Even if Sharon Gold was involved with Sprague, which I'm sure she wasn't, Jake isn't the kind of guy to go shoot him."

"What kind of guy he is don't mean shit," said Horowitz.

"I know," I said. "Maybe Jake held Sprague responsible for what happened to Brian. . . ."

"Yeah," said Horowitz. "That's good. But why? Why would he blame the chief? He ever say anything like that to you?"

"No. He told me he admired Sprague, considered him a friend. But maybe he got wind of that witness that Sprague didn't follow up on."

"There's your motive for murder, right there."

I shrugged. "Seems thin to me."

"Combine it with Sprague humping his wife."

"Sharon Gold wasn't humping anybody," I said, though as I said it, a worm of doubt wiggled into my mind. How well did I really know Sharon?

"I've been trying to connect all the dots, Roger," I said. "But I just don't see it."

Horowitz flashed his Jack Nicholson smile. "Of course you don't. I don't either. If one if us did, we'd be getting somewhere. That's why I bought this nice breakfast for you. See if the two of us could put our heads together, connect up some of them dots." He picked up a corn muffin, broke it in half, slapped on a big glob of margarine, and took a bite. "So, okay. Let's try again. These two kids drive into the river and die. Might've been witnessed. Might've even been another car involved. But as far as we know, the chief doesn't pursue it. Turns out, the boy had a pile of ripped-up money hidden in his trunk. The father finds it, runs off to fucking Route Nine, rents a cruddy motel room for a week, and next thing we know, the chief of police is dead in that room, and the professor's flown the coop. The fact that we don't see the connections don't mean there aren't any."

"I know," I said. "I've been trying to see them."

"We found Gold's car in the parking garage at Logan," he said.

"That's progress, I guess. I assume you're checking with the airlines."

He shrugged. "You know how tedious that is? Thousands of passengers every day."

"So you're not checking?"

"Of course we're checking. So far, zippo." He squinted at me. "My guess is he didn't fly anywhere. Left the car there to throw us off. Hopped in a cab or maybe had somebody pick him up."

"You saying he had an accomplice?"

"Makes sense, don't it?"

"But who?"

Horowitz arched his eyebrows.

"No," I said. "Not Sharon."

"Why not?"

I shook my head. "It just doesn't make any sense."

"Supposing the two of them blame Sprague for what happened to their son."

I nodded. "Interesting. But why would they blame Sprague?"

"That witness."

"I don't think so," I said. "They liked Sprague. Everyone liked him. When I was with Sharon yesterday, it was clear that she was very upset about what happened to him."

114

"Like maybe she *was* having a thing with him."

"No, for Christ's sake," I said. "Like any normal person would feel if a friend of theirs had been found shot to death in a motel room."

"Maybe she was just scared and guilty," he said. "Upset that way."

"I didn't read it like that at all."

He took a gulp of coffee. "I'm probably gonna have to drag her in, give her a proper interrogation. We went easy on her yesterday."

"She didn't exactly find you warm and sympathetic," I said.

He grinned humorlessly. "She ain't seen nothing yet."

"I doubt if you'll get anywhere playing the tough guy with her," I said. "Unless you're interested in upsetting a woman whose son just got killed in a car crash and whose husband has disappeared."

He shrugged. "Sometimes you gotta upset them."

"You'll do what you've got to do, Roger. It'd be nice if you could be a little sensitive to what she's trying to live with, though."

He waved the concept of sensitivity away with the back of his hand. "I'm betting she knows more than she's letting on," he said. "For starters, she's gotta have some idea where the professor would go."

"I spent the whole afternoon and evening with her," I said. "I don't think she knows anything."

"Sounds like she's got you bamboozled."

"I'm not above being bamboozled by pretty young women who are mourning the sudden death of their only son and the disappearance of their husband, all within a couple weeks. I admit it. But," I said, "if you're planning to question Sharon Gold as a suspect, I promise you she'll have her lawyer with her."

"That's fine with me," he said. "Whatever. Some of my best friends are lawyers." He grinned. "You better grab a muffin before I eat 'em all. Last thing I put in my stomach except for coffee was a fuckin' Big Mac last night sometime. I been burping ever since."

I picked up the last corn muffin and took a bite. "You're sure Jake killed Sprague, huh?"

"He takes the room under a false name, pays cash, hangs the Do Not Disturb sign on the door, and disappears after the deed. Sounds like a plan to me. Not a particularly sophisticated plan. But a plan." Horowitz shrugged. "It adds up to the professor, don't you think? Means and opportunity up the wazoo. We're still a bit speculative in the motive department so far, that's all."

"What about the gun?"

"It was a twenty-two. Long-rifle hollow points from about five feet away. Sprague was sitting right there in that chair where we found him when he got it. We figure the professor was sitting on the bed."

"Any way to trace the gun?"

"Nope. We find it, ballistics can match it up with the slugs they dug out of Sprague's chest. Otherwise it's not much help. The wife said Gold didn't have any guns."

"That's what she told me, too," I said. "She said Jake hated guns."

"Don't mean shit, of course."

"Of course."

Horowitz stood up and wandered over to the east-facing glass sliders. He stood there with his hands clasped behind his back, staring out at the harbor. "So whaddya think this homicide has got to do with that accident out there in Reddington?" he said, without turning to look at me.

"Damned if I know," I said.

"Gotta be a connection," he said.

I picked up my coffee mug and went over to stand beside him. The low-angled morning sun was streaming in on us, and puffy white clouds hung like balloons in the sky. It reminded me of the e. e. cummings poem—the one where the goat-footed balloonman is whistling far and wee and the world is mud-lucious and puddle-wonderful.

"It's just-spring," I said.

Horowitz turned and frowned at me. "Huh?"

I smiled. "A poem, that's all."

"Fuckin' Ivy Leaguer," he muttered.

We watched a tanker plow out toward the Mystic River Bridge and the gulls and terns wheel and swoop over the water.

"Jake called me from that motel," I said.

"Yeah, you told me that."

"He set up an appointment. Said he had something important to tell me."

"And he broke the appointment, right? So what?"

"I don't know," I said. "I'd like to know what he wanted to talk about."

"Yeah," said Horowitz. "Me, too. Tell you his plan, maybe."

"You really think he had the whole thing planned out?"

"How the fuck do I know?" he muttered. "I'm just trying to make scenarios. You're supposed to shoot them down."

"I don't see Jake Gold as a premeditated murderer," I said.

"Why not?"

I shrugged. "I've known him for almost twenty years. He's just not that kind of guy."

Horowitz snorted. "Compelling." He turned to me. "If he didn't premeditate it, what's he got a gun for? Why'd he call you?"

"We don't know he had a gun," I said. "I wish I could tell you why he called me."

Horowitz and I stood there looking down at the water and rehashing what we'd already talked about for another half hour or so. Neither of us came up with anything else.

My phone rang once, and I let the machine in my bedroom get it. Evie, probably. I'd call her as soon as Horowitz left.

Finally, a little after nine, he yawned and said, "We're goin' around in circles. I gotta go grab a nap."

"Sixteen ounces of coffee," I said. "You'll never sleep."

"Wanna bet?"

After Horowitz left, I went into the bedroom. The light on my answering machine was not blinking. Evie hadn't bothered leaving a message. She knew I'd call her anyway.

Which I did. And got her machine. She was probably in the shower. This time I left her a message. "Hi, honey," I said. "It's, um, nine-fifteen, and I'm here. It's the weekend. Time to play. Give me a call."

Then I took a shower, shaved, got dressed, made coffee.

Read the newspaper.

Did some laundry.

Ran the dishwasher.

Tied some flies.

Waited for the phone to ring.

It kept refusing.

At noon I tried Evie again. Got her machine again. Left no message.

Hmm.

I made myself a toasted cheese sandwich and ate it out on my balcony. It was a beautiful just-spring day. Not quite springlike enough to go fishing, but close. Damned if I was going to spend it sitting around my apartment waiting for the phone to ring.

I found Tory Whyte's business card where I'd stuck it in my wallet. I called her pager and left my number.

My phone rang twenty minutes later. "What's up?" said Tory.

"Can you talk?"

"No, sir."

"If I come out there, can we meet?"

"Yes. That would be fine."

"Where?"

"I go on patrol at two," she said.

"In front of the bank, two o'clock?"

"Make it two-thirty. Remember how to find it?"

"I'll be there."

THIRTEEN

I parked in front of the bank in Reddington at two-twenty. Five minutes later a black-and-white police Explorer pulled up beside me. Tory Whyte got out, opened my passenger door, and slid in beside me. She left the door of the cruiser open and the motor running.

The first thing she did was crank down the window beside her so she could hear her radio. Then she turned to me and smiled quickly. "We've gotta stop meeting like this," she said. "This is a small town. People will talk."

She wore tailored blue slacks and a short leather jacket with a fur collar over her blue uniform shirt and tie. She squirmed her hip against the car seat to adjust her revolver.

I hadn't seen her face very well in the darkness the previous night, and I'd forgotten how pretty she was.

"I just have a couple quick questions," I said.

"Go ahead."

"Do you know a local girl named Sandy?"

"Sandy who?"

"I don't know her last name. Heavy-set girl. Teenager. Black

119

hair. Looks dyed. She was a friend of Brian Gold and Jenny Rolando."

"Yeah, okay. That'd be Sandy Driscoll. What about her?"

"I want to talk with her."

"About what?"

I waved her question away with the back of my hand. "Any way I can get ahold of her?"

"I know she works at the camera store. She's probably there now." She looked at her watch. "They're open till five-thirty on Saturdays, I believe. Know where the camera store is?"

"I pass it on the way back to town, right?"

She nodded and pointed. "Just a mile or so up that way. It's on the left."

"One more thing," I said.

"Yes?"

"Where did Sprague live?"

"Big old fix-me-up farmhouse on the north side. Why?"

I shrugged. "Just wondering. Tell me about it."

"It was one of those handyman specials when he bought it, oh, ten or twelve years ago," she said. "He did a lot of work on it. Paid the local kids to help him in the summers. He knew about things like carpentry and masonry. Ed knew about a lot of things." Tory glanced sideways at me. "Nice big old barn, fifteen or twenty acres abutting the pond. He always had an open house around the holidays. Most of the town would show up. Used to have cookouts and swimming parties for the kids in the summer, square dances in his barn in the fall, things like that. This town doesn't have much for teenagers to do, and Ed tried to make up for it."

"Quite a guy," I said.

"Oh, yeah," she said. "Quite a guy, all right."

"So how do I find his place?"

"Look," she said. "I'm not sure—"

"You're not involved, Tory. But if you don't want to tell me, that's okay."

"Why do you want to know?"

120

"I'm just a snoopy kind of guy."

She smiled. "Everybody knows where Ed lived." She gave me the directions. It didn't sound complicated.

"I've been thinking I never should've stopped you last night," she said.

"I'm glad you did."

"Yeah, well, I think I might've opened a can of worms."

"Who, me? That's not a very flattering metaphor."

She smiled. "I didn't mean it that way. It's just, sometimes it's better to keep your mouth shut, let things play out."

"And sometimes keeping your mouth shut is irresponsible," I said.

"I don't even know you."

"I hope you trust me."

"I hope I can," she said. "See, the problem with opening a can of worms is, once they crawl out, you can never convince them to crawl back in again."

I reached over and took her hand. "Look, Tory," I said. "I'm not one of those hot-shot, fast-talking, big-money lawyers. I don't perform miracles. In fact, most people would probably say I'm a pretty average attorney. I'm only really good at one thing. Discretion. My clients trust me. I keep my word. Always. I am discreet and fair and honest, and for some reason, a lot of people seem to value that in their lawyer. All I'm saying is, I promised you I'd keep you out of it, and I will."

"Truly?"

"Truly," I said.

She reached over, gave my hand a quick squeeze, opened the car door and slid out. Then she bent down and peered in at me. "Happy snooping," she said. "Be careful, okay?"

I let Tory pull out of the lot before I started up my car. Then I headed back toward town, and a mile or so down the road on the left I spotted the Reddington Camera Shop.

I pulled up in front, got out of my car, and went inside.

Sandy Driscoll was down at the end of the counter, which ran the length of one wall. No one else was in the store. She was bent over with her back to me, and it looked like she was checking some things on the shelves. A cordless telephone rested facedown on the counter.

I stood there for a moment, then cleared my throat.

She whirled around, then rolled her eyes and smiled. "Geez," she said. "You scared me. Hang on a sec." She picked up the phone and said, "I'm sorry, it's not back yet. It should come in on Monday. Check sometime after noon, okay?"

After she clicked off the phone, she put both elbows on the counter, propped her chin in her hands, and frowned at me. "I know you, don't I?" she said.

"It was a few weeks ago. You were tossing daisies into the river."

She nodded. "Oh, right. What's up?"

"We were having a conversation. I don't think we finished it."

"What were we talking about?"

"Brian and Jenny. You were starting to tell me why they'd packed their clothes, where they were going."

Sandy glanced around. "Look, mister—"

"Coyne. Brady Coyne. I'm the Golds' lawyer."

"Right," she said. "Well, Mr. Coyne, I don't know what great story you thought I was gonna tell you, but the answer is, I didn't have anything to say then, and I still don't."

"Why?"

"Huh?"

"Why won't you talk to me?"

"I am talking to you."

"So tell me about Brian and Jenny."

"They died." She shrugged. "Everybody's trying to deal with it."

"There's more to it than that," I said. "And I think you know it. I think if Chief Sprague hadn't shown up when he did, you would've told me what you know. So now that he's dead—"

"I don't know anything," said Sandy quickly.

122

"You knew that those kids had packed clothes to bring with them. How did you know that?"

She shrugged. "Heard it, that's all."

"From whom?"

"I don't know. It's what people were saying, I guess."

I put my own elbows on the counter so that I was looking straight into Sandy's eyes. "It's *not* what people are saying," I said. "Those two duffel bags with clothes in them, the police didn't tell anybody about them. That day when I met you by the river, your chief of police told me they hadn't even told Brian's and Jenny's parents about those clothes. But you knew."

Sandy straightened up, turned her back on me, and pretended to examine the shelves behind the counter. "So what if I did know?" she said without turning around. "What difference would it make? Brian and Jenny are dead."

"Then why lie to me about it?"

She turned to face me. "Why shouldn't I?"

"Because your chief of police is dead now."

"What's he got to do with it?"

"I don't know. You tell me."

She shrugged. "Ed was our friend."

"He was murdered. What do you think of that?"

"What kind of stupid question is that?"

I nodded. "Okay, sorry. Look. All I'm trying to do is ease the mind of a couple of grieving parents, help them get on with their lives. They still have questions about what happened. Not finding Brian's body—that's been awfully hard for them. Jake and Sharon Gold are dear old friends of mine. I've known Brian from the time he was born. Do you know his parents?"

Sandy shook her head. "Not really."

"Brian's mother—Sharon is her name—she keeps having this dream," I said. "In Sharon's dream, she's standing outside a big plate-glass window and Brian's on the other side. His face is pressed against the glass, and he's clawing at it as if he's struggling to break through it, and he's calling to his mother. But she can't hear what he's saying, and when she tries to call back to him, the words stick in her throat. No matter how hard she tries to call to her boy, she can't make a sound. She wakes up crying. She's afraid to go to sleep, because she knows she's going to have that terrible dream, and she thinks she's going to have that dream for the rest of her life."

Sandy was staring at me. "Like he was trapped under the ice," she whispered.

I shrugged.

"That's an awful dream," she said. Her eyes were glittery.

"All I want," I said, "is to help Brian's mother get rid of that dream."

She brushed the back of her hand across her eyes. "I just can't—"

A bell jingled, and Sandy lifted her head quickly and looked over my shoulder.

I turned. An elderly woman had come into the shop. She was limping toward us with the aid of a cane.

"I got a customer," Sandy said.

"I'll wait," I said.

"Would you mind waiting outside?"

"Okay." I turned, smiled at the old woman as I passed her, and went out. I stood there on the sidewalk by the door and lit a cigarette.

The old woman came hobbling out a few minutes later. She nodded to me, then climbed into an ancient Jeep Wagoneer and drove away.

I shaded my eyes and peered into the camera store. Sandy was pacing back and forth behind the counter talking on the telephone. She was frowning and waving her hand in the air.

I continued to wait outside. After a while, Sandy tapped on the inside of the glass door and beckoned me in.

I went in.

Sandy stood there by the door. "I can't talk with you any-more," she said. "I got work to do."

I nodded. "I'm sorry I bothered you. I guess I was mistaken. I thought you might want to help ease the pain of some very nice, very sad people."

She blinked. "That's so unfair."

"Is it?"

She shook her head. "I can't," she whispered. "Please. Just leave me alone."

"That day by the river," I said. "I gave you my business card. Do you still have it?"

She shook her head.

"You lost it?"

"I—I threw it away."

I took out another card and put it on the counter. "Don't throw this away," I said. "You might change your mind."

She didn't look at the card. "Please," she said. "Just go away."

"Promise me you'll keep my card."

"Sure, fine," she said. She picked it up, glanced at it, and put it into her pocket. "Okay?"

"Thank you." I held out my hand to her.

She hesitated, then shook it quickly.

I turned and started for the front of the store.

"Hey, Mr. Coyne," said Sandy.

I stopped and looked back at her.

She hesitated, then shook her head. "Nothing," she said.

I sat in the front seat of my car outside the Reddington Camera Shop and smoked a cigarette. Terrific work, Coyne. Subtle. Intimidating teenage girls. Right up your alley, Counselor.

I couldn't figure out whether that was one step above ambulance chasing, or several steps beneath it.

It was all Evie's fault. I should have been spending this pleasant late-winter Saturday with her, minding my own business, intimidating nobody.

Except Sandy Driscoll knew something, and she was afraid to share it. It wasn't Sprague she was afraid of. He was dead.

Who, then?

Whom had she called on the telephone while I was waiting outside?

I finished my cigarette and flicked the butt out the window. It was almost three-thirty. There were still a couple of hours of daylight left.

I started up the car and headed for the house where the murdered chief of police had lived.

FOURTEEN

Tory Whyte's directions were good, and I found the long, sloping gravel driveway off the two-lane country road in the northwest corner of town. Sprague's driveway was bordered by a scrubby oak-and-pine forest on one side and a lumpy meadow on the other. Old snow blanketed the shaded ground under the pines, but the meadow had been swept clean by the wind. The driveway was made for a four-wheel-drive vehicle. In the spring when the ground thawed I wouldn't even try it in my BMW, but now it was solid under my wheels. It curled down and around the slope for about a quarter of a mile before it stopped at a turnaround in front of Sprague's house.

It was a typical nineteenth-century New England farm-house—white clapboards, an L-shaped porch across the front and one side, fieldstone foundation, three chimneys, bow window, a couple of oddly shaped dormers. Several rocking chairs were lined up on the porch, and some old-fashioned lightning rods sprouted from the peak of the roof. It looked like it had been painted fairly recently. Azaleas and rhododendrons, now dormant, grew against the foundation.

To the right of the house was a kidney-shaped in-ground

swimming pool. It had been drained for the winter. Beyond that was a fenced-in thirty-foot square of raw earth covered with hay, which I assumed had been Sprague's vegetable garden.

A big wooden barn with a tin roof stood off to the left. The sides had been left to weather naturally.

Ed Sprague interested me. He seemed to have been one of those people who are good at everything, the kind of guy who was captain of three varsity sports and president of his high school class, the boy most likely to succeed who'd grown into a man who inspired the admiration and respect—love, even—of those who knew him. He was smart and friendly and energetic. Too good to be true. A perfect human being.

Too good, it occurred to me, to be satisfied with being chief of a tiny rural police force. I've never known a perfect human being. I don't believe in them.

Neither did Tory Whyte. According to her, Chief Sprague preyed on his female underlings and tormented all of his officers.

Anyway, somebody had murdered him. That made at least one person who didn't admire, respect, and love him.

I climbed the three steps onto the porch, shielded my eyes with both hands, and peered in through the windows. The living room featured exposed beams, wide-plank flooring, a scattering of braided rugs, and a big fieldstone fireplace flanked by floor-to-ceiling bookcases. All the furniture was early American. I couldn't tell whether they were authentic antiques or good replicas, but either way it was tasteful and understated and expensive-looking.

The kitchen was modern, all stainless steel and inlaid tile and white birch. A beehive oven dominated the inside wall, and bunches of strung garlic and dried herbs and copper-bottomed pots and pans dangled from the center beam.

I wandered over to the barn. Probably where Sprague kept his car, maybe a riding mower and a snowmobile and a motorcycle. The only windows were high up under the peaks, and both the big sliding door in front and the regular-size door on one side were padlocked.

I went back to the house and sat on the front steps. It was a pretty spot Sprague had here on a little plateau about halfway down the gentle hillside. He'd cut away enough trees to open up a view of his pond, which was down in a little tree-rimmed bowl and now covered with ice. Plenty of seclusion and privacy for the chief of police when he wanted to get away from it all, and a good place for crowds to gather when he wanted company.

It was the kind of place where I'd like to live. I'd thought about getting the hell out of the city a million times, and when I did, I imagined a place very much like this. Trees and birds and fresh air, and my own pond a five-minute walk from my front door. I'd keep an old rowboat down there. No motor. Just a pair of oars and creaky oarlocks. There were probably bass and pickerel in that pond. Hell, I could stock it with trout.

I lit a cigarette. Okay, so Chief Sprague had himself a heavenly little spot out here in the country, and from all outward appearances, he kept it well maintained. Now what?

Now I should turn around, drive back to Boston, and call Evie. It was Saturday.

And if she didn't answer her phone, then what?

It took me five minutes to find the front door key. Just about everyone I know who lives in the country hides a spare house key somewhere. Under a doormat, in a flower pot, wedged under a shingle, on the ledge over the door.

Sprague had kept his under the cushion of one of the rocking chairs on the porch.

I unlocked the door, then returned the key to its hiding place. If anyone caught me inside, I'd say I'd found the door unlocked. That would eliminate the "breaking" half of a B and E charge.

I had no idea what, if anything, I was looking for. I just

wanted to get a feeling for Ed Sprague. Oddly enough, I didn't feel the slightest bit guilty, entering Sprague's house uninvited. He was dead. He wouldn't mind.

Furtive, maybe. It pumped some adrenaline. I liked the feeling.

Ed Sprague's living room reminded me of his office at the police station. Comfortable furnishings, outdoorsy paintings on the wall, big fireplace, lots of books. Tasteful and homey.

So was the kitchen. It appeared that Sprague liked to cook. There were two shelves of cookbooks, lots of utensils and machines, well-stocked cabinets and refrigerator.

He had a small office on the first floor off the living room. No early-American stuff here. This room was dominated by a two-wall L-shaped teak desk that was tangled with electrical cords and covered with computer hardware—a new top-of-the-line Apple Macintosh with a nineteen-inch monitor, a big box-shaped color printer, two scanners, and a few other mechanical gizmos I couldn't identify. Three digital cameras and two laptop computers sat on one shelf. Another shelf was crammed with CDs and boxed software. I'd never have guessed that Ed Sprague was a computer nerd.

A three-drawer metal file cabinet was unlocked, and I paged through everything. Sprague had been a meticulous record-keeper. He kept copies of bills and tax documents and insurance policies and mutual-fund statements and mortgage payments going back ten years. I added and subtracted the numbers in my head, and they were about right. Reddington paid him pretty well, and he seemed to have been living within his means.

There were two bedrooms upstairs, a small one and a big one. The small one was a spare, furnished with twin beds. The big one, which was about the size of his living room, was apparently Sprague's. King-size bed, neatly made, bedside table with an alarm clock and lamp, a pair of upholstered chairs with a pair of blue jeans lying over the back of one of them. Floor-to-ceiling bookshelves lined the wall at the foot of the bed. A big television and some audio equipment occupied several shelves. A small writing desk stood under a window.

The closet held police uniforms and suits and pants and shirts, with well-shined shoes lined up on the floor. Underwear and socks and sweaters lay neatly folded in the bureau.

No suspicious prescription drugs in either of the two back-to-back upstairs bathrooms or in the downstairs half bath.

The cellar had a dirt floor and two unshaded lightbulbs. Nothing down there except the oil burner and a big stack of firewood and a few old wooden chairs.

I went outside, fetched the key, locked the door, put the key back under the cushion, and sat in the rocking chair. I lit a cigarette and put my feet up on the rail. I'd spent a little more than an hour searching Sprague's house, however ineptly, and I'd learned nothing.

I was, in fact, quite impressed with how much I had not learned. Ed Sprague's place was clean and neat and utterly un-revealing.

Something kept nagging at me, though, and after a few minutes of smoking and rocking, I figured out what it was.

Nobody's perfect. Call me a cynic, but I don't believe there's a person on earth who has absolutely no secrets. A one-hour search of any normal bachelor's house—even by an amateur snooper such as I—would turn up something. Love letters from a married woman, pornographic magazines or videos, a carton of empty vodka bottles, a baggie of weed, a collection of Uzis, a drawer full of women's lingerie, a stash of hundred-dollar bills.

I kept my old *Playboy* magazines in a desk drawer—in case I wanted to reread the stories.

So where did Ed Sprague hide his secrets? In his office? On his computer? In a safe-deposit box?

Any of those places was safe from me.

The barn, maybe. I hadn't checked there yet.

I pushed myself up from the rocker, flipped away my ciga-

131

rette butt, and walked over to the barn. Both doors were pad-locked. Maybe Sprague had kept a key hidden somewhere, but I had no idea where to start looking for a barn key.

I followed a rutted old roadway around back and saw that this barn had originally been used for cows or horses. The ground sloped acutely away from the back, leaving a garage-door-size opening underneath. The hay and manure that the animals left on the barn floor would be swept through a hole down onto the ground underneath, and a truck could back up to this opening to lug it away and spread it on the gardens. Those old Yankee farmers knew all about recycling.

I stepped into the opening under the barn. It had probably been half a century since animals had lived upstairs, but down there I could still detect the faint, moist aroma of old manure. Not an unpleasant aroma, actually.

In the day's gathering gloom, it was pitch dark.

I went back to my car, got a flashlight from the glove com-partment, returned to the back of the barn, and went in.

I shined my light around and saw a ladder going up to the opening in the main floor of the barn. I squished my way across the cushiony layers of old manure and rotten hay, and as I placed my foot on the bottom rung of the ladder, my flashlight picked up something shiny way in the back corner of this big space under the barn.

I went over there. It appeared to be a vehicle of some kind. A tarpaulin had been thrown over it. My light had caught the reflection from a chrome bumper where the corner of the tarp had pulled away.

I lifted a corner, hesitated, then pulled off the tarp.

It was a mud-spattered red Jeep Cherokee, no more than a year or two old. Sprague, I assumed, had driven it here, as far out of sight as he could get it, and had then covered it with this tarp.

He'd hidden his car.

Why?

I shined my light around the inside of Sprague's Jeep. Aside from a few Coke cans and some McDonald's and Dunkin' Donuts trash on the floor on the passenger side and a couple of paperback books on the backseat, it was empty.

I started to walk slowly around it.

When I got to the front, I stopped. The fender on the passenger side was smashed in, and my flashlight revealed a long, deep dent extending halfway along the passenger side. The Jeep's red paint had been scraped away. I looked closer and saw a few smudges of blue paint.

Tory Whyte's witness had been right. There had been another vehicle there when Brian and Jenny went into the river.

And Chief Ed Sprague had been driving it.

It had been a hit-and-run. Tory's suspicion about that had been on target, too. Sprague had sideswiped those kids. Had he been drinking? Just driving too fast, the way cops sometimes do? Trying to pass those two kids on a narrow road, cutting it too close?

Whatever. Sprague had panicked and kept going. Then he'd hidden his car in a place nobody—except a snoopy Boston lawyer—would think to look.

No wonder Sprague had refused to follow up on Tory's witness. If he had, that witness, under careful questioning, might have been able to describe Sprague's red Cherokee.

Jake had somehow figured it out. That's what he'd been so excited about when he called me from Unit Ten at King's Motel on Route Nine.

He'd been right. It *would* have blown my mind.

I figured Jake had intended to tie up all the loose ends and bring them to me. He'd probably invited Sprague to his motel room, expecting a sorrowful confession.

Sprague had showed up. And then what happened?

Then Jake murdered him.

My first impulse was to jog back to Sprague's house and use his phone to call the cops.

My second, stronger impulse was to finish what I'd started. There was a whole barn to explore. Another hour wouldn't make any difference. Sprague's Cherokee wasn't going anywhere.

So I climbed up the ladder, pulled myself up through the opening, and found myself standing in the middle of the barn floor.

I shined my light around and saw that the barn had originally been for horses. Narrow stalls with shoulder-high doors lined one side. At the front end of the barn was an open stairway leading up to the hayloft.

The rest was a big open space with a rough plank floor. It was big enough to store reapers and threshers and mowers. Big enough for a square dance.

The odor up here was much more intense than down below where the old manure and hay were moldering.

This was a different odor—fresher and sharper and more nauseating.

In fact, it was almost overpowering.

One winter back in my married days when I was living with Gloria in our house in Wellesley, we were invaded by field mice. They left their droppings in the kitchen cabinets and behind the refrigerator and on the pantry shelves. When Gloria started finding mouse turds in the silverware drawer, she threatened to move out unless I got rid of the little buggers. So I baited some old-fashioned springloaded snap traps, and in a couple of nights I slew half a dozen of the poor critters.

A few days later, Gloria began complaining about an odor in the pantry. At first, I couldn't smell it. But it kept getting stronger, and after a week it was unbearable.

I eventually found the dead mouse up under the heating unit, where he'd dragged himself to die, along with the trap that had snapped down across his back.

This odor in Ed Sprague's barn reminded me of that dead mouse. Except this was worse.

I covered my mouth and nose with my handkerchief and started shining my flashlight into the stalls.

I found the body in the second stall from the front.

FIFTEEN

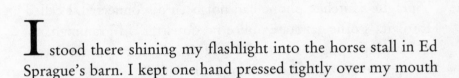

I stood there shining my flashlight into the horse stall in Ed Sprague's barn. I kept one hand pressed tightly over my mouth and nose.

It was a man's body, and it was hard to look at.

He'd been dead for a while.

He wore pants but no shirt. His skin was bloated and grayish green. He was sitting in a wooden armchair. His ankles were tied to the legs and his wrists were bound to the arms. A rope around his chest held him upright. His chin was slumped down on his chest so that I couldn't see his face, but I recognized him by his thick thatch of curly gray hair.

Sour bile rose in my throat. I swallowed it back and forced myself to kneel in front of him and shine my light on his face.

Jake Gold's cheeks, throat, neck, and chest were covered with round black scabs. His left eye was gone, leaving a socket full of crusty dried blood. The blood had run down his face, off his chin, and onto his shoulder and chest.

His wrists, where they were tied to the arms of the chair, had swollen around the baling wire that held them there. It looked like his hands would explode if you poked a needle into them.

I turned my head and puked on the floor.

I shined my flashlight away from Jake and knelt in front of him. I felt that I should say something comforting to him, but no words came to me.

After a minute or two, I stood up and got the hell out of there. I went back down the ladder, and when I got to the bottom I took a deep breath. The musky smell of old manure cleansed my lungs and throat. It was a relief.

I went over to the house and sat on the front steps. I hung my head between my knees and took several long, deep breaths. I didn't want to puke again.

After a few minutes I thought I had it under control.

I smoked a cigarette before I retrieved the key from under the cushion and went into the house.

Sprague's kitchen phone had not been disconnected. I called Horowitz's office at state police headquarters in Framingham.

"I am reporting a murder," I told the woman who answered. "I've got to speak to Lieutenant Horowitz."

"What's your name, sir, and where are you calling from?"

"My name is Brady Coyne. I'm an attorney. Find Horowitz and patch me through to him. I'll wait."

"Tell me where you are, sir."

"I know you can trace this call and figure it out eventually. But please trust me, Horowitz will have your ass if you don't find him and put him on."

"Just a minute."

I waited nearly five minutes before Horowitz said, "Okay, Coyne. What's this about a murder?"

"I'm at Ed Sprague's house in Reddington. Jake Gold's dead body is in the barn. Not only that, but—"

"Sit tight."

"Wait a minute—"

But he'd disconnected. Typical.

I sat on the front steps, and ten minutes later I heard sirens. Then a squad car crested the rise and came down the long driveway with its blue lights flashing. It crunched to a stop in front of the house, and a uniformed officer climbed out. The cruiser was one of the Reddington PD Explorers. The cop was Tory Whyte.

I wondered if I should pretend we hadn't met, but she came over to where I was sitting, looked down at me, and said, "Hello, Mr. Coyne."

I smiled up at her. "Hi, Tory."

Then another uniformed officer got out of the cruiser and came over. It was the big redheaded guy. McCaffrey. "You know this man?" he said to Tory.

She nodded. "It's okay," she said. "He's a lawyer."

"That makes it okay?" McCaffrey looked at me and smiled. Then he wandered back to the cruiser.

"We're just supposed to baby-sit you until the state police arrive," said Tory. "Make sure you don't get away."

"I'm not going anywhere."

"Feel like talking about it?"

"No," I said. "Thank you."

She sat on the steps beside me. I smoked another cigarette, and we both stared down toward the pond. A few minutes later another Reddington PD cruiser pulled in, and Gus Nash got out from the passenger side. He came over to where we were sitting and jerked his head at Tory. "I want to talk to him," he said.

Tory stood up, flashed me a quick frown—a reminder of my promise to her—and went over to her cruiser.

Nash stood in front of me with his arms folded over his chest. He looked down at me and shook his head. "So what in hell are you doing here?"

"Snooping."

He smiled. "I was under the impression you'd given up snooping."

"Once a snooper, always a snooper. It's a kind of addiction."

"Yes," Nash said. "I can see that. So what've we got here?"

137

"I found you a murder victim," I said. "Feather in your cap."

"Murders are never feathers in my cap," he said. "Who is it?"

"Jake Gold. Kinda screws up the case, huh?"

"How do you mean?"

"Well," I said, "unless Jake killed Sprague and then was feeling so distraught that he came out here, tied himself to a chair in the barn, shot himself in the eye, and then went and hid his gun, it looks to me like we've got another murderer running around."

Nash nodded and blew out a breath. "It looks that way to me, too," he said. He sat beside me on the steps. "Let's talk about it."

"No," I said. "I'm gonna wait for Horowitz to show up. I don't want to go through the whole thing twice."

He squinted at me for a moment, then shrugged. "Suit yourself."

Within fifteen minutes, four or five more vehicles had pulled into the dooryard. Among them was the gray Taurus that Horowitz and Marcia Benetti drive. Nash went over and started talking with Horowitz. After a few minutes, the two of them headed over to the barn.

Benetti came over and sat with me on the porch steps. "The lieutenant and the DA are getting things organized," she said. "We'll wait for them before we talk."

For the next hour or so, men and women trooped back and forth between the dooryard and the barn. By then, darkness had settled over Ed Sprague's farmyard. The flashing blue and red lights from all the vehicles and the swooping yellow beams from all the flashlights reminded me of something out of *Close Encounters of the Third Kind*.

After a while, an emergency wagon bumped over to the barn, and a few minutes later it returned and headed on up the driveway. It had its red lights flashing, but it seemed to be in no hurry.

One by one, people climbed back into their vehicles and drove away. Marcia Benetti and I sat on the steps and watched.

Finally Horowitz and Gus Nash came over. They both stood in front of us.

Horowitz crossed his arms and let out a long breath. "I damn near puked," he said.

"I did puke," I said.

He gave me his Jack Nicholson grin. "I saw it. Don't feel bad. The ME himself was gagging."

"You want to tell us why you came here, decided to break into the house and barn?" said Nash.

"I didn't break in," I said. "I used a key."

"Just tell us your story," said Horowitz.

It wasn't much of a story. I'd come out here, poked around, and found Sprague's red Cherokee and Jake's body.

"What exactly were you looking for?" said Nash.

"I don't know. I had this idea that Jake had blamed Sprague for Brian's accident, and that's why he killed him."

"Why?" said Nash. "Why would Gold blame Ed?"

I shook my head. I wasn't going to mention Tory Whyte's witness to him. "It struck me as a logical connection, that's all. Between that accident and Sprague's murder."

"Then you found Sprague's car," said Nash.

"Right. That seemed to clinch it."

"The question is," said Horowitz, "if Gold killed Sprague, who killed Gold?"

"You asking me?" I said. "Hey, you guys're the cops. I haven't got the slightest idea."

Horowitz was standing there with his arms folded, rocking back and forth on his heels. "He'd been tortured," he said.

I looked up at him. "Who? Jake?"

He nodded. "Looked like cigar burns all over him."

"Jesus," I whispered.

I followed Horowitz and Benetti in my car to Sharon's house. They parked in front, and by the time I'd pulled up behind their Taurus and got out, the two of them were standing on the sidewalk in the middle of an argument.

"Don't be ridiculous," Horowitz was saying. "It's my job."

"There's no sense upsetting her any more than necessary." Marcia said. She stepped close to him, planted her forefinger in the middle of his chest, and glared up at him. "You scare her. She doesn't like you. If she sees you at her door, she'll burst into tears. And you know how sensitively you handle weeping women. So, for once in your life, listen to me. You are *not* going in there. Mr. Coyne and I will do it. You wait here. Got that?"

He shrugged. "Yeah, fine, okay. Whatever."

Marcia turned to me and gave me a quick smile. "Come on, Mr. Coyne," she said, and started for the door.

I glanced at Horowitz. He rolled his eyes.

When Sharon opened the front door and saw Marcia and me standing there, her eyes widened, and she put her hand over her mouth and began shaking her head.

"We found Jake," I said.

I put my arm around her shoulder, led her to the sofa, and sat beside her. She clutched my hand with both of hers while Marcia squatted in front of her and told her that Jake had been murdered.

Sharon hugged herself and swayed back and forth. Her eyes filled with tears, and she let them run down her face without trying to wipe them away. "Why?" she whispered. "Who?"

"We don't know yet," Marcia said.

Marcia asked the necessary questions. Sharon's voice was soft but clear, and she answered them fully. No, she hadn't heard from Jake since he'd left on Sunday. She didn't know why he'd left or what he was doing or what he'd been thinking. She'd had no idea who'd want to kill him. She'd had no unusual phone calls or conversations since Jake disappeared.

Then Marcia put her hand on Sharon's knee, looked up into her face, and told her that she'd have to identify Jake's body and they'd probably want to ask her some more questions, but it could wait until tomorrow.

Sharon nodded and said she understood.

Marcia asked her who could come and spend the night with her, but Sharon said she didn't want anybody, she'd be okay. Marcia suggested there must be a neighbor or a relative. Sharon just shook her head. Really, she was all right, she'd half expected this, she was prepared for it, it was almost a relief to know and not to have to imagine it, and all she wanted was to be alone for a while.

"Call your mother, at least," I said. "Have her come back and stay with you."

Sharon smiled. "Oh, God. My mother. Just what I need." Then she nodded. "Yes, well, I'll have to call her, of course. Not tonight, though. I'm not up to it tonight."

"I could call her for you."

Sharon shook her head. "Please, Brady. No."

Finally Marcia looked at me. "Why don't you go ahead, Mr. Coyne," she said. "Leave us girls alone, okay?"

I nodded. I gave Sharon a hug and turned for the door.

As I opened it, I heard Marcia say to Sharon, "How about a pot of tea?" and Sharon said, "Tea. That sounds nice."

I played a Bob Seger CD on the drive back to Boston. I turned up the volume so that the music filled my car, and it helped me not to think about Jake and Sharon and Brian Gold.

"Wish I didn't know now what I didn't know then," Seger sang, and I sang along with him.

Sixteen

I got back to my apartment around nine-thirty. I immediately poured myself a shot of Rebel Yell, gulped it down, poured another, and took it into the bedroom.

My machine was blinking, as I'd hoped it would be.

I hit the button, it whirred and clicked, and then Evie's voice said, "Hello, dear man. It's me. It's about six o'clock in the afternoon, and I just walked in the door. Where are you? You better call me so I'll know you're not mad. I missed you horribly all day, and . . ."

I started dialing her number while the machine was still replaying her message.

She answered on the second ring with her usual cautious, "Yes?"

"Hi, babe. It's me."

She laughed. "Oh, geez. Thank God. I figured you were totally pissed at me and had decided to never talk to me again."

"I'm not pissed, honey."

"Are you home now? What time is it? Is it too late to—?"

"It's not even ten," I said. Certainly not too late on a Saturday night."

"I'm on my way."

"I'll go there if you'd rather."

"You sit tight," she said. "See you soon."

"Don't forget your nightie."

After we hung up, I sat on the edge of the bed, raised my glass, and drained it. Then I went to the kitchen, splashed in another few fingers of Rebel Yell, took a couple glugs straight from the bottle for good measure, and took the glass out to my balcony. My aim was to sit and relax and not think about Jake and wait calmly for Evie to arrive.

I knew it would be a while. When Evie says she's on her way, it means that she's only going to take a shower, wash and dry her hair, reapply her makeup, try on a few blouses and sweaters, and agonize over which lipsticks and items of lingerie to pack in her overnight bag.

Sometimes she says it's going to take her a little while, which means that before she showers and packs she intends to run the vacuum around her place, unload the dishwasher, call a few friends, and set her VCR to record something from the Discovery Channel.

I tried to focus on Evie. But in spite of my best efforts, the image of Jake Gold's bloated, tortured body kept flashing in my mind.

I finished my drink out on the balcony, went inside, took another big swig out of the bottle, and poured some more into my glass. Then I put on a Beach Boys CD. I played it loud. When Evie arrived, maybe we'd dance.

I practiced dancing. I hadn't rocked or rolled for many years, but I was groovin', man. "Little Deuce Coupe." "California Girls." "Good Vibrations." Happy, carefree music. Love those Beach Boys.

One of them drowned. A Beach Boy drowning, for Christ's sake. Imagine that.

Ironic, dude.

Catch a wave, you'll be sitting on top of the world.

My glass was empty. I had another drink.

Are you drunk?"

I opened my eyes. I was slouched in my armchair, and Evie was standing between my sprawled legs, leaning over me with her hands braced on my shoulders.

"Yes," I said, "I believe I am."

"I've never seen you drunk."

"Not a pretty sight, huh?"

She smiled. "It's a different side of you."

"I'm sorry, baby."

She leaned down and kissed me softly on the lips. I reached up and held her hips, and when she started to push herself away, I pulled her down onto my lap.

She sat there stiffly with one arm around my neck.

I stroked her leg. She picked up my hand and held on to it. I twisted my head around and kissed her throat. She didn't move.

"This was the worst fucking day of my life," I said.

"I'm sorry."

"Are you?"

She turned her head to look at me. "Huh?"

"Honey—?"

"I don't want to talk about it," she said.

I nodded. "Did you have a nice day?"

"Yes," she said. "Yes, I did. I had a lot of fun."

"Good," I said. "That's nice. I'm glad."

"Are you?"

"Am I what?"

"Glad I had fun."

"No."

She smiled. "So tell me about your day."

I shrugged. "Typical Saturday. Read the paper. Did some laundry. You disappeared. Found Jake Gold. His dead old body. Poor guy got murdered. Came home. Listened to the Beach Boys. Got a little drunk."

145

"*What?*"

"The Beach Boys," I said. "You wanna dance?"

"What'd you say about Jake Gold?"

"I found his body in Ed Sprague's barn. He'd been dead for a while. Very smelly. He'd been tortured. Went and broke the news to Sharon. Then I came home and got drunk. Now aren't you sorry you didn't spend the day with me?"

Evie slumped against me. She tucked her face into the hollow of my shoulder, snaked her arms around me, and held me tight. "Talk to me," she whispered.

"You want the long version or the short one?"

"The long one."

"Then I think I need another drink."

"You better get me one, too," she said.

It was nearly two in the morning when Evie and I staggered into the bedroom. By then I was beyond drunk, and I passed out before my head hit the pillow.

A dream woke me up. I was sweating. I forgot the dream instantly, but the weird, disorienting panic of it stayed with me. I slipped out of bed, stumbled into the bathroom, peed, splashed cold water on my face, and swallowed four aspirins.

When I glanced at my watch, I saw that I'd been sleeping for only about an hour.

I hadn't been truly drunk in years.

Never again.

When I slipped back under the covers, Evie was lying on her side facing away from me. She was breathing quietly. I slithered over beside her and pressed the length of my body against hers from behind. She was wearing a short silky nightgown. It was bunched up around her waist. She wore nothing underneath it. I buried my face in her hair, put an arm around her hips, and snuggled up against her. Her body was very warm. A little humming moan came from her throat. She took my hand,

146

moved it up so that it was cupping her breast, and held it there. Her butt wiggled back against me. She sighed.

We slept that way, and I don't think I had any more dreams.

It was nearly ten in the morning when my eyes popped open. I staggered naked out into the kitchen and got the coffee going.

Somebody was driving nails into my eyeballs. He was wielding a heavy hammer, and each blow clanged in my brain. Somebody else was doing sit-ups inside my stomach.

I had a long hot shower while the coffee was brewing, and after I got dried and dressed, I poured a mugful and brought it to Evie.

I sat on the edge of the bed and kissed her bare shoulder. She groaned. "Jesus," she mumbled. "Don't touch me."

"I got coffee," I said. "Happy Sunday."

She rolled onto her back and blinked at me. "What time is it?"

"Around ten."

"*What?*"

"Ten o'clock on a pretty Sunday morning."

"Oh, shit," she said. "Gimme the phone."

I passed the phone to her. She sat up, brushed her hair away from her face, and pecked out a number. While it rang she frowned up at me. Then her eyes shifted and she smiled. "Hi. It's me. I'm kind of under the weather this morning. I'm gonna be a little . . . No, I'm feeling better. Something I ate, is all . . . Oh, about eleven?" She ducked her head so that her hair fell like curtains around her face. "No, really," she said softly. "I'm okay now. . . . That's sweet, but I'm fine." She was smiling. "Yes, you, too," she said. "Thank you."

She turned and handed the phone to me.

I gave her the mug of coffee I'd been holding. "What's up?"

She shook her head, bent to her mug, and took a sip.

"You got a date or something?"

She shrugged. "Something like that."

147

"Lucky you," I said, and I stood up and went into the kitchen.

I set the table, mixed an omelette, poured two glasses of orange juice, and sliced some English muffins while Evie took her shower.

When she came into the kitchen, she had her coat on.

"I made breakfast," I said.

She shook her head. "I gotta get going. Thanks, anyway."

"It'll only take me a minute to cook," I said.

"I'm not feeling that hot."

"You can't leave on an empty stomach."

"Yeah," she said. "I can." She put her coffee mug in the sink, then brushed my cheek with a kiss. "Have a nice day."

By the time I said, "You, too," the door had slammed and she was gone.

Have a nice day?

I cooked the omelette and ate it at my kitchen table with the sports section of the *Sunday Globe* for company. Then I took the rest of the paper into the living room. I read it all, even the business section.

There was no mention of finding Jake Gold's tortured body in Ed Sprague's barn in Reddington, of course. That would have to wait for the Monday paper.

I tried calling Sharon in the middle of the afternoon. Her machine answered. She hadn't changed her message. Her voice was still cheerful and carefree. "Sharon, Brian, and Jake aren't here right now," she said, without irony.

I tried not to think about Evie. But my place felt empty without her. It was Sunday afternoon, dammit. She should've been there.

Evie and I had made no agreements, no commitments. We'd met back in September. We'd exchanged house keys only a couple of months ago. The life stories we'd exchanged were skeletal. She knew I'd been divorced, had two grown boys, and

148

had lived alone for a long time. She knew about Alex, my most recent love, knew that I'd blown that relationship and still regretted it.

I knew even less about her. Just that she'd been involved with several men. She didn't like to talk about them, and I didn't push it.

It was still early times in our relationship. Evie and I were two grown-ups who'd lived some life, and we'd both grown some scar tissue around our hearts. I figured that was part of the attraction for both of us. We didn't have to explain ourselves to understand each other.

We'd lapsed into the comfortable habit of spending weekends together. We always had fun. We cooked and ate and watched old movies and played cards and board games and made love. We laughed a lot.

Evie had joined the rhythm of my life.

So what the hell was she doing?

A date? I'd asked her.

Something like that, she'd said.

Huh?

The more encounters I had with women, the more mysterious and frustrating they became. It reminded me of a conversation I'd had with Charlie McDevitt the last time we had lunch together.

There were some things, he'd said, that men should say to women, but none of us ever did.

Such as:

1. If you think you might be fat, you probably are. Don't ask us.
2. Learn how to work the toilet seat. If it's up, just put it down.
3. Don't ever cut your hair.
4. If you ask a question you don't want an answer to, you should expect an answer you don't want to hear.
5. Sometimes we're not thinking about you. Live with it.

149

Charlie and I had fun with it. We came up with a dozen other things we wished we had the balls to say to women.

Charlie said that pissing accurately while standing up is harder than pissing from point-blank range, and they ought to accept the fact that even the best shots will sometimes be off target.

I suggested that men who own two or three pairs of shoes at the most are poor judges of which ones go with which outfit.

Charlie added that men didn't bother matching their shoes with their wallets.

I said that the ugliest, most evil-tempered dog is a better friend than the cutest, sweetest cat.

We agreed, of course, that telling women exactly what we were thinking was guaranteed to ruin a relationship forever.

Had I said something to ruin my relationship with Evie? Probably. I'd been drunk. I couldn't remember what I'd said.

I decided I wouldn't call her. I'd wait for her to call me.

If she didn't, that would tell me everything I needed to know.

SEVENTEEN

I spent that Sunday afternoon moping around my apartment
feeling sorry for myself, and when the phone rang a little after
four o'clock, I figured it was Evie, full of explanations and apol-
ogies.

I thought about not answering. Show her a thing or two.

Childish, of course.

When I picked up the phone, there was a hesitation on the
other end. Then a woman's voice I didn't recognize said, "Is
this Mr. Coyne?"

"Yes," I said. "Who's this?"

"It's Sandy. Sandy Driscoll."

It took me an instant to connect the name with the chubby
black-haired girl from the camera shop in Reddington. "What's
up, Sandy?"

"I was wondering if I could talk to you?"

"Of course."

"No. I mean, not on the phone. I'm at the shop. We close
at five."

"I'll be there," I said.

I pulled up in front of the camera store in Reddington at about quarter of five. I sat there and smoked a cigarette, and at exactly five the lights in the shop blinked out.

One minute later, Sandy Driscoll opened my car door and slid in beside me.

"I don't know if I'm doing the right thing," she said.

"Whatever it is," I said, "you can trust me."

"Can I?"

"Absolutely."

She was looking out the side window. I couldn't see her face. "You've got to promise me," she said. "No matter what, you won't tell anybody unless I say it's okay."

"I promise."

She turned to face me. Her eyes were watery. "I can't get Mrs. Gold's dream out of my mind," she said. "Then today, when I heard that Brian's dad . . ."

I nodded.

"So," she said after a minute, "so I decided . . . God, I hope I'm doing the right thing."

"Sandy," I said, "what is it?"

She stared out the window for a moment, then reached up and snapped on her seat belt. "Drive," she said.

I turned on the ignition. "Where to?"

"Head for Boston."

Sandy told me to get on the Mass Pike and take the Kenmore Square exit. Then she found an FM station on my radio that played what they called "classic rock," and she sat there beside me in the darkness of my car, gazing out the side window and saying nothing.

I resisted the almost unbearable urge to ask her what the hell was going on.

At Kenmore, she directed me to the Fenway, and a little past the Museum of Fine Arts she told me to look for a parking space.

I found one off a narrow side street under a PERMIT PARKING—RESIDENTS ONLY sign.

We got out of the car. Sandy looked around, as if she was orienting herself, then started up the sidewalk.

I caught up with her and touched her arm. "Don't you think it's time you told me what's up?"

"You'll see," she said. "Just remember your promise."

I followed her onto one of those myriad one-way side streets that connect Huntington and Columbus avenues on the fringes of Northeastern University. Cars were parked against dirty old snowbanks, leaving barely enough room for a vehicle to creep past. Here and there we stepped around a tipped-over trash can that had spilled newspapers and beer bottles and pizza crusts onto the sidewalk. Music blared from inside the buildings.

Sandy walked slowly, peering at the doors of the identical dirty-brick four-floor walkup apartments.

Finally she stopped. "Wait here for a minute." She went into the building. I could see her inside the little entryway. She appeared to be talking on the intercom.

A minute later she opened the door and beckoned me up.

She was holding the inside door open. We went in, and I followed her up a curving flight of stairs to the second floor.

There were just two apartments there, twenty-one and twenty-two. Music came from behind both doors.

She banged on the door of number twenty-two, and a tall young man with a blond ponytail and a wispy goatee opened it. He and Sandy hugged each other, and then she turned and pointed to me. "This is him," she said. "He's a lawyer. We've got his word."

I held out my hand to the boy. "Brady Coyne," I said.

He gripped my hand firmly. "I'm Jason," he said, and left it at that. He turned to Sandy. "I'm not sure about this."

"I'm not, either," she said. "But I don't see as we've got a choice."

Jason nodded, then looked at me. "C'mon in, then."

I followed him and Sandy into a tiny room with a high ceiling and tall windows that looked out onto the building across the street. It was furnished with a ratty old sofa, a couple of mismatched wooden chairs, and a low coffee table. The table and floor were strewn with Coke cans and dirty dishes and pizza cartons and newspapers and textbooks. A television set sat on a plank that was supported by a couple of cement blocks. A stereo system was playing what I thought I recognized as hip-hop music. It was very loud.

"Where is he?" said Sandy.

Jason pointed down a narrow hallway. "Last door on the left."

Sandy took my hand and led me down the hallway. At the last door on the left, she stopped, blew out a quick breath, and knocked.

A voice from inside said, "Yeah? Who is it?"

"It's Sandy," she said. "Let me in."

"It's not locked."

Sandy pushed the door open.

It was a tiny room, not much bigger than my bathroom, and it was dark except for the streetlight outside the single window.

A figure was curled on the cot-size bed, facing the wall.

"What do you want?" The voice was muffled.

Sandy went over, sat on the edge of his bed, and touched his shoulder. "I brought someone to see you," she said gently.

"Who? I told you—"

"It's all right," she said. "He won't tell anybody."

The figure on the bed pushed himself up onto his elbows, turned, and looked at me over Sandy's shoulder.

I'd forgotten how much he looked like his mother. Same shiny black hair, same dark, frightened eyes.

"Hello, Brian," I said.

Brian Gold blinked at me. "Uncle Brady?"

I nodded.

He flopped back onto his bed. "Please," he said. "Just leave me alone."

Sandy stood up, backed away from the bed, and arched her eyebrows at me.

I went over and squatted beside Brian. "It's awfully good to see you," I said to him. "Your mother—"

"No," he said. He rolled onto his side, putting his back to me.

"She thinks you're dead," I said.

"That's fine," he said.

"She deserves to know you're okay," I said. "She's grieving terribly."

"She'll get over it."

"Brian," I said, "your father . . ."

"I heard." His voice sounded strangled. "That's my fault, too. Just leave me alone. Mind your own business, Uncle Brady. Go away. Both of you. Just forget about me."

"At least tell me what happened."

"Ask her," said Brian. "Ask the traitor. Ask my former friend who said I could trust her. She'll tell you all my secrets."

I glanced at Sandy, who was leaning back against the door. She was hugging herself. She looked at me with wide eyes and nodded once.

I turned back to Brian. "At least call your mother."

He curled himself into a ball, as if he were trying to disappear, and said nothing.

I bent over him and gripped his shoulder. "Brian, listen—"

Sandy tugged at my jacket. "Leave him alone. Can't you see he wants to be left alone?"

I sighed and straightened up. "Okay." I touched Brian's cheek. "I'm sorry about your dad."

He jerked away from my hand and hugged his knees.

Sandy and I didn't speak until we were back on the Mass Pike, heading outbound to Reddington.

Then I said, "Talk to me, Sandy."

"I've been ready to explode," she said softly. "It's been so awful, having this secret, not being able to tell anybody. He made me promise. When you told me about his mother, it was bad enough. Then I heard about his father. . . ." She was silent for a minute. Then she said, "You knew, didn't you?"

"No," I said. "I hadn't figured it out but I should have. The day after the accident, when you and Mikki were tossing daisies into the river, you said they were for Jenny. Not Jenny and Brian. You didn't mention Brian until I reminded you. Right then, it passed through my mind that you thought Brian was still alive. But I figured it was wishful thinking on your part. They hadn't found his body, so there was still hope. So, no, I didn't know."

"I guess I blew it, huh?"

"What, bringing me in to see Brian?"

"Yeah. I promised him I wouldn't tell anybody."

"You did the right thing, Sandy," I said. "There are times when breaking a promise is better than keeping it."

"*You* better not tell anybody," she said. "You promised me."

"How can I not tell Brian's mother that her boy is alive?"

"He will himself," she said. "When he's ready. You heard him. He's got his reasons."

"Do you know what his reasons are?"

"No," she said. "Anyway, it's not up to me to talk about Brian's reasons."

"What do they have to do with the murder of Chief Sprague and Brian's father?"

"I don't know," she said. "Honestly."

"Sandy—"

"I can't talk about it," she said.

We rode in silence for a while.

"Sandy," I said, "at least tell me what happened that night. Brian said you'd tell me that."

"He called me a traitor."

"You did the right thing, bringing me to him," I said. "You

156

had a hard choice, and you made the right one. Now you've got me to share your secret with."

"If I tell you what happened that night—?"

"I'll keep that a secret, too, if you want me to."

EIGHTEEN

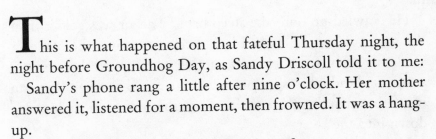

This is what happened on that fateful Thursday night, the night before Groundhog Day, as Sandy Driscoll told it to me:

Sandy's phone rang a little after nine o'clock. Her mother answered it, listened for a moment, then frowned. It was a hang-up.

The next time it rang, Sandy got there first.

"It's Brian," he said. His voice was soft. He sounded scared. "Please. Come and get me. Don't tell anybody. Not even your mother. Just come. Hurry."

She told her mother she was going to a friend's house to do some homework and needed to borrow the car. Her mother was watching television. She waved a hand without turning around and told her to drive carefully.

She followed Brian's directions to the abandoned factory building by the dam on the river. Brian was hiding in a door-way. When she stopped her car, he sprinted out and slipped in beside her. "Go," he said.

He ducked his head when a car came toward them from the opposite lane. "Turn up the heat," he said. He was shivering.

She reached out to touch him. He was soaking wet.

He told her to drive to Jason's apartment. Jason was a freshman at Northeastern, a Reddington boy who'd played soccer with Brian. Sandy and Brian and some of the other Reddington kids had been to a couple of parties at Jason's.

When Sandy asked him what happened, Brian started crying. They were forced off the road, he said. Jenny lost control, and they went over the bank, rolled over, and landed upside down in the river.

Brian hadn't been wearing his seat belt. His door sprang open, and the next thing he knew he was in the river. He was groggy and disoriented. He'd hit his head and banged his knee. He started swimming. He ended up on the other side of the river about fifty yards downstream from where the car went in.

He crawled up onto the steep bank. The air was colder than the water. When he looked back across the river, he couldn't see Jenny's car. But there was another car stopped there on the street. Its headlights were on, and Brian could see the silhouette of a figure standing there at the top of the embankment, looking down into the river.

He was shivering uncontrollably. He was dizzy and dazed. He couldn't think straight.

Jenny was dead. He knew that.

He started running. He knew he had to keep moving. He didn't know where he was going or what he was going to do. All he knew was, he had to get away from Reddington.

He was scared. They'd killed Jenny. They'd tried to kill both of them.

When he found the pay phone, he called Sandy.

He could trust Sandy.

He didn't know anyone else he could trust.

When Sandy finished, I said, "Why didn't Brian think he could trust his parents?"

160

"I don't know," she said. "I asked him that. I told him I should just take him home. He yelled at me."

"You said he was confused. He'd banged his head."

"He wasn't confused about that," she said. "He was very emphatic about that. I was to tell nobody that I even knew he was alive. Not even his parents. Nobody."

"He said they tried to kill him? As if it was on purpose?"

She shrugged. "That's what he said. I don't know if that's what he meant."

"What else can you tell me?" I said.

"Nothing. That's it. That's the whole story. I drove him to Jason's and left him there. Now you know everything I know. So what are you going to do?"

"I don't know," I said.

I took Sandy back to the camera shop. She'd driven her mother's car to work. It was a little after eight o'clock. I asked her if her mother would be worried. She said she'd called her before I picked her up, told her she had some things to do, wouldn't be home for a while.

Sandy sat beside me in the car for a minute. Then she turned to face me. "Thank you," she said.

"For what?"

"For sharing my secret." She opened the door. "I think Brian knows who murdered Ed and his father, don't you?"

"I think he's got an idea," I said.

"So what are you gonna do?"

"I don't know."

"If you try to see him again . . ."

"I understand," I said.

I got back to my apartment around nine. I poured a finger of Rebel Yell into a glass, took a sip, nearly gagged, and dumped it out.

I picked up the phone and put it down half a dozen times.

Finally I took a deep breath and dialed Sharon's number.

Her machine answered.

I disconnected without leaving a message.

It felt like a reprieve.

I was sitting in my office staring blankly at some legal documents on Monday afternoon when Horowitz called.

"Thought you'd like to know," he said without preliminary. "The ME got a good fix on Professor Gold's time of death. Figured he'd been dead four days as of Saturday night, give or take about eight hours."

"So that's . . ."

"Sometime Tuesday night, early Wednesday morning last week."

I thought for a minute. "Jake called me on Tuesday. We set up an appointment for the next day. He didn't show up."

"Of course he didn't," said Horowitz. "He was already dead by then."

"Jake died before Sprague," I said. "So he couldn't have killed him." I thought for a moment. "Okay, I get it," I said. "Sprague killed Jake, then. But who—?"

"Just shut up and listen for a minute," said Horowitz. "Professor Gold had been tortured with a cigar butt. Judging by the number of burns, he held out for quite a while. But it looks like he finally gave 'em what they wanted, because they Moe Greened him. Quick and humane."

"Huh? They did what?"

"Moe Greened him. Remember *The Godfather*? One shot in the eye. They dug the slug out of his brain, gave it to ballistics. It was a—"

"A twenty-two hollow-point," I said. "Same gun that killed Sprague. Right?"

Horowitz chuckled. "You'd probably of made a better cop than a lawyer, Coyne. Right. Gold didn't kill Sprague, and Sprague didn't kill Gold, either. Someone else killed 'em both."

I lit a cigarette and swiveled around to look out my office window. It was a brisk late-winter day out there—bright sun, high puffy clouds. A sharp wind was swirling around Copley Square, and the girls were hunching their shoulders and pressing their skirts against their legs as they walked across the diagonal pathways.

"Roger," I said after a minute, "I appreciate your telling me all this. It's unlike you to share. Usually you make me tell you things, and then you refuse to reciprocate."

"Yeah," he said. "I must be gettin' soft."

"Somehow I doubt that," I said. "What's going on?"

He let out a long breath. It hissed into the phone. "Truth is," he said, "I'm off the case."

"Why? Did you—?"

"Gus Nash pulled some strings."

"Politics, huh?" I said.

"Ah, I don't blame him." Horowitz paused for a moment. "This is a helluva hot case for a DA, especially one who might be looking ahead to a career in elective office. Chief of police runs a couple of teenagers off the road and into the river, then gets himself murdered in a cruddy motel room? College professor from the same dipshit little town, father of one of the dead kids, ends up tortured and murdered in the chief's barn? Delicious stuff. Helluva case."

"Yeah," I said, "But—"

"If I was in Nash's shoes," said Horowitz, "I wouldn't want to work with me, either. Nash knows how I work. I don't take shit from any DA, is how I work. Fuckin' DA's got his job, but it ain't running a murder investigation."

"That sucks," I said.

"Yeah, well, I got plenty of cases. Don't feel sorry for me."

"I don't," I said. "I feel sorry for Sharon Gold and for the people of Reddington. They deserve to have this thing investigated, not milked for its PR value."

"Oh, Nash ain't like that," said Horowitz. "He'll do a good job."

163

"So what's going to happen? I mean, it's still a state-police case, isn't it?"

"Nash has got Chris Stone working with him."

"Stone?" I said. "Your old partner?"

"Ah, Stone's okay," said Horowitz. "He's a good cop."

"Stone's an ass kisser," I said. "That's why you got rid of him."

Horowitz snorted. "And he got promoted a year later. How it goes."

"How's Marcia taking it?" I said.

"Blew her stack. I explained how it works. Good lesson for her. She'll be okay."

"Well," I said, "if you hear anything else . . ."

"I'm not gonna hear anything," he said. "I'm off the fuckin' case, remember?"

"Well, if I hear anything—"

"You gotta talk to Stone or Nash," he said quickly. "I expect one of them'll be coming around to talk to you. Don't lose track of what's important here."

"Finding out who killed Jake."

"Yes. And Sprague."

"Roger," I said, "are you okay?"

"Me? One less case to drive me crazy, keep me from spending time with my wife? Don't worry about me."

"Okay," I said. "I won't."

After I hung up with Horowitz I tried calling Sharon again. Her machine picked up, and I didn't leave a message.

I thought of calling Evie, but I didn't. I didn't know what to say to her. Something was going on. But if I asked her what it was, she'd say nothing, she was fine, and if I pushed it, she'd get annoyed.

I pulled my stack of legal papers back in front of me. Julie had instructed me to get through them by the end of the day. I knew they were all perfect. I never found a mistake in anything Julie drew up.

I'd plowed through about half the pile when Julie buzzed

me. I glanced at my watch. It was a few minutes after five-thirty. Normally she'd have the office machines shut down and be on her way out the door by five-thirty on a Monday afternoon.

I picked up the phone. "How come you're still here?"

"Brady," she said, "can you come out here for a minute?"

"Sure. What's the problem?"

"I need to show you something."

I got up from my desk and went out into the reception area. Julie's desk backs up to the inside wall, facing the door. She was sitting stiffly behind it, and it took an instant for my mind to register what I saw.

A man was standing behind her. He was gripping Julie's hair in his left hand, and he was pressing the muzzle of a small-caliber automatic handgun against the side of her neck.

NINETEEN

—✦————————————✦—

He wore creased black jeans and a fawn-colored suede jacket over a powder-blue turtleneck sweater. A slender guy, medium height, with short black hair cut military style, squinty eyes, and a slit for a mouth. His face was long and thin, all planes and angles except for an incongruous round piggy nose.

His eyes were as pale as a hot blue flame, and they were boring directly into mine.

"Get your hands off her," I said.

His lips pulled back over small, pointed teeth into an entirely humorless smile. "Go over there, lock the door," he said. He gave Julie's hair a tug for emphasis, and she squeezed her eyes shut and grimaced.

I did what he said, then turned back to him. "What do you want?"

"That envelope in your safe."

"What envelope?"

He yanked Julie's hair again. It lifted her halfway out of her chair, and she took a quick breath. He kept his gun rammed into the soft place under her jawbone. "Right now, pal. It's in your office."

"Let her go," I said. "She's just a secretary. She doesn't know anything."

"Sorry," he said.

He jerked Julie to her feet. His grip on her hair forced her to arch her neck and bend her head back against him. Her eyes were wide and watery. He pushed her around the desk.

"Okay," I said. "Don't hurt the girl. I'll get the envelope for you. I'll be right back."

I turned to head into my office.

"Wait," said the guy.

I stopped.

"We all go in together," he said. "And if you think I'll hesitate to shoot her, try me."

"Sure," I said. "We'll do it your way. Just don't hurt her."

I went back into my office, and the thin guy pushed Julie in behind me.

"Now what?" I said.

"Open the safe."

"Which envelope is it you're interested in?" I said.

He gave Julie's hair another tug and jammed the muzzle of his weapon into her breast.

She closed her eyes and said, "Oh."

"Don't fuck with me," he said.

"I'm not fucking with you," I said. "I've got a lot of envelopes in my safe."

"The one the professor gave you. Big manila envelope."

"Ah," I said. "That envelope."

"Do it," he said.

The framed black-and-white blowup of Billy and Joey, aged seven and five, hung on the wall behind my desk, about shoulder high. I went over there, pushed the photo aside, and spun the knob through the six-number combination. Billy's birthday, then Joey's.

I glanced over my shoulder. The guy had come to the other side of my desk. Now he had the muzzle of his gun pressed up under Julie's chin. Her head was tilted back and her eyes were squeezed shut.

The man's gun looked like a .22 to me. The only person who knew about the envelope in my safe was Jake Gold—plus whoever had tortured him in Ed Sprague's barn before shooting him in the eye with a .22.

I turned the handle, pulled the door open, and reached inside the safe. As my hand touched Jake's envelope, it brushed against the cold barrel of my .38 S&W revolver.

I peered into the safe and rummaged around as if I were looking for the right envelope, and I got my hand around the revolver's grip. The hammer was down on an empty chamber, the way Doc Adams had told me to keep it. I cocked it with my thumb, and as I did, I coughed loudly to cover the click that would echo inside the safe.

"Come on," said the guy. "The fuck are you doing?"

"Finding the right envelope," I said.

I got the cocked gun in my hand and wedged Jake's ten-by-thirteen envelope against the side of it with my thumb. Then I slid the envelope and the gun out of the safe with my back to the guy, and with my back still to him, I rotated my hand so that the envelope was on top with the gun hidden underneath it.

I turned around and held the envelope to him.

He let go of Julie's hair and pushed her to the side.

When he leaned across the desk to reach for the envelope, I shot him in the middle of his chest.

The explosion of the gunshot was followed almost instantaneously by the softer report of his little .22 automatic and the simultaneous thunk of a slug smacking into the wall beside my head.

He toppled backwards onto my carpet, moaned and twitched for a few seconds, then lay there motionless. His eyes stared up at the ceiling. The automatic pistol fell out of his outstretched hand.

I went over and kicked the gun away, then turned and took Julie in my arms.

"You shot him," she mumbled into my chest.

"Yes. He would've killed us."

"Is he dead?"

"I think so," I said. "Are you okay?"

I felt her head nodding against my chest. "Who is he?" she said.

"I don't know his name," I said. "I think he's the same man who killed Jake Gold and Chief Sprague."

"But why—?"

"I don't know."

"We should get an ambulance," she said. "And the police. I'll go call 911."

"No," I said. "Call Lieutenant Horowitz. Don't talk to anybody else. Just Horowitz."

"But—"

I was still holding her against me. I could feel her trembling. "Call Roger Horowitz, honey," I said gently. I stroked her hair. "Just tell him I shot a man, and he appears to be dead. Don't mention the envelope. Don't mention the safe. Don't explain anything. Okay?"

"But what if—?"

"Horowitz won't ask a lot of questions," I said. "If he does, just say a man came in here with a gun. He shot at me, so I shot him. You were frightened. It's all a kind of blur. Act hysterical."

She looked up into my face. Her eyes were wet, but she was smiling. "I *am* hysterical."

I patted her back. "You're doing fine."

She nodded, then stepped out of my hug and frowned at me. "What's going on here, Brady?"

"It's better if you don't know. You've got to trust me, okay? The police will be here. They'll ask you questions over and over. Keep it simple. All you know is, this man came in and held a gun on you. He demanded our money and our jewelry.

170

He grabbed your hair, jammed his gun barrel into your throat and breast, dragged you into my office. I got my gun out of my desk—I keep it in my desk, that's our story—the top right-hand drawer—and when he saw it, he fired at me, so I shot him. He shot first. Stick with that story. You were very frightened. It happened so quickly. You don't remember exactly what was said. It's all kind of a jumble. Play it like that. Okay?"

"You want me to lie to the police?"

"Yes."

"Brady . . ."

"I'm a lawyer, kiddo. Don't worry about it."

She smiled and rolled her eyes. "Right. Of course. You're a lawyer. Nothing to worry about."

"Trust me on this."

"No ambulance? No 911?"

"Horowitz will ask if you called them. Tell him no, I told you to call him. I'm pretty shook up, too, tell him. He'll take care of the rest of it."

She shrugged. "I assume you know what you're doing."

"Of course I do."

"What's in that envelope, Brady?"

"I don't know. I haven't looked. It doesn't belong to me. Forget the envelope. Don't mention the safe. There was no envelope, okay?"

Julie nodded, gave me a quick hug, and went back out to her desk in the reception area. I closed my office door and knelt beside the guy sprawled on my carpet. He hadn't moved since he went down. His eyes were glazed over, and a dark stain the diameter of a softball had seeped over the front of his powder-blue turtleneck. I felt for a pulse under his jawbone and, as I expected, found none.

My office smelled like the indoor handgun range at Doc Adams's gun club. I realized I was still holding my .38. I put it on my desk. Then I picked up Jake's envelope from the floor where I'd dropped it, took it over to the sofa, sat down, and opened it.

171

It held about a dozen eight-by-ten black-and-white photographs. They were grainy and imperfectly focused and printed on cheap paper, but there was no mistaking what they depicted.

Brian Gold was in some of them. A pretty young girl with long pale hair and a slender childlike body was in the others.

They were naked in all the photos.

They looked painfully young, those two kids. More like children than teenagers. Brian had a sturdy little athlete's body, but his skin was smooth and hairless, and he had the face of innocence.

The girl had tiny little breasts and boyish hips. It was Jenny Rolando. I remembered her from the soccer-team photos on the wall in the Reddington police station.

In some of the photos, Brian and Jenny were together—just the two of them in one shot, these two naked children, coupling on a bed. In a few others, the two of them were with a third person. In the rest of the photos, it was either Brian or Jenny with somebody else, different people in each photo, it looked like, some male and some female. Except for Brian and Jenny, all the other figures were adults, many of them half-dressed, and all the adult faces were turned away from the camera.

The photos were hard to look at. These two children on their knees with their arms wrapped around the hips of fat, hairy men with their pants down around their ankles, with their heads between the legs of flab-thighed women, on their hands and knees with a man wearing a T-shirt mounted behind them, with a big-butted woman with her dress bunched up around her hips sitting astride them, sandwiched between two middle-aged people, one male and one female . . .

No wonder Brian had fled. No wonder he was ashamed and guilt-ridden. No wonder he couldn't face his mother.

I heard a deep voice from Julie's office. I hastily crammed the photos back into the envelope, took it over to my safe, shoved it in, shut the door, twisted the knob, and adjusted the framed picture of Billy and Joey over it.

I was back sitting on my sofa smoking a cigarette when Horowitz came in.

He stopped in the doorway, stared down at the dead body on my floor, then looked at me. "Jesus Christ, Coyne," he muttered.

"You recognize him?"

He squatted beside the dead guy and frowned down at him for a minute, then looked up at me. "Yeah," he said. "I know who this is. You've done mankind a great service."

"Who is it?"

"Name of Bobby Klemm. Freelancer. Started out with the Capezza mob down in Providence, got himself a reputation, went independent, oh, eight or ten years ago. Been working all over New England. He's slick. Uses twenty-two long-rifle cartridges. Slices a big X on the tips of his slugs. Nastier than hollow-points. That's his signature. We figure him for about a dozen hits from Burlington to Springfield to New Haven. He's been picked up a few times, but no one's ever had enough on him to go for an indictment."

"If he was that slick," I said, "he wouldn't be lying there looking up at my ceiling."

"Don't kid yourself, Coyne," said Horowitz. "He got careless, underestimated you, and you got lucky." He stood up, then nudged Klemm's leg with his toe. "Wish you didn't have to kill him, actually."

I nodded. "He could've explained it all, probably."

Horowitz nodded, gave Klemm's leg another halfhearted kick, then came over and sat on the sofa beside me. "I called it in a few minutes ago. I figured you wanted to talk to me first. Boston homicide's on their way, and when they get here it'll be their case, so you better talk fast. This has gotta be connected to the Sprague thing, and assuming it is, Gus Nash'll be all over you like a full-blown case of genital herpes."

I told him what had happened, about the envelope Jake had given me for safekeeping, how Klemm had known about it, known that it was in my safe.

Horowitz puffed out his cheeks and blew out a long breath. "The professor told him," he said. "The business end of a cigar butt'll do things like that to a man. So what was in that envelope the guy was so hot to get ahold of?"

I told him.

"Jesus," he muttered. "Kiddie porn." He glanced over at Klemm's body. "Fuckin' scum. He died too easy. You shoulda aimed lower."

I nodded. "I'm sorry I didn't."

"What a world," he said. "You're gonna have to give Nash that envelope, you know."

"Like hell I am," I said.

He cocked his head and frowned at me. "Whaddya mean, like hell?"

I shrugged. "I'm not showing those pictures to anybody."

"You better not get all moral and honorable on us here, Coyne," he said. "You just killed a guy, don't forget."

"No one sees those pictures," I said. "It's the least I can do."

"Show 'em to me, at least."

I shook my head. "Nope. Not even you."

"Just lemme see them," he said.

I hesitated. "You'll give them back?"

"If you insist."

"And you won't mention them to anybody?"

"If I can see them," he said, "maybe I'll recognize something. I can do some checking. I won't have to tell anybody where I saw 'em."

I considered it for a minute, then went to the safe, took out the envelope, and handed it to Horowitz. "I'm trusting you on this, Roger," I said.

He thumbed through the photos, peering hard at each one, then gave them back to me. I returned them to the safe.

"So?" I said.

"Vile," he said.

I nodded.

"There's only two identifiable people in them. The Gold boy's one of 'em, huh?"

"Yes."

"Who's the girl?"

"Jenny Rolando," I said.

"That accident?"

I nodded.

He looked at me. "Maybe it wasn't an accident," he said. "Maybe Sprague intended to kill them."

"I've been thinking the same thing."

"Well," he said, "it's a start. I'll pursue it. What're you gonna do?"

"I'm not going to tell anybody about the photos."

"You're gonna lie about it?"

"I didn't lie to you," I said.

He nodded. "That's because I'm not on the case. What about Nash?"

"I'm not telling Gus Nash. My story is that it was a robbery. The guy said he was after money and jewelry. What the hell do I know? Probably some cokehead. Scared the shit out of me. He was very rough with Julie. Took a shot at me, so I shot him. Self defense. If I have to talk to Gus, yes, I'll have no problem lying to him."

"Nash ain't stupid," said Horowitz. "He'll recognize Klemm, know it was no robbery. He'll connect it to the Sprague thing."

"I assume he will," I said. "That's fine. But I'll play dumb. Let him think what he wants. I'm not telling Gus Nash or anybody else about those pictures. Those photos are between you and me."

Horowitz shook his head. "You're puttin' me in a tough spot. You realize that, don't you?"

"You're a tough guy, Roger."

He nodded. "True." He narrowed his eyes at me. "So you got this figured out?"

"Not really," I said. "But for starters, I assume Bobby Klemm's pistol is the one that killed Jake Gold and Ed Sprague, and if it is, I don't think I'm in trouble for this."

"Well, let's hope so." He looked toward my door. There were voices out there. "Sounds like the Boston cops're here," he said. "This one—" he nodded toward Klemm's body "—is their case. Tell 'em whatever the hell you want. I'll verify it was what you told me. You and me need to talk some more."

"I thought they took you off the Sprague case," I said.

"They did," he said. "Fuck 'em."

He stood up, started toward the door, then stopped and turned back to me. "You okay, Coyne?"

"Sure. Why?"

He shrugged. "You just killed a man."

"I'm fine," I said.

He looked at me for a minute, then shrugged and left my office.

I *was* fine. I felt calm and clear-headed and under control.

It would probably hit me later.

After Horowitz left, two men came in. Both wore dark suits and dark mustaches and had shields pinned on their jackets. The taller of the two had streaks of gray in his hair. He introduced himself as Lt. Dominic Gillotte, Boston homicide. The other guy was Sergeant Michaelson. I shook hands with both of them.

They took me out into the reception area. Julie was sitting at her desk talking to a uniformed female officer. Several other people who were standing around out there, including Horowitz, went back into my office.

Gillotte and Michaelson sat me down in one of the waiting-room chairs on the opposite side of the room from Julie's desk and asked me to tell my story, which I did, the way I'd told Horowitz I intended to tell it. Gillotte asked a few perfunctory questions, which I answered, then he repeated them in such a way that I understood they weren't perfunctory at all.

I stuck to my story, and after about half an hour, Gillotte

went back into my office. Michaelson stayed with me. He didn't ask any more questions, and I didn't say anything to him.

I lit a cigarette, and about the time I was stubbing it out, Gillotte and Horowitz came out. Gillotte had my .38 in a plastic bag.

"This is yours, right?" he said.

"Yes. It'll have my fingerprints on it, and you'll find that it's the gun that killed that person in there."

"You got a license for it?"

"Of course."

He nodded. "Assuming everything checks out, we'll get it back to you in a couple days." He looked at Horowitz. "Anything else, sir?"

Horowitz shrugged. "It's your case. Seems pretty straightforward to me."

Gillotte nodded, and he and Michaelson went back into my office again.

Horowitz sat beside me. "They'll put two and two together pretty soon," he said quietly. "Soon as they ID Bobby Klemm and do their ballistics on that twenty-two, they'll connect this with Sprague and Gold. You should expect to hear from Nash and Stone before long, and I doubt they'll be as gullible as Gillotte. I covered for you here, but I can't do anything for you with Nash."

"I can handle it," I said.

Horowitz grinned. "That was a good shot you made."

"He was all of five feet from me. Hard to miss."

"You'd be surprised. I've seen experienced police officers miss from five feet."

"Go for the body mass. That's what Doc Adams always told me."

"Well," he said, "you done good, Coyne. He woulda killed you and Julie. He let you see his face. That means he was planning to kill you."

I nodded. "That's what I figured."

177

He patted my leg. "If this was my case, I'd grill you like a Fenway hot dog, you know."

"Last time I was at Fenway, they steamed the dogs."

"Yeah," he said. "Good point." He stood up. "I'll be in touch," he said. "We'll have to put our heads together on this."

I looked up at him. "Thanks, Roger," I said. "I know you're putting yourself on the line here."

"I ain't doing it for you, Coyne," he said. "This is the first time I ever got taken off a case, and it stinks."

TWENTY

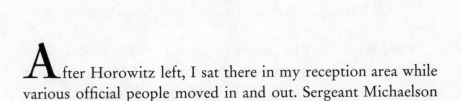

After Horowitz left, I sat there in my reception area while various official people moved in and out. Sergeant Michaelson sat stolidly beside me. He didn't say anything, but I understood that I was supposed to stay put. I was his prisoner, and I didn't like the feeling.

After a while, two men pushed a gurney into my office, and they came back out a few minutes later with a zipped-up body bag on it. Julie had been sitting behind her desk the whole time with the same female officer baby-sitting her. She kept glancing my way, and whenever she did, I smiled and nodded at her. She nodded back to me. She was sticking to our story.

Finally Lieutenant Gillotte came back. "You can go home now, Mr. Coyne," he said.

"About time."

He frowned at me. "You okay?"

I nodded. "I guess so. I don't shoot people every day."

He cocked his head. "Back in eighty-seven you shot a guy. You were in your apartment. Used that same gun, if I'm not mistaken."

"Yes," I said. "Same gun. They called that guy Rat. He was

179

some kind of small-time mobster. He'd already killed a few people, and he was going to kill me and my girlfriend."

Gillotte nodded. "Most people don't shoot anybody in their whole life. I'm a fucking homicide cop, and I never shot a guy. You've shot two."

"I'm a lawyer," I said. "That probably explains it."

He smiled. "Anyway, why don't you get the hell out of here. We'll be in touch with you. And you better plan on taking the day off tomorrow. Your office is a crime scene."

"Okay," I said. I got up and went over to Julie. "They told me I can leave."

She nodded. "Me, too. I called Edward. He's coming to pick me up."

"Hey," I said, "you might as well take the day off tomorrow."

"Since they won't let us in here anyway?" She smiled. "Just so it doesn't count against my vacation time." She cocked her head and frowned at me. "Are you all right, Brady?"

"Sure. You?"

"I'm okay."

I hugged her, then left.

A uniformed officer was standing stiffly outside my office door. I nodded to him, and he nodded back. Then I went down to the end of the corridor and got into the elevator. I'd walked to work, so I'd have to walk home.

I looked forward to it. The wintry air would clear my head, and the long stroll down Boylston Street, across the Public Garden and the Common, through the financial district and Quincy Market and along Atlantic Avenue to my apartment over-looking the harbor—it would give me time to do some think-ing. Maybe I'd stop off at Skeeter's on the way, have a burger and a beer, watch a basketball game on the TV over his bar. It would be fun to watch a good college basketball game, have a beer or two, talk sports with Skeeter, think about something else besides dead people and pornographic photographs of a boy I'd known since he was a baby, a boy who still called me Uncle Brady.

The elevator stopped at the lobby and the doors slid open. I stepped out . . . and lights started flashing and a mob of people with cameras and microphones closed in on me. They were shoving and elbowing each other and yelling all at once.

"How'd it feel to kill a man?"

"Was he a client?"

"A few questions, Mr. Coyne."

"Who was he?"

"Got a license for that gun?"

"Did he rape your secretary?"

"Was he on drugs?"

". . . Reddington?"

". . . Professor Gold?"

Somebody grabbed my arm. I tried to shake him off, but he didn't let go. "Come with me," he growled.

It was Horowitz. He held up his shield so the mob could see it and yelled, "Move out of the way or I'll arrest every goddamn one of you."

Surprisingly, they stepped back. Horowitz shouldered his way through them. I followed along behind him, out of my office building and onto Boylston Street.

We stopped on the sidewalk and looked back. The mob of reporters had followed a short distance behind us. They stood there uncertainly, and Horowitz glared at them.

"Hey, thanks," I said.

"You got a car?"

"No. I was going to walk."

"They'll follow you. Come on."

He led me to his Taurus, which was parked in the loading zone around the corner. We got in. He slapped his magnetic portable blue flasher onto the roof, and we pulled away and entered the flow of evening traffic on Boylston Street, heading east.

I smoked a cigarette as Horowitz maneuvered through the traffic, and we didn't talk all the way to my apartment on Lewis Wharf.

When he pulled up in front, he leaned toward me. "I wouldn't say a damn thing to the media if I were you."

I nodded. "I wasn't going to. Advice of counsel."

He grinned. "I was gonna tell you to get yourself a lawyer, too."

"I already got one."

"Any lawyer who tries to defend himself has a fool for an attorney, don't forget," said Horowitz.

"So I've heard." I opened the door, slid out, then leaned in. "Thanks again. Thanks for everything."

He waved me away. "Ah, you're a pain in the ass, Coyne."

"I try."

"I got some things I need to do," he said. "I'll get in touch with you. I ain't done with this."

"Neither am I."

The first thing I did when I got up to my apartment was go into the kitchen, take down my jug of Rebel Yell, and pour myself a double shot. I thought maybe I'd get myself blitzed again. Two nights in the same week. That would be a personal best, if you didn't count college.

I took my drink into the bedroom, shucked off my office clothes, and climbed into jeans and a sweatshirt.

The red message light on my answering machine was blinking like a toddler with a cinder in her eye. I pressed the button. The machine whirred for a long time as the tape rewound through a dozen or more messages. Then it clicked, beeped several times, and a voice said, "Mr. Coyne, this is Melissa DuPont at Channel Seven news, and—"

I hit the button. The next voice belonged to Dan Hutchins at the *Globe*, and the one after that was the eleven o'clock news anchor from Channel Four.

I turned the machine off, sat on my bed, lit a cigarette, and took a long gulp of Rebel Yell.

And then it finally hit me.

Both of my hands started trembling, my stomach lurched, and I couldn't catch my breath. I put my drink on the bedside table, stubbed out my cigarette, and lay back. I took several deep breaths. The booze burned in my stomach.

I closed my eyes. Pictures began flashing and whirling in my head.

Bobby Klemm's cruel eyes.

The black hole of his gun's muzzle.

The look of pain and fear in Julie's eyes.

The patch of dark, shiny blood on Klemm's powder-blue turtleneck.

Lieutenant Gillotte's skeptical smile.

The shrunken, lifeless lump inside that black body bag.

Brian Gold's naked childlike body in those grainy black-and-white photographs—

The phone beside my head bleated. I started to pick it up, then pulled my hand back.

I'd turned the answering machine off, so the phone just kept ringing.

After a minute, I reached over and unplugged it.

Then I let my head fall back on my pillow.

I didn't really sleep, and it certainly wasn't restful, but when I opened my eyes and looked at my watch, I saw that it was after ten o'clock. I'd stopped shaking, and my stomach was no longer flip-flopping.

I took my unfinished glass of whiskey out to the kitchen and dumped it down the sink. Then I made myself a fried-egg sandwich. I ate it standing over the sink. I realized I was famished. I made another sandwich, ate that one, then had a banana. I found a bag of oatmeal-and-raisin cookies and ate half of them.

Then I got a Coke from the refrigerator and took it into my bedroom. I picked up the phone and started to dial Evie's number before I realized I had no dial tone.

183

I plugged the phone in and tried again.

She picked up on the second ring.

"It's me," I said.

"Oh, God," she said. "Where are you? What's going on? I've been trying to call you all night. Are you all right?"

"I'm okay," I said.

"I saw it on the news. Is it true?"

"I killed a man today. Yes. What are they saying?"

"Nothing, really. They interviewed some police detective, and all he'd say was that you were not under arrest at this time, and that the victim was a known criminal. They showed a mug shot of him on the television, one of those head-on police pictures. He looked like a nasty man."

"*At this time?* Is that what they said?"

"Yes." Evie hesitated. "Brady, about the weekend . . ."

"Don't worry about it."

"I'm sorry," she said softly. "I was—I don't know. Upset with you."

"I figured you were."

She was silent for a minute. Then she said, "Sometimes I don't think it's working."

I didn't say anything.

"I didn't want to be with you," she said.

"You were with me when I needed you."

"Yes. Of course I was."

"Then, in the morning, you couldn't get away from me fast enough."

"I'm not sure I can explain it," she said.

"That's okay. You don't have to."

"I would if I could. It's just . . ." She laughed softly. "We do have some fun, don't we?"

"I know I do," I said. "Sometimes I'm not so sure about you, though."

"I had a date," she said. "Both days."

"Whatever," I said. "We've got no commitment."

She laughed quickly. "No, we don't, do we?" She hesitated. "Her name is Mary."

"Mary," I repeated. "Jesus. Don't tell me—"

"Oh, Brady. Not that." She chuckled. "Mary's an old friend, for heaven's sake. She and I used to hang out a lot."

"Before I came along."

"Yes. Saturday we went to the MFA. We always used to go to the museum on Saturdays, then go treat ourselves to dinner in a fancy restaurant. We spent all day Sunday dumping quarters into the slots down at Foxwoods." She hesitated. "Would you ever spend a Sunday at Foxwoods with me?"

"Not if I could help it."

"See," she said, "sometimes I like to do things like that."

"I don't like casinos," I said. "Crowds, noise, glitz. Everybody after your money. Such an intense, desperate quest for pleasure. It depresses me. I don't like shopping, either, or lying around on a beach, or ballet or opera or rock concerts. I don't like paying money to be entertained. I can entertain myself."

"What about Red Sox games?"

"That's different," I said.

She laughed. "Anyway," she said, "I know how you are. So I went with Mary. I had to get away, that's all."

"Away from me," I said.

"I guess so. I like to go places sometimes, and it's no fun going with somebody who's miserable."

I lit a cigarette. "I'm not very good at talking about this stuff."

"Yes," she said. "Don't I know it."

"Relationships," I said. "How I *feel*. I don't like to analyze those things. It doesn't seem to get me—us—anywhere."

She was quiet for a long moment. Then she said, "I felt guilty the whole time I was away, you know."

"That was dumb."

"It felt like I was cheating on you."

"I thought of that, actually," I said.

185

"That I was cheating on you?"

"Like I said—"

At that instant somebody started banging on my door. It was loud and insistent, and a man's voice was calling my name.

"Someone's here," I said to Evie. "It better not be more reporters. Hang on."

I took the phone out to the door and peeked through the peephole. It was Horowitz.

I opened the door for him, and he pushed past me. "Okay, Coyne," he said. "We gotta—"

"I've got a buzzer, you know."

He shrugged. "Figured you'd think it was a reporter and ignore me."

"You're right." I pointed at the telephone I was holding. "Make yourself at home. Be right with you."

I went back into the bedroom. "It's Lieutenant Horowitz," I told Evie. "I've got to go talk to him."

"Sure," she said.

"I'll call you."

"Not tonight," she said. "I've been worrying about you all evening. It's past bedtime, and you're okay, and now I've got to get some sleep."

"I meant I'd call you later in the week," I said. "We'll have ourselves a nice weekend. Maybe go somewhere. I don't mind museums."

"I'll call you," she said. "Let's leave it that way."

I looked at the phone for a minute after she disconnected. Then I put it back on its cradle and unplugged it again.

Twenty-One

After I hung up with Evie, I went out to my living room. Horowitz was standing at the glass sliders with his hands clasped behind his back, staring down at the harbor. The ferry was on its way out and some kind of barge was on its way in. Both craft were brightly lit. Their lights made wavy reflections on the wind-riffled water.

I stood beside him. "Kinda pretty, huh?"

He shrugged. He needed a shave, and his eyes were red, and his thinning black hair stuck up in clumps on the back of his head.

"You look like shit," I said.

He rubbed his whiskery cheek with the palm of his hand. "You got a drink?"

"Sure," I said. "I quit drinking, myself."

"Yeah? Since when?"

I looked at my watch. "Little over an hour ago."

He shrugged. "I want one. I don't give a shit if you have one or not."

"An hour is long enough," I said. "I'll join you."

187

He followed me to the kitchen and slouched into a chair at the table. I poured each of us a drink, then sat across from him.

Horowitz held up his glass. "Pretty, ain't it? The way the light comes through?"

"I never noticed," I said.

He took a gulp, held it in his mouth for a moment, then swallowed. He closed his eyes and sighed. Then he looked at me. "You're probably thinking you killed the bad guy today. Mystery solved. Case closed."

I shrugged. "I've been trying *not* to think about it, to tell you the truth."

"As soon as their ballistics boys match up that slug they dug out of your office wall with the ones they found in Sprague and the professor, run a couple bullets through Bobby Klemm's gun, that's how they'll play it."

"How will they explain Klemm's motive?" I said.

Horowitz shrugged. "They won't. They don't have to. Why bother? They don't have to prosecute him. He's the killer, now he's dead."

"So it's over," I said.

"Good chance of it. Officially, anyway." He arched his eyebrows at me.

"But—?"

"But that'll just be for public consumption, to give the media something, let everybody know they did their job, solved a multiple murder." Horowitz dipped his finger into his drink, then touched it to his tongue. "They ain't going to leave it lay, though. Chris Stone might be an asshole, but he ain't stupid, and the same goes double for Gus Nash. It won't sit right with either of them. Why the hell would Klemm assassinate a mild-mannered college professor in a barn, plug a chief of police in that very same professor's motel room, and then try to rob a lawyer in his own office at gunpoint? Especially when the professor's kid just died in a car crash, and the professor happened to be that lawyer's client and lived in the same town as that chief?"

"Because Klemm was dealing in kiddie porn and those three people found out about it," I said.

"Yeah, if you shared those photographs with them, that's maybe how they'd see it."

"Well, I'm not going to do that," I said. "The hell with motive. The bad guy's dead. That's good enough."

Horowitz took another sip from his drink. Then he put it down on the table and leaned toward me. "Bobby Klemm was no child pornographer, Coyne."

"Then who—?"

"I don't know. But I talked with some people this evening. People who knew Klemm."

"Who?" I said.

He shrugged. "Don't matter who. Klemm was strictly a free-lance gunslinger. Worked for hire. Killed people. That was his job. You want somebody dead, you pay Bobby Klemm, he'll do it. He was pretty good at his job, but he never had an original idea in his life. People I talked to, they laughed when I hinted at kiddie porn. Not Klemm. He wasn't smart enough."

"So you're saying the real bad guy is some mysterious pornographer, and he hired Klemm to—"

"To kill the people who found out about it," said Horowitz.

I nodded. "Okay. I get it. Jake Gold found those photos in his son's bedroom and went to his friend Ed Sprague. Sprague did some investigating, got a line on whoever it was, and—"

"Sprague's the one who killed those kids, don't forget," said Horowitz.

"Right," I said. "So Sprague was in on it."

Horowitz nodded. "But he was sloppy. That accident made a mess for them. So they hired Klemm to clean things up. Didn't just whack the two of them, though. First he tortured the professor, who told him about giving you those photographs. Then Klemm set up Sprague in Gold's motel room. Then he went after you."

"So I *was* right," I said. "Klemm would've killed me."

"No doubt about it. You and Julie both. Like I say, that was his job. Killing people. First he had to retrieve those photos."

"But he failed."

Horowitz nodded.

"Which means," I said slowly, "whoever hired Klemm isn't done with me."

"Not as long as you're holding on to those pictures." He arched his eyebrows at me.

"You're saying I should just give them to Gus Nash?"

He shrugged. "Make him agree to tell the media that you've turned over important evidence in the case. Bad guys hear that, maybe they'll leave you alone."

"Yeah," I said. "And maybe not." I shook my head. "I'm not gonna do it."

"You might not have a choice."

"What do you mean?"

"Look," he said. "Nash and Stone know damn well Bobby Klemm doesn't walk into some law office to commit robbery, okay? Nothing random about this. It was *your* office he went into. You're Professor Gold's lawyer. Klemm had to be after something. Nash and Stone'll hound you for it."

"Let 'em," I said. "I'll play dumb. Those photos are staying in my safe. Nobody knows they're there except you, me, and Julie."

Horowitz gave me his Jack Nicholson smile. "I figured you'd say something like that. Just remember, there's a hundred Bobby Klemms out there. Nothing special about him. Whoever hired him will hire someone else."

"You trying to scare me?"

Horowitz nodded.

"You're doing a good job of it," I said.

"I figure you got a few days to play with," he said. "It'll take 'em that long to find a replacement for Klemm, and it might take Nash and Stone that long to connect the dots and figure out you got something the bad guys want. You better hope it's the cops who come after you first."

"Then what?" I said.

"Then you probably ought to come across with those photos."

"And if I don't?"

He shrugged. "You get too stupid and stubborn, Coyne, you'll have to deal with me."

"You promised," I said.

"Yeah, well, I had my fingers crossed."

"Wait a minute—"

"I'll give you a few days," he said. "See what happens. After that, fuck it. I'll come and get them photos myself."

Horowitz held up his glass. It was empty. I took it, poured him a refill, and handed it to him.

He swirled the whiskey around in his glass. "I been working my ass off this evening," he said. "Made a million phone calls, talked with some of my colleagues. Had a very interesting conversation with a couple guys in vice." He took a sip, then peered at me. "I asked 'em about the kiddie porn industry in Massachusetts."

"I bet it's thriving," I said.

He shook his head. "Internet's the way to go these days. They can upload, download, in, out, and offload this shit. Photographs, films, live stuff, even, whatever, buy and sell, hard as hell to trace." He waved his hand. "Anyway, point is, from what the vice boys're telling me, no new players in New England have come into the game in the past year or so."

"Did you describe those photos to your colleagues?"

He shrugged. "A description wouldn't do much good."

"But you're saying these photos aren't being sold or traded?"

"Those photos are worth shit. Still photos, black-and-white, lousy quality? You seen the stuff you can rent at your local video store?"

I shook my head.

"A few years ago," said Horowitz, "those photos might've been worth something. How old are they?"

"They're all recent pictures of Brian," I said. "Okay, so what happens next?"

"So far, we got four murders," said Horowitz. "Five, counting what you did today. Who's next, do you figure?"

"Me, I guess."

He grinned. "That'd be my guess, too. You prepared to die to protect the reputation of a kid who's already dead?"

Brian, I thought, isn't dead. But I wasn't going to reveal that. Not to Horowitz, not to anybody.

"Of course I don't want to die," I said.

"Then maybe you oughta—"

I shook my head. "You said I've got a few days. I only just saw those photos this afternoon. I haven't had much chance to think it through. It's all pretty confusing right now. But this is what feels right to me, okay?"

He looked at me blearily, lifted his glass, drained it, put it down on the table, then stood up. "You've always been a stubborn bastard, Coyne. No sense even talking to you." He put both hands on the tabletop and shoved his face close to mine. "So, okay," he said. "It's about time you started *thinking* and stopped going on what fucking *feels* right. Think about what I been telling you. You don't turn over those photos, and make damn sure the entire world knows you don't have 'em anymore, there isn't much I can do for you."

I looked up at him. "Oh, I'll do some thinking. I guarantee that."

"Just don't go doing something stupid."

I smiled. "I can't guarantee that."

TWENTY-TWO

It was after midnight when Horowitz left.

I waited fifteen minutes to be sure he was gone. Then I put on my jacket, took the elevator down to the parking garage, and climbed into my car.

It occurred to me that I could be followed, and I didn't think it was paranoia. Whoever had hired Bobby Klemm knew that he'd failed. They weren't done with me.

Nor were the Boston police. Safe to assume that they considered me a suspicious character. After all, I had killed a man.

For that matter, I wouldn't have put it past Horowitz to stick somebody on my tail.

I didn't want to lead anybody to Brian Gold.

Traffic was predictably sparse on the Boston streets at half past midnight on a Monday night in February. I kept my eye in the rearview mirror as I wandered up and down and in and out of the hilly one-way streets in the North End, and I kept looping back around on myself until I was satisfied that nobody was following me.

Then I found Cambridge Street, hopped onto Storrow Drive, headed west, and took the Fenway exit.

It took me as long to find a parking space after I got there as it did to drive from my place on Lewis Wharf to the apartment behind Symphony Hall where Brian was holed up.

I figured somebody would still be awake. If I knew college kids, the night was young.

I found the building, went into the foyer, and squinted at the rows of buttons beside the mailboxes. I pressed number twenty-two.

A minute later the door buzzed. I pushed it open, climbed the stairs to the second floor, and knocked on the door at apartment twenty-two.

Jason, the kid who'd been there before, pulled it open, releasing a blast of amplified guitar into the hallway. He blinked at me. "Oh," he said. "It's you."

"You were expecting somebody else?"

"I certainly wasn't expecting you."

"Sorry. Can I come in?"

He shrugged. "I guess so." He stepped back, and I went into the apartment.

Two young women were sitting on the sofa. A blonde and a brunette. They were holding beer cans and watching MTV and jiggling their knees.

I smiled at them. They both smiled at me.

Jason went over and sat between them. "He's in his room," he said. "He's probably asleep."

"How is he?"

Jason shrugged. "I don't know. He hardly ever comes out of there."

"I've got to talk to him."

"That's up to him, I guess."

I went down the hallway and knocked on Brian's door.

"What?" he called from inside.

"It's Uncle Brady," I said. "We need to talk."

He said nothing.

"Brian," I said, "please. It's important."

"Go away," he said.

194

I tried the doorknob. It was locked.

"Listen to me," I said through the door. "I know about the photographs. I know why you're scared. I know why you don't want to talk to your mother. Let me help you, okay?"

"Leave me alone," he said.

"Dammit, Brian," I said. "Pay attention. I know Sprague tried to kill you. He killed Jenny, and he wanted to kill you, too. You two were running away, right?"

Brian was silent.

"Help me get the bad guys," I said. "It's time to talk to the police. You've got the answers. What do you say?"

What he had to say was nothing.

"We'll talk to your mother together," I said. "Think of how happy she'll be to see you, to know you're okay. Come on, kid. Let's do it. You and me."

There was no response from inside the room.

I waited a minute, then pounded on his door. "Brian, I swear if you don't answer me I'll break down this door and drag you out of there."

I felt a hand on my shoulder. I turned.

Jason was standing there glaring at me. "Leave the poor kid alone," he said.

"Do you know what's going on?" I said to Jason.

He shrugged. "He wants a place to stay, he doesn't want anybody getting on his case. He obviously doesn't want to talk to you. So you better just go."

"You haven't got a clue," I said.

"Maybe not. None of my business. But if you don't get out of here, I'm calling the cops."

"Look," I said. "I'm a lawyer, and—"

"I don't give a fuck what you are," he said. "You come barging in here, start threatening my friend, and I want you out. I'm gonna give you one minute."

I looked at him, then nodded. "Okay. You're right. I'm sorry." I took out one of my business cards and slipped it under the bedroom door. "I just put my card under your door," I called to Brian. "Think about what I said. You can call me any time. Okay, Brian?"

He did not reply.

I turned to Jason. "If you're his friend," I said, "you should encourage him to call me."

"He's in some kind of trouble, huh?"

"Yeah, you could say that."

I followed Jason back out to the living room, nodded to the two girls, and left.

As I drove back to my apartment on the waterfront, I replayed the scene in my head.

I definitely could have handled it better.

I paced around my apartment for a long time after I got back from my abortive visit with Brian Gold. Bobby Klemm, I figured, would surely have killed Brian if he'd been able to find him, and since he hadn't, it meant that Brian was safe where he was, at least for a while. As far as I knew, Sandy and Jason and I were the only ones who knew that Brian was alive and hiding out in a Northeastern University student apartment.

Sooner or later, whoever had hired Klemm to kill me and fetch those photos would hire somebody else. I didn't know what to do about it. Horowitz was on the case. That was comforting. So was Gus Nash. They were pros.

After a while, I almost convinced myself that I'd done everything I could do.

When I finally went to bed, I read a whole chapter from *Moby Dick*. Melville's complex prose and richly detailed narrative cleared my brain and exhausted me. After I turned off the light, I smoked a cigarette in the dark and wondered whether Melville or Hawthorne or Henry James or Jane Austen could even find a publisher in these Stephen King and John Grisham times.

Snowflakes the size of quarters were drifting down from a slate-colored sky when I woke up around nine-thirty the next morning. I stood behind my glass sliders sipping my coffee and watched the snowflakes swirl around over the black water before they touched down and the ocean ate them. Judging by the white mounds on the docks, nearly half a foot had fallen while I slept.

According to the folklore of Yankee farmers, big soft snowflakes mean a short-lived storm, but along the coast you can't tell. Inland, the flakes might be small and dense.

When I'd finally drifted off to sleep the previous night, I had dreams. In the only one that stuck with me, Bobby Klemm was lying there on the carpet in my living room. In my dream, Klemm was naked. He had the smooth, hairless body of a child, and blood was gushing like a Yellowstone geyser out of a softball-size hole in his bare chest. When I knelt beside him, he smiled and winked at me.

It was, I guessed, some kind of wish-fulfillment dream. According to Freud, they all are, although recalling it the next morning filled me with the same terrible dread and sadness I'd felt when I'd dreamed it, and I couldn't figure out what wish it fulfilled.

I liked the way the snowflakes dissolved when they hit the water, and I watched them for a long time.

When my mug was empty, I went back to the kitchen and refilled it, then took it into the bedroom, plugged in my phone, and called Julie at home.

Edward, her husband, answered. When I asked for Julie, he said, "Brady, can I talk to you for a minute?"

"Sure," I said. "What's up?"

He hesitated. "Well, I don't like this." His voice was soft, as if he didn't want Julie to hear him. "She's—both of us, actually—we're frightened."

"I understand," I said. "I was frightened, too. But it's over now."

"Actually," he said, "she's handling the—the shooting thing

197

pretty well. No, I mean the lying. You know how loyal to you Julie is. But she doesn't understand why you want her to lie, and neither do I. You can't lie to the police."

"I've tried not to tell her anything, Edward," I said. "The less she knows, the better. And I can't explain it to you, either. You both have to trust me."

"I think she should tell the police the truth, Brady. I think you're wrong to ask her to do this."

"Well, I can't stop her," I said. "All I can do is advise her." I lit a cigarette. "Look, Edward. She can't get into trouble unless she lies under oath in court, okay? Then it's perjury. If it ever gets to that, I'll be the first to insist that she blame me for misguiding her, and we'll both tell the whole truth."

"Well, you're a lawyer, but—"

"You know I'd never do anything to hurt Julie," I said.

"I know that."

"Please trust me, Edward. Some very nice, very innocent people could be terribly hurt if it all gets out too soon."

He hesitated for a minute, then said, "My concern is my wife, who also happens to be a very nice, innocent person."

"Listen," I said, "If I told you what I know, you'd agree with me. I know you would."

"Lying to the cops, though," he said. I heard him blow out a breath. "I don't know."

I didn't say anything, and after a few seconds, he said, "Well, I guess you called to talk to her."

"Yes. Thank you."

"Hang on."

A minute later, Julie said, "I've been trying to call you all morning."

"I unplugged my phone," I said.

"Reporters?"

"Yes."

"I guess I should consider myself lucky," she said. "Anyway, I wanted to know what we should do about your appointments today. When I couldn't reach you, I accessed our computer, downloaded our schedule and phone directory, and took the liberty of rescheduling. I hope that was all right."

"You're the boss," I said. "And a most efficient and cybernetically clever boss at that."

"Yes, I am." She laughed softly. "It worked out well. Megan got a snow day from school. We're going to make cookies."

"Julie—"

"It's okay," she said quickly. "Edward's upset, but I'm not. I told those police officers what you told me to say. I trust you. Lieutenant Horowitz assured me he was in our corner."

"I can't explain it to you," I said.

"I understand. I don't want to know."

"I assume we'll get our office back tomorrow."

"That's what I figured," she said. "I've lined up a busy day for you."

"Maybe that's what I need," I said. "A busy day talking with rich people about their money."

"It would be nice if you put in a full day of billable hours for a change, separated those rich people from some of their money."

"I'll do it," I said. "But you won't. I want you to take the rest of the week off."

"But—"

"Don't argue with me," I said. "I will not dock your vacation or your sick leave time. Stay home or go shopping or go to the Caribbean. Just don't come to the office. Okay?"

She hesitated. "What's going on, Brady?"

"I'll tell you all about it when I can."

"Will you be all right?"

"Sure."

"Be careful."

"Of course I'll be careful. I'll talk with you. Give Megan a hug for me."

I spent the rest of the day reading and tying flies and watching it snow. I tried calling Sharon Gold several times, but I kept getting her answering machine. After the third try, I decided to leave her a message. "Hope you're doing okay," was all I said. "Give me a call."

Maybe she'd decided to go stay with her mother for a while. I hoped so. It would be good for her to get away from Reddington. I assumed the police would keep Jake's body for at least a week. Until they released it, there was no reason for Sharon to hang around in that house full of ghosts and echoes.

And until Brian decided he was ready to confront her, I would just have to sit on my secret.

I had only two phone calls all day—both reporters. I told them I'd been advised not to talk to the media, and they didn't push it.

I figured by now the lawyer-shoots-intruder story was old news anyway.

The snow stopped in the middle of the afternoon. Then the clouds broke up and blew away, and the sun came out just in time to set. Tomorrow would be a pretty winter's day.

Wednesday was the last day of February. As I'd predicted, it was a cold, cloudless, sky-blue day. The sun cut through the thin air so sharply that I had to squint when I looked out my office window.

I saw clients all morning and had Chinese food delivered for lunch. I ate it off the coffee table in my office with plastic utensils and Coke. Julie always mocked me for eating fried rice with a fork. She was a chopsticks-and-green-tea gal.

It felt strange to be at my desk without Julie right outside my door, poised to nag me.

Boston homicide detective Dominic Gillotte called from his car around three-thirty and showed up a few minutes later. We stood there in the reception area. He leaned against Julie's desk and declined coffee.

"So how you doin'?" he said.

"Okay," I said with a shrug. "Busy, you know? So is this a social call?"

He smiled quickly. "Never is, is it?" He reached into the briefcase he was carrying and pulled out a plastic bag. It had my revolver in it. "Wanted to return this to you," he said. "It's unloaded. Here." He gave me the gun and dumped a handful of cartridges into my palm.

"Thanks," I said. "So what'd you learn?"

"What you told us. This gun fired the bullet that killed Bobby Klemm. It had your fingerprints on it."

"So where do I stand?" I said.

He shrugged. "I don't know. Turns out Klemm's gun killed two other people outside my jurisdiction, so the state cops are involved in the case. Needless to say, they're not sharing a helluva lot with me."

"Lieutenant Stone?"

He nodded. "And the DA. Mr. Nash. I expect they'll be calling on you."

After Gillotte left, I went back into my office. I took my gun out of the plastic bag, reloaded it, and started to open my safe. Then I paused, thought about it, and put the gun into the upper right-hand drawer of my desk.

TWENTY-THREE

———————————————

District Attorney Gus Nash and state police detective Christopher Stone showed up just as I was rinsing out the coffeepot at the end of the day. I ushered them into my inner office.

They made a Mutt and Jeff team. Gus was wiry and gray-haired and studious-looking behind his rimless glasses. Chris Stone had played tight end for B.U. back in the days before the university abandoned its football program, and he looked like he could still play. He'd gotten his master's in criminology at Northeastern, and while he had the dark, scowling look of a dumb tough guy, I knew he was shrewd and clever and ambitious.

"You guys want coffee?" I said. "I can put on a fresh pot."

Stone started to nod, but Nash said, "No, thanks. We're fine."

Stone gave a little shrug and shook his head.

So that's how it was. Nash was in charge. Stone had always been an ass kisser.

"So how're you doing, Brady?" said Nash.

"I'm fine, Gus. You?"

He smiled. "Me? Oh, I'm okay. I understand you had quite an experience."

"Yes. It was quite an experience."

"You know Detective Stone, I believe."

"Yes. We've met." I looked at Stone. "How's it going, Chris?"

"Pisser," he said.

"So what can I do for you guys?"

Nash jerked his head at the sofa in my conference area. "We need to talk."

I arched my eyebrows. "About what?"

"Come off it," growled Stone. "You know damn well—"

Nash touched Stone's shoulder. "Relax, Lieutenant. Brady's a good lawyer. He knows how it works."

"He's an officer of the fucking court," said Stone. "Good lawyers don't lie."

I poked my finger at Stone's chest. "Are you accusing me of lying?" I said.

"You're goddamn right. I—"

"Cut it out," said Nash. "Both of you." He touched my elbow. "Come on, Brady. Let's go sit. We need to get this straightened out."

I glared at Stone for a minute, feigning anger and outrage, which wasn't that hard, since I'd always disliked and distrusted him. Then I shrugged and allowed Gus to lead me over to the sitting area. I slumped onto the sofa. He took one of the armchairs across from me. Stone came over and stood beside Nash's chair.

I lit a cigarette, then looked at them. "So what am I supposed to be lying about?" I said.

"Why don't you just tell us what happened yesterday," said Nash.

"I already told those Boston cops. Don't you guys share?"

Nash nodded. "Humor me."

I shrugged. "Okay. Glad to help." And I proceeded to tell them the same story I'd told Gillotte, the Boston cop—that

Klemm had held Julie and me at gunpoint demanding our money, and when I'd slipped my revolver out of my desk drawer, he'd taken a wild shot at me and I'd reflexively pulled the trigger, hitting him in the chest.

As I talked, Gus nodded and smiled and asked for an amplification here and there. Stone scowled at me and said nothing.

When I finished, Nash said, "Bobby Klemm—that man you shot—he wasn't a thief or a burglar. We don't think he came here to steal your money."

"No?"

"We need to know what he was after."

I shrugged. "Money and jewelry. That's what he said."

"Listen, Brady," he said. "Bobby Klemm was a gun-for-hire. That twenty-two automatic he brandished at you and Julie is the same gun that killed Ed Sprague and Professor Gold."

I widened my eyes. "Jesus," I whispered. "Are you saying that man came here to kill me?"

Stone smacked his fist into his palm. "God*damn* it, Mr. Nash. He's yanking your chain. I told you he wouldn't cooperate. We're wasting our time. I say we haul his ass down to the station, read him his fucking rights, and stop pussyfooting around."

Nash looked up at him. "Oh, I don't think there's any need for that, Lieutenant. Brady wants to cooperate." He turned to me. "Right?"

"Of course," I said. "I'm an officer of the court, as the lieutenant has reminded me. I just don't know what you want me to say."

"So why'd you call Horowitz?" said Stone.

I shrugged. "He's a policeman. Friend of mine, as you know. First thing that came to my mind. I had no way of knowing you guys would be interested."

"Why not dial 911 like any other citizen would do?"

"I'd just shot a man," I said. "Maybe I wasn't thinking straight, I don't know. I've seen a lot of Lieutenant Horowitz lately. We're old friends. I trust him."

"Old friends," growled Stone. He looked at Nash. "This stinks," he said. "Fuckin' Horowitz—"

"You said you keep your gun in your desk drawer?" said Nash quickly.

I nodded. "So?"

"I understand it's been returned to you," he said. "Can I see it?"

I waved in the direction of my desk. "It's in the top right-hand drawer," I said, "where I always keep it. Help yourself."

Stone went over to my desk, opened the drawer, looked in, then closed it. "It's there," he said to Nash. He came back to where we were sitting and stood in front of me. "Horowitz's been coaching you, huh?"

I looked from Stone to Nash. "What's he talking about?"

Nash waved his hand. "Forget it, Brady. There's bad blood between the two of them. They used to be partners, you know."

I nodded. "Yes, I know. Horowitz is a good cop. He and Stone were therefore incompatible."

Stone's hands bunched into fists. "Goddamn it, Mr. Nash, so help me—"

Gus reached out and grabbed the sleeve of Stone's jacket. "Lieutenant, why don't you go back out there to the reception area, read a magazine or something."

Stone glowered at me, then looked at Nash. "He's playing games with us," he said.

"Go on," said Nash.

Stone turned and headed for the door.

"Don't steal any of my magazines," I said to him.

He narrowed his eyes at me for a moment, then threw back his head and laughed.

After Stone left, I said to Nash, "You guys've got the good-cop bad-cop thing down pat. Very impressive."

"You got it wrong, Brady," he said. "Chris isn't playing any role. He really and truly doesn't like you."

"Because I'm friends with Horowitz?"

206

"Because he knows you don't respect him."

I nodded. "I didn't realize he was smart enough to figure that out."

Nash smiled. "You don't have to antagonize him."

"It's not that difficult," I said.

He leaned back, propped an ankle over a knee, and fingered the crease on his pants. "Here's how we figure it," he said. "Klemm tortured Professor Gold before he killed him. We believe Gold told Klemm something that brought him here, to you. It has to be either something you know—maybe something about the professor—or something you have, like some kind of documents. Whatever it is, he wanted it. We figure, if you tell us what Klemm was after, we'll be able to understand what those two murders were all about."

"What makes the difference?" I said. "If Klemm killed Jake and Ed Sprague, you've got your murderer. Case closed, right?"

Nash shook his head.

"I get it," I said. "You think somebody hired Klemm. That's who you're after."

"Right. We got bigger fish to fry. That's why I need to know what Klemm wanted."

I spread my hands. "I wish I could help you, Gus. But if Klemm was after something other than my money and Julie's jewelry, he didn't tell us what it was."

"You saying you shot him before he had a chance to tell you?"

I shrugged. "I'm saying, if he was after something else besides our money and jewelry, he didn't say what it was."

Nash leaned forward. "The thing is, Brady," he said, "I'm in agreement with Lieutenant Stone. I think you're holding out on me."

"Why would I do that?"

"I don't know," he said. "But I intend to find out."

"You gonna turn into a bad cop on me, Gus?"

He smiled. "Did Klemm ask you any questions?"

"No."

"Any hint he thought you knew something about Gold or Sprague?"

I shook my head.

"That he thought you had information that would incriminate somebody?"

"Listen, Gus—"

He waved his hand. "Yeah, I know. That sort of information could be privileged. I'd like to look in your safe."

"My safe?"

"We spent all yesterday morning here in your office, Brady. We know you've got a wall safe behind that picture of your two boys. I figure if Professor Gold gave you something so important that somebody would send Bobby Klemm here to get it, you'd keep it there, in that safe."

"You're right," I said. "That's where I keep my absolutely confidential stuff."

"So open it for me," he said.

I shrugged. "I'd like to do that for you, Gus. But I can't, of course."

"Of course you can."

I shook my head. "I don't need to lecture you, Gus, of all people, on the sanctity of the attorney-client privilege."

"In this case," he said, "the client in question is Professor Gold, and he happens to be dead. That changes everything."

"In this case," I said, "the client's spouse remains alive, so even if I did have something of Jake Gold's in there, I couldn't show it to you."

"Even if it meant solving a double homicide?"

I shrugged. "Protecting my clients is my job. Solving homicides is yours."

"You're going to force me to get a court order?"

"Do what you have to do. I'm the only one who knows the combination to that safe, and I'm not going to open it, court order or not."

208

"You'd be willing to go to jail for this—this abstract principle?"

"Sure. I'm a noble guy, Gus. You know that. Anyway, it's hardly abstract."

He shook his head. "I don't know why you're refusing to cooperate with me, Brady. All I want to do is figure out why your client was tortured and murdered and a hired gun came here to kill you. I'm on your side on this thing."

"Maybe you should get Stone back in here, have him knock some sense into me."

Nash stared at me for a minute. Then he smiled quickly and stood up. "I was hoping you'd be sensible about this," he said. "I didn't want to have to play hardball with you."

"You don't," I said. "All you've got to do is believe me."

"Well," he said, "that's the problem. I don't." He started for the door, then stopped. "You'll be hearing from me, Brady."

I nodded. "Any time. It's always a pleasure, Gus."

He shook his head, then smiled, lifted his hand, turned and left.

After the door shut behind him, I went over to my desk, took my gun out of the drawer, and put it back into the safe where it belonged.

TWENTY-FOUR

I worked alone in my office all day Thursday. I heard nothing from Gus Nash and Chris Stone, but I wasn't fooled. I figured the two of them were digging around, looking for some way to confront me with a contradiction, spring an embarrassing tidbit of evidence on me, nail me in a lie.

I didn't hear from Horowitz, either, also no surprise. Even if he'd come up with something, it wasn't like Roger Horowitz to think of sharing it with me. He'd get ahold of me if he needed me for something.

The last time I'd talked to Evie, she said she'd call me, which meant that she didn't want me to call her. So I didn't.

Something was bugging her. Me, I assumed. I didn't like it, but when I tried to be objective about it, it wasn't hard to understand. I wanted to hear it from her, get a handle on it, talk it out with her, get our lives back. I didn't like not having a weekend with Evie to look forward to.

But she didn't call. Normally, I wouldn't notice. We rarely talked much during the week. But for the past few months, our weekends together had been a given. We didn't have to discuss them or plan them. We just assumed we'd spend them together.

Before she spent that Saturday at the Museum of Fine Arts with her friend Mary, and then Sunday down at Foxwoods in Connecticut, Evie and I had spent at least one day and night of every weekend together since around Thanksgiving.

I started to pick up the phone to call her a dozen times, and each time I resisted the impulse.

So when my phone rang Thursday night just after I'd finished my Melville bedtime reading and turned off the light, I grabbed it fast before she could change her mind.

"Hi, honey," I said.

There was a momentary silence, then a soft laugh. "Sorry to disappoint you. It's just me." It was Sharon.

I propped myself up in bed and got a cigarette lit. "How are you? Are you okay?"

She hesitated. "I guess it's all relative. Aside from being afraid and depressed and really, *really* angry, sure. I'm okay."

"Dumb question," I said.

"No, it's okay. Believe me, I've been dealing with a lot dumber stuff than that lately."

"Are you home?"

"Oh, yes. Back in my haunted house."

"You've been away," I said. "I've tried to call you several times."

"I've been at my mother's in Wisconsin. It was easier to go than to argue with her. I just got back this afternoon." She cleared her throat. "So why were you trying to call me? Is anything new?"

I couldn't say anything about Brian, as much as his secret was burning a hole in my heart.

And I didn't want to tell her about Bobby Klemm. That would raise questions I didn't want to lie to her about. I figured the Wisconsin newspapers hadn't carried the story.

"Nothing's new," I said.

"I'm wondering about Jake . . . his body . . ."

"I don't know, Sharon. I guess the police will be in touch with you when . . . when they're done with him."

She was quiet for a minute. I stubbed out my cigarette in the ashtray on my bedside table.

"Hey, Brady?"

"Yes?"

"Would you do me a favor?"

"Of course."

"Have dinner with me tomorrow?"

"Tomorrow?"

"I really need to talk about things."

"Okay," I said. "Sure. I'd like that."

"It's a Friday night, you know."

"I know."

"Aren't you—?"

"I'm free," I said. "Dinner would be great."

"I'll cook," she said.

"You don't have to do that. Why don't we go to a nice restaurant, let people wait on us."

"No," she said. "I'd like to cook. I'm a pretty good cook, you know."

"Well, if you insist."

She laughed. "I absolutely insist."

"I can be there around seven," I said.

"Wonderful. I'll see you then."

After we disconnected, I stared up at the ceiling in my dark bedroom.

March had come in like an angry beast. Friday was the second day of the month, and for the second day in a row, a cold, insistent wind blasted icy pellets of frozen rain against my office window.

When my phone rang in the middle of the morning, my first thought was Evie. My second thought was that I already had a date for the evening. I couldn't break it if I wanted to, and I wasn't sure if I wanted to.

I grabbed the phone on the second ring, cleared my throat, and said, "Brady Coyne."

213

There was a moment of hesitation. Then a male voice said, "I hope to hell you're satisfied."

"Huh? Who is this?"

"It's Jason."

It took me a minute. "Oh," I said. "Jason. Brian's roommate."

"Yeah," he said. "Make that former roommate."

"What're you talking about?"

"He's gone."

"What? Gone?"

"Disappeared, man. Flown the coop. Skipped town. Outta here. Gonzo."

"Where—?"

"If I knew where, you can be damn sure I wouldn't tell you, so you could go there and scare the shit out of him again. I don't know where he is. He left and he took all his stuff with him."

"When did this happen?"

"Sometime Wednesday when I was at class. The day after you were here. I didn't think much about it at first. None of my business where Brian goes. But two days and two nights he's been gone now, and I figure he wants to be someplace where you can't get at him."

"Jason," I said, "did Brian talk to you about any of this? Why he's been staying with you, why he's so upset?"

"I know his old man got murdered, if that's what you mean."

"He was with you before that happened, wasn't he?"

"Yeah. He was."

"But he didn't—"

"No. I don't know why he wanted to stay here. He was hiding out, that's all I know. I didn't ask, and he didn't tell me. I figured it was stuff with his parents. All he said was, he needed a place to crash for a while."

"And you don't have any idea where he'd go?"

"No."

"You understand that he could be in danger," I said.

214

"I guess I was thinking that, yeah."

"So if you know where he is—"

"I don't know, man."

"If you do, or if you figure it out, you've got to tell me."

"Why? You're the one who scared him off."

"I don't think it was me," I said. "I think it was the . . . the situation."

"Well, I don't know where he went."

"Do me a favor," I said. "No. Correct that. Do Brian a favor. If you hear from him, or if he shows up, let me know."

"He's in some kind of danger, huh?"

"Yes," I said. "It's serious stuff, Jason."

"I'll think about it," he said.

I saw clients and conferred with attorneys for the rest of the day and tried to keep thoughts and speculations about Brian Gold's ominous disappearance out there on the fuzzy fringes of my consciousness.

I'd done what I thought was the right thing, I told myself, and it had apparently backfired. It was useless to second-guess myself.

I did it anyway, of course.

It was chaotic without Julie there to run things, get the decks cleared on a Friday afternoon, and I ended up staying late to clean up the leftover paperwork, write myself some reminders, and in general clear my conscience so that I wouldn't feel I had to come in over the weekend or lug my briefcase home with me.

I had more important things to do on the weekend.

When I looked at my watch, it was nearly six-thirty. I'd never get to Reddington by seven, so I called Sharon and told her I was running a little late.

"No problem," she said. "Take your time. The driving might

be bad." I heard music in the background. It was The Band, singing "The Weight."

"I'll be careful," I said.

She hesitated. "If you don't want to . . ."

"I'll be there."

I stopped at a florist on Newbury Street, debated roses, decided they might imply something I didn't intend, and bought a mixed bouquet of what they called "spring blooms." Then I went to the gourmet wine shop next door and took the salesman's advice on a midpriced bottle of white and one of red.

I drove home, changed out of my office pinstripe into Dockers, shirt, sweater, and boots, and checked my answering machine.

No messages.

Friday evening, and Evie still hadn't called.

TWENTY-FIVE

The frozen rain was turning to snow, and it swirled in my headlights on the Mass Pike, where the speed limit had been reduced to forty. The plows weren't keeping up with the snow, and it was accumulating on the pavement, but the idiots still passed me going seventy. They threw slush against my windshield, blinding me while my wipers struggled to catch up, and I kept expecting to come upon a car in the median strip heading in the wrong direction with his headlights aimed at a cockeyed angle into the sky.

Where were the speed traps when you needed them?

I pulled up in front of Sharon's house in Reddington a few minutes before eight. I lugged the flowers and wine to the front door and rang the bell.

She opened the door a moment later. She was wearing a red sweater and blue jeans. Her feet were bare. She had her black hair pulled back in a loose ponytail and tied with a red-and-black silk kerchief. She wore pale pink lipstick and had done some subtle things to her eyes that didn't quite disguise the dark circles under them.

She smiled when she saw me, but the sadness showed in her

eyes. She tiptoed up, kissed my cheek, and hugged me quickly. "It's wonderful to see you," she said.

I was holding the flowers in one hand and the bag with the wine bottles in the other. My return hug was awkward.

When she stepped away from me, I held out the flowers. "Spring blooms," I said. "Pushing the season a bit optimistically."

She smiled and poked her nose into them. "They're beautiful," she said. "Thank you."

"And wine," I said, holding up the bag.

"Nice," she said. She blinked several times.

Please don't cry, I thought. *This is going to be hard enough for me.*

I lifted my nose and ostentatiously sniffed the air. "Umm, yum," I said. "Apple pie, huh? Smells good. I'm hungry."

She smiled. "Me, too." She turned and headed for the kitchen.

I took off my coat, hung it in the hall closet, and followed her.

She was standing at the counter cutting the ends off the flowers and fitting them into a vase. "You know," she said softly, "I can't remember Jake *ever* bringing me flowers."

I had nothing to say about that. I sat on a stool and watched her. She took her time arranging the flowers.

"I shouldn't have said that," she said after a minute. "About Jake. He tried."

"He loved you," I said stupidly.

She looked up at me. "I know. Why don't you open the wine, let it breathe."

"Which one?"

"We're having shrimp. I hope—"

"I love shrimp," I said. "The white, I guess."

I got the wine open, and Sharon finished arranging the flowers. She put them on the dining room table, and then we went into the living room.

"How about a drink?" she said.

"I gave up booze the other night," I said. "Fell off the wagon about an hour later. I think next time I might make it for two hours. Bourbon and a handful of ice cubes would be great."

She went over to a sideboard and poured drinks. "Want some music?"

"Wasn't that The Band you were playing when I called?"

"Yes."

"Play it again."

She put my drink on a napkin on the coffee table in front of me, then went to the corner and turned on her stereo. The Band started singing "Up on Cripple Creek."

Sharon came over and sat at the opposite end of the sofa from me. She tucked her bare feet under her and held up her drink. I picked mine up, leaned over, and clinked glasses with her.

"Tell me the truth," I said. "How are you?"

"Actually," she said, "it was probably a good thing, spending time with my mother. She's just one little bundle of gray-haired energy. We went shopping and we cleaned her cellar and she had people I haven't seen since high school over for dinner, and I even convinced her that I really did want to talk about Brian and Jake. She surprised me. She listened and she understood and she didn't insist I talk to her priest. I think I'm . . . coming to grips with it. I'm starting to realize I've got a life to live and I might as well start doing it." She sighed and shook her head. "I have my moments, still. It's going to take a while. I know that."

The Band was singing "It Makes No Difference," a very beautiful, very sad love song that always got to me. I found myself thinking about Evie.

"I'm okay about Jake, I think," said Sharon after a couple of minutes. "I saw—I had to identify his body. They wanted me to look at a video, but I told them, I said I want to see him, not a picture of him. So I know Jake is dead, you see? But Brian . . . ." She shook her head. "I still can't . . . ."

I hitched closer to her and took her hand. *Don't give up on*

219

Brian, I wanted to tell her. *I'm going to bring him home to you if it's the last thing I do.*

But I said nothing. I wasn't sure if it was the right thing to do, and I felt like a hypocrite, sitting there sympathizing with her about her dead son when I knew he was still alive. But I'd given my word.

"What about you?" said Sharon after a minute. "How are you doing?"

"Me? Oh, I'm fine."

"So why aren't you with your lady tonight?"

I smiled. "Because I'm here."

She nodded. "You men all think you've got to be so damned stoic. Jake was that way. So was Brian. Just fifteen, and he had already learned to keep it all inside."

"Keep what inside?" I said.

She shrugged. "I don't know. Whatever was bothering him. Nothing particular, I guess. Kids that age, they think everything is so important, you know?"

I nodded. "Was anything different before—?"

"Before he died?" She smiled quickly. "It's okay, Brady. You can say it." She shook her head. "To answer your question, I don't know. Yes, maybe. I thought he was, you know, just being a teenager. Noncommunicative. Not telling us where he was going or where he'd been or what he was doing. Staying out late. Locking his bedroom door. I tried to get him to talk, but he made it clear he didn't want to, at least not with his mother. I didn't think too much about it. Everybody I know who has teenagers always says the same thing. You just have to get through it. It used to make Jake crazy. Of course, Jake was the last person on earth Brian would talk to." She cocked her head and frowned at me. "Why are you asking?"

Because your boy is still alive, I wanted to tell her. *Because he has a secret, and he thinks it's so terrible that he'd rather you believed he was dead than have you hear it.*

I waved my hand. "No particular reason," I said. "What about the girl? Jenny? What was she like?"

220

"I hardly knew her," Sharon said. "Brian brought her home a couple times. I kept asking him if he'd like to have her for dinner or something, but he wasn't interested in that. She was almost two years older than Brian. She looked about twelve, but I had the impression that she was ten times more mature than he was. I used to think about them—you know, together. Petting. Her seducing him. Having sex."

I sipped my drink and remembered the photos. "Remember when you were that age?" I said.

She smiled. "God, do I. I hate to think I'd ever forget." She shook her head. "It was so strange, coming home last night. It felt like I'd been away forever. I expected it to be hard. You know, like Brian would be here, and Jake. But it wasn't like that. The house was empty, but that wasn't it . . ."

I waited, and when she didn't continue, I said, "What, Sharon?"

She shrugged. "Nothing, I guess. It's just—it felt like someone had been here. I don't mean like ghosts." She turned to me and put her hand on my arm. "Brian's bedroom door was ajar."

"Yes?"

"I've kept it shut ever since—since he died. I didn't want to see in there. Jake used to go in, but I didn't. I would've sworn I shut his door when I went to my mother's."

"You probably left it unlatched. A draft or something blew it open."

She nodded. "I guess so. It just felt spooky. When I saw it open, I had this overwhelming feeling of panic. Like Brian had come back, and if I looked in there, I'd see him, hunched over his desk doing his homework." She tried to smile. "I know. I'll have times like that for a while. I'll hear something, think it's one of my men coming in the room, or the phone will ring, or the floor will creak, and . . ." She waved her hand. "Well, anyway. About ready for dinner?"

"I'm famished."

"I've just got to sauté the shrimp. They'll only take a few minutes." She pushed herself to her feet. "You relax, enjoy your drink, sing as loud as you want to the music. I'll call when it's ready."

"Actually," I said, "I need to use your bathroom."

"Off the downstairs hallway or top of the stairs. Your choice." She turned and went into the kitchen.

I went upstairs. The bathroom was next to Brian's room, which was my actual destination. Sharon had latched his door. I opened it, went in, and closed it behind me. The room looked the same as it had last time I'd been there.

I knelt in front of the steamer trunk at the foot of his bed, lifted the top, pulled out the blankets, removed the false bottom, and peered in.

The scraps of torn-up money were gone.

My first thought was Brian. He'd slipped into his house while his mother was away to remove the last evidence of his shameful secret.

The money and the photos, hidden away in his trunk. He'd been paid to pose for those evil pictures. Or to keep his mouth shut about them. Dirty photos, dirty money.

Brian had ripped up the money.

I wondered why he hadn't destroyed the photographs, too.

Jake had found the photos and brought them to me for safekeeping, and then he'd gone looking for the people who'd corrupted his son.

He'd found them, too. Or else they'd found him. They'd watched while Bobby Klemm tortured Jake until he told them everything he knew. Then they'd had Klemm kill him, and they set about to clean up after themselves.

They sent Bobby Klemm to kill Ed Sprague, and then Klemm went to my office to retrieve the photos . . . and to kill me.

Then somebody came here, to Sharon's house.

Maybe it had been Brian.

It wasn't Bobby Klemm. He was already dead.

I realized that any vague thought—or hope—I might've still had that Bobby Klemm had been acting alone was wrong. As both Horowitz and Gus Nash insisted, Klemm was just the hired gun. This was not over with yet.

Jake had probably carried a house key in his pocket. They'd taken it when they killed him—whoever "they" were—and they used it to slip into Sharon's house. Maybe they came specifically for that ripped-up money. Maybe they had to be sure that all the photographs were gone. Fortunately, they'd come while Sharon was at her mother's.

I fitted the false bottom back in the trunk, returned the blankets, and shut it. Then I closed Brian's door behind me, went into the bathroom, and flushed the toilet.

I washed my hands and splashed water on my face. Should I tell Sharon that whoever had hired Bobby Klemm to torture and kill Jake might have a key to her house? If I did, I'd have to explain about the money scraps in Brian's trunk, which meant I'd have to tell her how her son had earned that money, and about the photographs, and I'd have to tell her about Bobby Klemm, and why Jake had been killed, and why Klemm had come to my office, and what I had in my safe.

And I'd have to tell her that Brian was still alive, or at least he had been a couple nights ago, but now he had disappeared again, thanks to my bumbling.

I decided to tell Sharon nothing.

If that turned out to be the wrong decision . . .

I couldn't allow myself to think about it.

I went downstairs. Sharon had replaced The Band with Dave Brubeck. A pair of tall candles flickered on the dining room table, and the vase of spring blooms sat in the middle. She'd set places with heavy silver and linen napkins. My open bottle of white wine sat in a pewter ice bucket.

I followed the aroma of garlic and butter into the kitchen. Shrimp scampi, with wild rice and asparagus.

Sharon was at the stove with her back to me. She was wearing an old-fashioned flowered apron tied in a bow behind her waist.

"Smells awesome," I said.

She smiled over her shoulder. "Go sit. I'll bring the salads."

I went into the dining room but didn't sit, and a minute later she came in with a salad bowl in each hand. She put them at our places, then said, "Help me with the apron?"

She turned her back to me and bowed her head. I untied the apron, lifted her hair, and eased the loop over her head. She turned to face me, holding out her arms, and I slid the apron off.

I held her chair for her, filled our wineglasses, then sat at my place across from her.

She lifted her glass. I did the same.

"To life," she said. "To the future. To everything that's good. Good friends, especially."

I nodded, tried to smile, and sipped my wine.

The salad featured avocado with cherry tomatoes, scallions, and ripe pitted olives on Bibb lettuce and a light vinaigrette dressing.

The candlelight danced on Sharon's face across from me. She kept looking up at me and smiling.

She was trying hard to be happy.

No way would I spoil that. I'd keep my secrets as long as I could.

"I don't remember the last time we sat down like a family and ate in here," she said quietly. "Brian was always off somewhere, and Jake hardly ever . . ."

She let the thought slide.

When we finished our salads, Sharon got up to clear away the bowls. I started to push back my chair to help, but she put her hand on my shoulder. "Please," she said. "Relax. I want to wait on you."

"I'm not comfortable," I said, "being waited on."

"You'll just have to suffer, then."

After we ate, we took slabs of hot apple pie and coffee back into the living room. I prowled through Jake's collection of

224

CDs and found Erroll Garner's *Misty* album, an old favorite of mine.

When it began, I realized that under the circumstances, this slow, sad song of love and loss and regret had been a monumentally stupid choice.

Sharon, sitting down at the other end of the sofa, was humming softly.

Look at me. I'm as helpless as a kitchen up a tree . . .

"I'm going to change the music," I said.

"No, please," she said. "I like this."

. . . never knowing my right foot from my left, my hat from my glove . . .

Sharon's eyes, I saw, were indeed misty.

We ate our pie without talking. Then I lit a cigarette, and we sipped our coffee.

After a few minutes, Sharon cleared her throat. "Brady," she said softly, "you've been avoiding the subject."

"Jake?"

"Yes. And Ed. And Brian, of course. And that man you killed."

"Oh," I said. "I didn't know you heard about that."

She nodded. "I talked on the phone to one of my neighbors when I was at my mother's. She told me."

"I don't know what's going on," I said. "The police are working on it."

She shook her head. "Please. I'm not stupid. You can't put me off like that. This has to be connected to Jake and Brian. You know something, and I have a right to know, too."

I nodded. "I agree that you have a right to know. But suspicious and speculations wouldn't do you any good. That's all I have now."

"They are connected, aren't they? All those—those deaths?"

"It looks that way."

"Brian, too?"

I shrugged.

She narrowed her eyes at me. "You're not going to tell me anything, are you?"

I shook my head. "Not until I know. Please trust me. When I know something, I'll tell you."

"Do you promise?"

"Yes. I promise."

"Even if you think it will hurt me?"

"Yes," I said.

"I have a right to that," she said. "And you have no right to protect me from the truth."

"I agree."

"I consider this a solemn vow, Brady Coyne."

"So do I."

"You do whatever you need to do to find out the truth for me. Okay?"

"I intend to," I said. "For both of us."

She nodded and settled back on the sofa.

We finished our coffee and listened to the music, and an hour or so later I looked at my watch and said, "Well, I should probably get going."

"So soon?" said Sharon.

"It's after eleven. It's been a long week."

She followed me to the front door. I slid into my coat, gave her a hug, and stepped out onto the porch.

The snow on the porch steps came up to my boottops and was swirling in the streetlights. Sharon's street had not been plowed, and my car was a snow-covered lump in her driveway.

I turned back to the door. Sharon was standing in the foyer, watching me through the storm door. She pushed it open for me. "Bad, huh?"

"No way I can drive," I told her. "I better crash on your sofa. Do you mind?"

"You can use the guest room upstairs," she said. "The bed's all made up."

"I don't want your neighbors talking."

"Actually," she said, "it would be comforting, not being

226

alone. This house feels awfully empty at night. And the hell with the neighbors."

I remembered that somebody might be running around with a key to Sharon's house. I saw no reason why he'd come back. On the other hand, there were a lot of things I didn't understand.

"I'll try not to snore," I said.

"I'd find that comforting, too," she said.

TWENTY-SIX

❧━━━━━━━━━━━━━━━━━━━━━━❧

Sharon's guest room doubled as Jake's office. It was lined with gray metal file cabinets, sagging book shelves, and an old oak desk with a Macintosh computer and an ink-jet printer and a rack of meerschaum and briar pipes on it. A twin bed was pushed against one wall. I wondered how many nights Jake had slept here instead of down the hall with his wife.

I kept the light on for a long time after I said good-night to Sharon. I flipped through some of Jake's books, smoked a couple of cigarettes, and thought about Evie, wondering if she'd tried to call. When I finally turned off the light, I lay there listening to the icy snow rattle against the side of the house and watching the light and shadows from the streetlight outside the window play on the ceiling.

The house groaned in the storm.

I thought of Sharon. She was trying desperately to get used to being alone. I wished I could tell her that her boy was alive, that one day soon she wouldn't be alone. But I didn't know how or when that was going to happen.

I hoped Evie was safely tucked in her bed.

And Brian. I hoped he was sleeping somewhere warm and

229

safe, missing his mother, understanding that nothing he had done could diminish her love. I hoped he was deciding that it was time to come home.

Maybe I dozed off, though it didn't feel as if I had, when I heard a floorboard creak outside my door. Then the knob turned and the latch clicked and the door squeaked as it opened.

I closed my eyes and breathed slowly.

I heard a faint silky rustle approaching my bed. Sharon's scent filled the room.

I pretended to sleep.

I sensed her standing beside me. My stomach clenched against the tension that was rising almost unbearably in my groin.

The candlelight, the music, the flowers, the food and wine. Sharon's perfume, her bare feet. It had all felt profoundly intimate. A prelude to something.

I realized I'd been repressing it all evening.

I risked slitting open my eyes. She was standing beside my pillow, so close I could've reached out and touched her. She was wearing a floor-length diaphanous gown. I could see the shape of her legs outlined against the light from the window.

I closed my eyes again and waited.

She stood there for a long minute. I sensed her bending over me, and then I felt her hand touch my cheek, hesitate, then move to my shoulder. She let out a soft, ragged breath. I thought she might be crying.

Her hand rested lightly on my shoulder for just a moment, but it seemed like much longer.

Then her touch was gone, and an instant later the door closed softly behind her.

I lay awake for a long time.

The aroma of bacon woke me up the next morning. When I walked into the kitchen, Sharon was unloading the dishwasher.

She was wearing sweatpants and a T-shirt and white cotton socks. Her dark hair hung loose down her back.

She smiled at me over her shoulder. "The coffee's ready." She jerked her head at the electric pot.

I poured myself a mug and sat at the table.

"How'd you sleep?" she said.

"Great," I lied. "Like a baby."

"So did I," she said.

I figured she was lying, too.

Scrambled eggs, corn muffins, bacon, orange juice. A fisherman's breakfast. It would get me through the whole day.

Afterward, I helped her clean up, and then we had more coffee at the kitchen table. Sharon was quiet, and I didn't have much to say.

I finished my coffee, stood up, and put my mug in the sink. "Well—"

"Brady?" she said quickly.

I looked at her.

"I want to tell you something," she said.

I sat down again.

"Last night," she said. "It was . . ." She lowered her eyes, avoiding mine. "It was nice."

I nodded but didn't say anything.

"I'm trying to fight it," she said, still looking down at her hands, which were gripping her coffee mug, "but I'm not as . . . as tough as I thought I was. I'm feeling very alone, very vulnerable, very sad, very angry. Sometimes I manage to put it out of my mind, but then it all comes smashing down on me. This almost unbearable feeling of despair."

"It's going to take a while," I said. "You really should talk to somebody. You shouldn't fight it. You should confront it."

"That's what Officer Benetti said. She gave me some names."

"You should call one of them."

"I know." She looked up at me. "I came into your room last night."

231

I nodded.

"You knew?"

"Yes."

"I thought all I wanted was a hug," she said. "But if you'd just looked at me, or—or touched me . . ."

I shook my head. "That's the last thing you need, Sharon."

She reached across the table and put her hand on top of mine. "I know. You're right, of course."

"You don't know how tempting it was," I said.

She smiled. "That's sweet. Thank you for saying that."

"It's the truth." I glanced at my watch. "Well . . ."

"Yes," she said. "You should go."

She hugged me at the door.

"Every day will be a little better," I said.

She shrugged. "That's what I keep telling myself. You'll keep in touch with me?"

"Of course."

"Come for dinner again?"

"Sure."

The two-day storm had passed during the night. The sun was bright and warm. Clods of wet snow were falling from the trees and shrubs in Sharon's front yard. They hit the ground with a muffled thump, and the branches that had been bent over were springing back up.

I brushed the snow off my car and managed to ram it through the pile the plow had left at the end of the driveway and drove out into the street.

It was a little after ten on this Saturday morning. I drove over to the camera shop. Sandy Driscoll was behind the counter toward the back of the store talking with a white-haired man. A middle-aged woman stood beside her, talking on the phone.

When Sandy saw me, she frowned. I arched my eyebrows at her, and she shook her head.

I looked at the display of camera bags and tripods, and a few minutes later the white-haired man left the store. Sandy came around the counter and stood beside me. She darted a quick glance at the woman behind the counter, then said, "Can I help you with something, sir?"

"I need—"

"Oh, right," she said quickly. "You wanted an album. This way, please."

She led me to the front of the store, pulled a photo album off a shelf, and handed it to me.

I pretended to examine it. "I need to talk to you," I said quietly.

"Please. Leave me alone."

"Brian has disappeared again. We've got to talk."

She shook her head. "No way."

"I'm sorry, Sandy," I said softly. "But I'm prepared to go to the police, tell them that Brian's alive and you know where he is. It's not what I want to do. But you're not leaving me any alternative. Is that what you want?"

She shook her head.

"Talk to me, then."

Sandy glanced over her shoulder. The woman behind the counter was still on the phone. She was looking at us.

"I don't want her to recognize you," Sandy murmured. "It's almost time for me to run out for coffee. It'll be about ten minutes if we don't get a gang in here. Leave now. I'll meet you out front."

"Fine," I said in a normal voice. "Thanks, anyway."

I went outside and waited in my car.

About fifteen minutes later, Sandy came out and slid into the passenger seat. "Drive somewhere," she said.

I pulled out onto the road. "Which way?"

"Left, I guess," she said. "Head for the college. I'll get coffee at Drago's."

"Do I make you nervous?" I said.

"It's a small town, Mr. Coyne. You were on television a few nights ago."

233

"I was?"

"You killed a man. They showed you coming out of your office."

"Oh, that."

"I know about Brian," she said.

"Where is he?"

"Oh, no," she said. "You scare him."

"He's okay?"

"He's alive, if that's what you mean. He's depressed and frightened."

"He called you the other day, right?"

She nodded. "I picked him up at Jason's. He's pissed at me for telling you where he was. He doesn't want anybody to know where he is now, and I'm not saying anything else about it."

"But you know where he is."

"I told you—"

"Okay," I said. "I'm sorry." I blew out a breath. "Sandy, just tell me, what's going on around here?"

She laughed quietly. "You want me to tell you things that nobody in this town wants to know. When it all comes out, I don't want anybody connecting it to me."

"So you *will* tell me?"

She hesitated. "I've been thinking about it. Thinking I should tell someone. You've got to promise—"

"You can trust me," I said.

"Yeah, well, you promised you'd leave Brian alone. I trusted you on that."

"Things changed."

"That man you killed?"

"Yes. But I've kept your secret. Yours and Brian's. I had dinner with his mother last night. She has a right to know that he's okay. But I didn't tell her. That was painful for me."

She was quiet for a minute. Then she said, "Most of what I know is secondhand. Hints I've gotten, things kids've said to me. Secrets, Mr. Coyne. I don't know how it all fits together."

234

"Let me ask you something about photography," I said.

"Photography?"

"I have these photos," I said. "They're kind of grainy, and they're printed on paper that seems thinner than regular photo paper. Not what you'd get if you took a film to your shop to be developed."

"Maybe someone printed them in a home darkroom," she said. "Maybe they're photocopies. Or they could've been scanned on a computer or taken with a digital camera and loaded into the hard drive. Then you could print them out on any kind of paper."

"I don't know anything about that technology," I said. "Would that make them grainy and blurry?"

"Depends on the equipment and the quality of the paper," she said. "Maybe the photos were poorly exposed in the first place."

I remembered what I'd seen in Ed Sprague's office. A computer. Digital cameras. Scanners and printers. "I want you to tell me about Chief Sprague," I said to Sandy.

I heard her let out a long breath. I glanced at her. She was looking out the side window.

"From my personal experience," she said softly, "he was just a nice man who cared about kids. It's not like we were friends or anything." She hesitated. "But that's because I'm not—not young-looking and attractive and skinny and athletic. Some of the kids . . . he was, um, closer with."

"Like Brian Gold?" I said.

"Yes. Like Bri. And Jenny and Mikki. There were a few others. His favorites."

"What do you mean, he was closer to them?"

"He had them over to his house all the time. He had a swimming pool, they had cookouts, they paddled his canoe around his pond. Their parents thought it was cool. What better place for kids to be than the chief of police's house? There's nowhere in Reddington for kids. We don't even have a mall. Ed's house was a place where kids could go, relax, have fun. Nothing organized. Ed let them do anything they wanted."

"What do you mean?"

"He just left them alone," she said. "Except he didn't allow drugs or booze. He said he'd arrest anybody who was breaking the law."

"So what do you want to tell me, Sandy?" I said.

She exhaled deeply. "You remember Mikki?"

"Sure. The girl who was with you that day by the river."

"She told me that Ed didn't mind if the kids . . . used his bedroom."

"What are you saying?"

"What do you think?"

"You mean he let them have sex in his house?"

She nodded.

"Is that it?"

"Okay," she said. "Mikki told me they sometimes had group sex. Like orgies, okay? I don't mean Ed. But sometimes friends of his were there."

"Adults, you mean?"

"Yes."

"And the kids didn't mind that?"

She mumbled something I didn't hear.

"What did you say?" I said.

She cleared her throat and turned to face me. "Mikki said they got paid."

"For doing what?"

"For—for performing."

"You mean Sprague's friends would watch?"

"Sometimes they just watched. Sometimes they'd . . ."

"Have sex with the kids?"

"Yes. That's what Mikki told me."

"Who paid them? Sprague?"

"His friends, I think. Mr. Coyne, you can't tell anybody I told you this. Please."

"You have my word." I paused. "How long has this been going on?"

"Not long, I don't think. A couple months? Mikki mentioned something about Christmas vacation."

"Who else knows about these—these orgies?"

"I don't know. Mikki told me. We're best friends. I don't think anyone else knows. Can you imagine if their parents found out about it? This town would explode."

Like Jake, I thought. Jake knew. He found those photographs, and he exploded.

"So what do you think happened?" I said.

"To Jenny and Bri, you mean?"

"Yes."

She was quiet for a moment. "It's pretty obvious, isn't it?"

"Tell me what you know."

She sighed. "I don't know anything, really. Brian—that night I picked him up, the night Jenny . . . when she died . . . he didn't say much to me. But the other night, after you—you went there and scared him—he told me he and Jenny had decided to run away."

"And Sprague went after them, ran them off the road."

"Yes."

"Brian told you that?"

She nodded. "They were good kids, Mr. Coyne. They got into something they shouldn't have, and they wanted to stop, and he wouldn't let them."

"He was afraid they were going to tell somebody," I said.

Sandy shrugged. "I don't know. I guess so."

"So who killed Sprague?"

"Bri's father, I thought."

"No," I said. "Somebody else. The same person who killed Sprague also killed Jake Gold. That was the man I shot the other day. Somebody hired him. I want to know who."

"I don't know," she said. "Honestly."

I pulled into the parking area at Drago's. There were only a few cars in the lot on this Saturday morning. I parked off to the side away from them, and we sat there in silence for a few minutes.

"Want some coffee?" said Sandy.

"Thank you. Black." I took out my wallet and gave her a five-dollar bill.

She was back ten minutes later. We sat there, sipping our coffee.

"You should've told me this before," I said.

"I figured it was all over," she said. "When Ed died, I mean."

"It's not over." I looked at her. "Sandy, were you ever there?"

"At Ed's?"

"Yes."

She shrugged. "I told you. I was there a few times. Ed didn't care who was there. But I stopped going when I realized what was going on. And I never..." She looked at me. Her eyes were brimming.

"It's okay, Sandy," I said.

"I'm not into sex. Anyway, I'm too fat."

"You're not too fat," I said.

She shrugged. "His friends, they liked the skinny, young-looking kids. Like Brian and Jenny. Jenny hardly had breasts."

"Did you meet any of Ed's friends?"

She looked out the side window and said nothing.

"What about that man I shot?" I said. "His picture was in the paper, on TV. Did you recognize him?"

She shook her head.

"Come on, Sandy. People have been murdered. Brian's in trouble."

"I didn't recognize that man." She turned to look at me. "Please, Mr. Coyne."

"You did meet some of Sprague's friends, didn't you?"

She shrugged. "Sort of."

"Would you recognize them if you saw them again?"

"I don't know. I don't think so. Look, I really shouldn't be talking to you."

I told you—"

"I know. But I don't want to talk about it anymore, okay?"

"Sure. I'm sorry."

We drove back to the camera store in silence. When I pulled up in front, Sandy turned to me. "I've told you everything."

I nodded.

"So don't come around again, okay?"

"Okay."

"If I think of anything else," she said, "I'll call you."

"The last thing I want to do is make trouble for anybody," I said.

She peered at me for a moment. "It's a little late for that, don't you think?" She laughed quickly, then got out, slammed the car door shut with her hip, and walked directly into the camera store without looking back.

I pulled away and headed back to Boston. I had to do some thinking.

I got home a little after one in the afternoon. I went directly into my bedroom. The red light on my answering machine was blinking steadily. One message.

Evie.

I sat on my bed and pressed the button.

"Hi, Brady." The soft feminine voice belonged to Sharon, not Evie. "I just wanted to thank you again," she said. "The flowers, the wine. The . . . the sympathetic ear. It was all so sweet. I had a lovely evening. I meant it about doing dinner again, you know. I hope you did, too." She paused, then laughed quietly. "I think I'm feeling a wee bit better today. One day at a time, huh? Anyway, that's my message for today. I just wanted to thank you for everything. I hope you'll keep in touch with me."

The machine rewound itself and beeped.

I sat there and stared at it. I wondered if Sharon would thank me if she knew what I wasn't telling her.

I went to the kitchen, made some coffee, and took it out onto my iron balcony overlooking the harbor. I leaned my elbows on the railing and savored the summerlike breeze. The snow on the docks below me had nearly disappeared.

Sandy's story whirled in my head. Evil secrets in a small town. It made me want to puke. It made me want to strangle somebody.

I thought about Evie. Where the hell was she? She had said she'd call me. I needed her.

Maybe I'd misunderstood. Maybe she was waiting for me to call her.

Hell, I wasn't proud. I had to talk to her.

I dialed her number. When her machine answered, I hung up without leaving a message.

I showered, shaved, and pulled on a pair of jeans and a flannel shirt. Then I went into the kitchen and heated up a can of Progresso lentil soup. I ate it at my table and thought about what Sandy had told me.

By the time I finished my soup, I knew what I had to do.

I waited until five o'clock to leave. I wanted it to be dark when I got to Reddington.

I pulled on a dark blue ski parka, my Herman's Survivor boots, a black knit watch cap, and thin leather gloves. I checked the batteries in my little cigar-size flashlight, stuck it into my jacket pocket, then took the elevator down to my car and drove over to my office in Copley Square.

When I got there, I went directly to my safe, took out the envelope of photographs, and spread them out on my desk.

They'd been printed on some kind of flimsy photographic paper with a shiny surface. They were as hard to look at this time as they had been before. But I forced myself to study them.

Brian and Jenny were easily identifiable in each of them. The other naked and seminaked bodies appeared to belong to several different people, both male and female. None of them was young. All of the faces except Brian's and Jenny's were averted from the camera. No help there. If there were tattoos or birthmarks or distinctive scars on any of those adult bodies, I couldn't make them out.

The surroundings were blurrier than the faces, but I could see that there was a patchwork quilt under the bodies, a lamp with a square shade on the table beside the bed, the corner of a window with no curtain, half of a picture frame beside the window.

There had to be other photos. Photos that showed faces besides those of the kids. I wanted them.

I slid the prints back into the envelope and returned them to the safe.

My hand hesitated when it brushed against the .38 Smith & Wesson. I took it out, held it for a minute, curled my finger around the trigger, hefted its weight.

I remembered the way Bobby Klemm had slammed backward onto the floor when I shot him, the way the blood had soaked his sweater, the way his eyes had stared up at the ceiling, seeing nothing.

I wondered if I could use my gun again.

Then I thought about those vile photos. I remembered Jake's dead body, spotted with cigar burns. I remembered Brian, curled fetally on a bed in a darkened room in Boston, telling me to go away. I thought about Sharon, her terrible dreams, her brave smiles, and I thought about Sandy Driscoll, and Mikki, and the other Reddington children, the unspeakable secrets that were haunting them.

Could I use my gun again?

I slipped it into my jacket pocket.

Damn right I could.

TWENTY-SEVEN

***

Sharon's porch light glowed a warm, welcoming orange. When I climbed the steps, I heard the sounds of television voices from inside. She opened the door before I took my finger off the doorbell.

She blinked, then smiled. "Oh," she said. "Brady. How nice." She pushed the storm door wide open. "Come on in. It's chilly out there."

I stepped into the little flagstone foyer. Sharon gave me a quick hug.

"I need you to do me a favor," I said.

"Of course," she said. She frowned, then took my hand and led me into the living room and turned off the TV. She was wearing tight-fitting black leggings and a man-size red-and-black checked wool shirt. The sleeves were rolled up over her elbows and the tails flapped down nearly to her knees. One of Jake's shirts, I guessed.

She turned to face me. "You've got that serious look," she said.

"I want you to drive me over to Ed Sprague's house," I said, "and I don't want you to ask why."

"Ed's?"

I nodded.

"Now?"

"Yes."

She shrugged. "Well, sure. Okay. Got time for a drink first? Or coffee?"

"No. I want to go right now."

"I'll get my coat."

I drove her car over the dark country roads. Sharon sat silently beside me. When I stopped at the end of Sprague's long sloping driveway, I looked at my watch. "It's seven twenty-five," I said. "Pick me up right here at nine-thirty."

"What if you're not here?"

"Go home and come back an hour later."

"This seems awfully . . . clandestine," she said.

"Oh, not really," I said. "I just don't think my car can get back up this driveway with all this snow, and I don't want to leave it on the street."

"Because you don't want anybody to know you're here."

"It's a crime scene," I said.

She was silent. She was remembering, I guessed, that the crime had been Jake's murder. "So you're going to break the law," she said after a minute.

"Technically, I guess."

"But you're not going to tell me why."

"No." I reached over and touched her cheek. "See you in two hours, okay?"

"I've got a better idea," she said. "Just call me when you're ready." She touched my arm and put something into my hand.

I held it up to the light. It was a cell phone. It wasn't much bigger than a thin deck of cards.

"Julie keeps telling me I should get one of these things," I said. "So I can keep in touch, she says. The truth is, most of the time I like being out of touch."

"They can be handy," said Sharon.

I slipped the little phone into my pants pocket and climbed

out of the car. Sharon got out the passenger side and came around, and I held the door for her. She slid in behind the wheel. "Well," she said, "see you later."

I nodded and closed the door, and she drove away.

The sliver of a new moon hung low in the star-filled sky. It was a clear, cold late-winter's night, and the fresh snow seemed to gather the starlight. It lit up the countryside with a pale bluish glow, and I didn't need my flashlight to navigate.

Sprague's driveway hadn't been plowed since the recent storm. The snow had melted and settled during the warm day, but the driveway was still covered with three or four inches of new snow. As I started toward the house, I found myself following the tracks of a large deer. They went about halfway down the slope before they abruptly veered off into the piney woods on the left.

When I got to Sprague's house, I fished my flashlight from my pocket and turned it on. A strip of yellow police crime-scene tape had been strung across the front porch. I ducked under it and found the key under the rocking-chair cushion. There was an X of tape over the front door, too, along with a cardboard sign that read: POLICE CRIME SCENE. The tape was flapping loose. I guessed the storm had torn it away from the doorway.

Actually, the crime scene itself had been the barn, not the house.

I unlocked the front door and put the key back. Then I ducked around the loose tape and went inside.

I followed the narrow beam of my flashlight directly to Sprague's office and sat down in front of his computer.

For years, Julie had kept insisting that I should learn how to use our office computer. I'd held out as long as I could. She called me "Old Man Technophobe," which I didn't take as any kind of insult whatsoever. I kept telling her that if I knew how to use the computer, I wouldn't need her anymore.

Finally, just a couple of years ago, I surrendered. Our office Mac was surprisingly simple to operate. I rarely used it myself,

245

but I liked being able to drop words like *megs* and *RAM* and *download* into casual conversation as if I knew what I was talking about.

I shone my light on the keyboard, pressed the key to turn it on, then shut off my flashlight and watched the icons pop up on the screen.

I'm not sure what I expected. Maybe a file labeled "dirty pictures." But no such luck.

I clicked on the icon called "hard drive," and a moment later a list of folders appeared on the screen. None of them was labeled "dirty pictures" or "kiddie porn" or "Brian Gold." I scrolled through the list. There seemed to be hundreds of items, many of them coded with numbers and letters that meant nothing to me.

It would take me hours to examine all of it. I clicked randomly on several of the folders and opened the documents inside them. All I came up with was text, stuff that Sprague apparently had downloaded from the Internet—statistical crime reports, articles about juvenile delinquency, Supreme Court decisions, studies from the FBI and the DEA, descriptions of experimental crime-prevention programs, speeches on crime and enforcement. Just the sort of thing a conscientious police chief would store in his computer.

No photos. Nothing that appeared remotely related to pornographic pictures of children.

All I wanted were some faces. One face would be enough.

But if Ed Sprague had stored his photos in his computer, he'd hidden them well. It would take time—and someone geekier than I—to dig them out.

I turned off the computer, turned my little flashlight back on, and made my way upstairs.

The upstairs hallway ran across the front part of the house, and two bedrooms occupied the full dormer on the back. I looked into what I assumed was the guest room, the smaller of the two. It held a pair of twin beds, a desk and chair, a shoulder-high chest of drawers, bookshelves. I remembered the photographs. They had not been taken here.

Between the two bedrooms was a small bathroom that opened into the hallway. I shone my flashlight into it—a mirrored medicine cabinet over the sink, toilet, shower stall, linen closet, and on the rear wall a door that opened into a larger bathroom, the one that adjoined the master bedroom.

I went into Sprague's bedroom. Those photographs, I instantly saw, had been taken here. I recognized the patchwork quilt. In a couple of the pictures, Brian and his partner had been lying on top of it. In others, the quilt had been thrown back. The bedroom window beyond it had no curtains. A framed watercolor painting of sailboats on what looked like a salt pond hung beside it. The lamp on the bedside table had a squarish shade.

I moved around the room, trying to find the angle from which those photos had been taken. I ended up with my back against the tall mirror that hung against the inside wall beside the door that opened from the bedroom into the master bathroom.

I went into the master bathroom. It had a Jacuzzi, two sinks, and a double-wide linen closet. I opened the closet door, and when I pulled a stack of towels off a shelf, I found myself looking into Sprague's bedroom. The bed was right there, and the window and the framed watercolor painting were beyond it.

I was looking through a one-way mirror.

Sprague had entered this bathroom from the hallway through the other bathroom without the people in the bedroom knowing it. He braced his camera on the closet shelf and clicked away.

The photos in my safe matched up perfectly with the view through this one-way mirror.

I put the towels back on the shelf and closed the closet doors. Now what?

One voice in my head—a strong, logical, sensible voice—told

247

me to get the hell out of there, call Horowitz, and dump it all on him.

But another voice kept reminding me that I hadn't snooped thoroughly enough, that I should learn everything I could, that once it was out of my hands, there was no way I could control what would happen.

What I needed was buried in Sprague's computer. I had to figure out how to ferret it out. Horowitz couldn't do that. He was off the case.

I stepped out of the bathroom and paused in the hallway. I heard a faint rustling sound behind me, no more of a noise than a mouse would make scurrying across a carpet. Before I could turn around to shine my light on it, something heavy slammed into the back of my legs.

My flashlight went flying, and I toppled forward. My head crashed against the wall, and I went down on my stomach.

He was on top of me instantly. Fists smashed against my head and shoulders. He was grunting, pounding away at me. Fists like pistons, bouncing off my skull, my arms, my back.

I curled into a ball, braced myself, and heaved, and he went flying.

I went after him in the dark, scrambling on all fours. I got ahold of his leg, yanked at it, pulled him down, grappled with him, got him in a bear hug.

I squeezed him as hard as I could. He wasn't very big, but he was kicking and straining against me.

I tried to get my forearm around his throat. He had his chin tucked down.

Then he got my wrist between his teeth.

"Ow!" I said. "Shit."

I ripped my wrist away and punched at him in the dark. I hit him in a soft place, and I heard the breath whoosh out of his mouth.

I threw myself onto him. He was lying there, limp and gasping for breath.

My flashlight was lying a few feet away. Its narrow beam

was shining against the wall. I grabbed it and shone it on my assailant.

It was Brian.

His face was streaked with tears and he was wheezing and panting.

"It's me," I said to him. "Uncle Brady." I shone the flashlight on my own face.

He looked wide-eyed at me. "I thought . . ."

"Did I knock the wind out of you?"

He nodded.

"You got me pretty good, too," I said.

He tried to smile. "I didn't know who you were. I'm sorry."

I reached for him, pulled him against me, and hugged him. "I'm not going to let you get away this time," I said.

I felt his shoulders shaking.

"You've been here since you left Jason's?" I said. "Sandy brought you here?"

"Yes," he whispered.

"Are you ready to go home now?"

"I guess so."

"First, we've got to—"

At that moment, a car door slammed out front.

TWENTY-EIGHT

I put my finger to my lips, and Brian nodded.

I flicked the flashlight off.

Voices came from outside the house.

The Reddington police, probably, on routine patrol, keeping their eye on their dead chief's vacant place.

I didn't want them to find me here. I didn't know if I could trust anybody on the Reddington police force. Sprague had been their chief. Maybe some—or all—of the Reddington officers had been involved in Sprague's sick business. Lucas McCaffrey, the redheaded cop, was ambitious. I'd seen him with Sprague. Tory Whyte claimed to despise him. But she'd been sleeping with him. I didn't know anything about the other Reddington cops.

I didn't know whose faces were on those photographs.

The only person I could trust was Horowitz.

Well, they'd be gone in a minute.

Then I remembered that the crime-scene tape had been ripped away from the front door.

Shit! I'd also left footprints in the new snow. They led from the road, down the middle of the driveway, up onto the front porch and into the house. It wouldn't take Daniel Boone to follow my tracks.

Maybe they'd chalk it up to nosy kids.

Wishful thinking, Coyne.

There was no upstairs window on the front of the house, so I couldn't look outside. But I figured the first thing they'd do would be to walk all the way around the house, looking for footprints leading away.

Of course, they wouldn't find any. Then they'd know I was still here, and they'd come in for me.

If I tried to hide, they'd keep looking until they found me.

Maybe I should just go downstairs and say hello to them. I could try to bluff my way out. Brian could hide upstairs. He could slip away later.

Or I could explain in a general way why I was here and insist they call Horowitz.

Except I didn't dare trust them.

Anyway, they wouldn't buy it. They'd arrest me.

They might not arrest me. They might shoot me. Jake and Sprague had been shot. It wouldn't be hard for a dirty cop to make up a plausible story that would justify killing a burglar— an armed burglar at that—who'd violated a crime scene.

Our best bet was to try to sneak away. If Brian and I could get out of the house, we'd head for the woods, loop around to the road, and call Sharon to come get us.

If we got caught . . . well, then our only choice would be to try to talk our way out of it.

We had to move fast. They didn't know about Brian, but once they checked for departing footprints in the snow and realized I was still inside, they'd probably call for backup.

"Come on," I whispered to Brian. "Stay right behind me. We've got to make a run for it."

I didn't dare turn on my flashlight, and the inside of the house was totally black. Brian kept ahold of my jacket. I felt my way along the wall until I found the railing. I stopped at the top of the stairway. I heard nothing.

252

We started down the stairs. Brian stayed close behind me. We paused at each step. It felt like it took an hour to reach the bottom of the stairs.

Then we were in Sprague's big open downstairs living area. The windows made it light enough down here that I could make out the shapes of furniture and walls and doorways.

"Stay right there," I whispered to Brian. I moved to the front of the house and slid along the wall until I could peek out a window.

The vehicle was a four-wheel-drive SUV. I didn't recognize it. It had no light bar on the roof, no logo on the door. Friend or foe?

The problem was, I didn't know who were the friends and who were the foes. It didn't look like anybody was inside the truck. And I saw nobody outside the house.

Push open the front door, slip out, and run for it?

If they spotted us, it would be all over. Even if they didn't shoot us and we made it to the woods, they'd call in backup. Hell, they could call in helicopters and dogs. They'd follow our footprints in the snow wherever they went.

But if we could just get back to the road without being seen, we'd call Sharon and be in the clear. It was our best chance.

My hand found the doorknob. I turned it slowly. The click of the latch sounded like a gunshot inside the dark house.

That's when the lights went on.

State Police Lt. Christopher Stone was standing barely ten feet from me. His left hand was on the light switch. His right hand held his square automatic weapon. It was pointed at my chest.

I glanced toward the foot of the stairs, then around the room. Brian had disappeared.

"Well, well," said Stone. He was grinning at me. "If it isn't the asshole attorney."

"Hello, Chris."

"Somehow, I'm not surprised."

"Listen," I said, "I've got—"

"Shut up," he said. "Clasp your hands behind your fucking neck."

I did.

He came over to me, grabbed my shoulder, spun me around, and slammed my face against the wall. The muzzle of his gun rammed into my ribs. His other hand was patting me down.

When he found the .38 in my jacket pocket, he reached in and took it out. "Oh, boy," he said. "Let's see. We got at least an armed B and E at a crime scene. You'll need more than your buddy Horowitz to get you out of this one, pal."

"Chris, for Christ's sake—"

His fist slammed into my kidneys, and I went down on my hands and knees. I hung my head, gasping for breath, fighting the urge to puke.

"Don't say a fucking word," said Stone. "Spread-eagle yourself and put your hands behind your back. Open your mouth again and I'll kick in your teeth, which is what happens when an armed criminal resists the lawful arrest of a police officer. You got that?"

I lay there on the floor with my arms behind me and my legs spread out.

He reached down and clamped handcuffs onto my wrists. Then he bent over and ran his hands up the insides of my legs and over my body. When he found Sharon's cell phone, he slipped it from my pocket and tossed it onto the sofa.

Then he took a two-way radio off his belt. "I got him," he said. "Just like you thought."

A minute later the front door opened and Gus Nash stepped inside. He was wearing a three-piece suit under his camelhair topcoat. He looked down at me and shook his head. "You okay, Brady?"

"This miserable excuse for a peace officer punched me in the kidneys," I grunted. "I am not all right."

Stone handed Nash my gun. "I had to disarm him, Mr. Nash."

Nash put my .38 into the pocket of his topcoat.

"He punched me *after* he took my gun," I said.

Nash reached down, took my arm, helped me to my feet, and led me to the sofa. I collapsed onto it and sat there awkwardly with my hands cuffed behind my back.

I hoped Brian had managed to slip out the back door and was hightailing it through the woods.

Nash sat in an armchair across from me. He leaned forward with his forearms on his thighs and peered at me. "You going to be all right, Brady?"

"Will you take these cuffs off me?"

"Of course." Nash turned to Stone. "You didn't need to do that. That's no way to treat a friend."

Stone frowned. "But Mr. Nash—"

"Uncuff him, Lieutenant."

Stone glared at me, then came over and took off the cuffs.

I rubbed my wrists. "I've just about got this figured out," I said to Nash.

"Want me to call it in, Mr. Nash?" said Stone.

Nash waved his hand at Stone without taking his eyes off me. "Not yet, Lieutenant," he said. "Let's hear what Brady has to say."

Stone came over and stood beside Nash's chair. He kept his gun pointed at me. "Mr. Nash," he said, "really, the correct procedure here is—"

"Lieutenant Stone," said Nash, "will you please shut up."

Stone recoiled as if he'd been slapped. He blinked a couple of times, then resumed glaring at me. The muzzle of his gun never wavered from my sternum.

Nash smiled at me. "Okay, now, Brady. Let's have it. I've got a feeling this is going to make heroes of all of us."

I shook my head. "I'd rather talk to Horowitz."

He spread his hands. "I understand," he said. "But this isn't Lieutenant Horowitz's case. So let's focus on what's important, which is figuring out who murdered Professor Gold and Chief Sprague. Isn't that what we're both interested in?"

I shrugged.

"However you want to play it," he said. "Horowitz is not involved. This—" he jerked his head at Stone "—is our case, and we're going to solve it. So what do you say?"

"I guess I don't really have a choice," I said.

"No," he said, "you really don't."

So I told Nash about the photographs Jake had brought to me, and how I'd figured out that Ed Sprague had taken them with his digital camera through the one-way mirror in his bathroom and stored them in his computer. I told him that Bobby Klemm had been hired by somebody to murder both Jake and Sprague, and I assumed that person's face would appear on some of those photos.

"Dig those photos out of Sprague's computer," I said, "and you'll have everything you need."

"So who have you shared these theories with?"

I flapped my hands. "Nobody. Just you. I only got it figured out tonight."

Nash was nodding. "Well, that's terrific deducting, Brady," he said. "So you figure the photos are in Sprague's computer, huh?"

"I'd bet my life on it."

He smiled. "Oh, you shouldn't do that," he said. He glanced up at Stone. "Help Brady up, Lieutenant."

Stone glanced at Nash, then shrugged. He came over to me, took my arm, and yanked me to my feet. I gasped from the sharp pain in my kidneys where he'd punched me, and a wave of dizziness swept over me. I leaned on him for a moment, swallowed a couple of times, and took a deep breath.

"You okay?" said Nash.

I nodded.

"Okay," he said. He pushed himself up from his chair. "Let's go in, take a look at that computer."

We went into Sprague's office.

"You know how to work that thing?" said Nash.

"I can turn it on," I said. "I already looked at it. I couldn't find any photos. You'll need someone who knows more about it than I do."

"Why don't you sit down, turn it on again for us."

I did, and the icons started popping up on the screen. Nash bent over, studying it. "I don't know a damn thing about computers," he said. He turned to Stone. "How about you, Lieutenant?" He laughed quickly. "No, somehow I doubt you're a computer wizard."

Stone shook his head. "Not me, Mr. Nash. I write my reports on them. That's about it."

Stone was standing there beside me. His gun was still pointed at me.

"Aim that thing somewhere else," I said to him.

"What I'd like to do—"

"Behave yourself, Lieutenant," said Nash.

Stone shrugged and lowered his arm so that his gun was pointed to the floor.

Nash frowned at the computer screen for a minute, then shrugged. "Well, I guess you're right. We'll have to take care of this later. Come on. Let's get out of here."

I pushed the chair away from Sprague's computer, stood up, and started for the living room.

"Hold on a minute, Brady," said Nash.

I stopped and turned to face him.

"Okay, Lieutenant." Nash nodded at Stone. "Now you can shoot him."

TWENTY-NINE

———————————✦———————————

Stone's eyes darted toward Nash. "Huh?"

Nash jerked his head at me. "I said shoot him."

Stone nodded. His gun slowly came up until I was looking into the black hole at the end of its muzzle.

"I always hated you," he said.

"I never liked you much, either, Chris," I said. "But I never thought you were a bad cop."

"Ah, it was always you and Horowitz," he said. "You two smart guys, and me, tagging along, running out for the fucking coffee. Horowitz thought he knew everything. Always took all the credit. I worked my ass off for him, and—"

Suddenly Brian came flying out of nowhere. He plowed his head into Stone's chest, and both of them went down in a tangle of arms and legs.

Stone's gun spun out of his hand.

I lunged for it.

Nash's voice stopped me. "Hold it, Brady," he said quietly. "Freeze, or I'll kill the kid."

I froze.

Nash was holding my .38 in both hands. It was aimed at

Brian. I could see that the hammer was cocked. He meant business.

I held up my hands, palms out. "Okay, Gus," I said. "You're the boss."

"Stand up, young man," said Nash to Brian.

"You better do it, Brian," I said.

Brian crawled away from Stone and stood up. He was panting and glowering at Nash.

Stone got to his feet, hunched his shoulders inside his jacket, then bent and picked up his weapon. He motioned with it for Brian and me to stand beside each other. Then he arched his eyebrows at Nash. "Who the hell is this?"

"This," said Nash, "is Brian Gold." He smiled at Brian. "You were supposed to be dead, son."

Brian glared at him.

"So Ed was right," said Nash. "It bothered him, never finding your body."

"Gus," I said, "let the boy go. He doesn't know anything."

"Yes, I do," said Brian.

Nash smiled at him, then turned to me. "Thanks, Brady," he said. "This helps us with another loose end."

"Fuck you," I said.

Nash turned to Stone. "Okay, Lieutenant," he said. "Let's get it over with."

"The kid, too?" said Stone.

"Coyne first," said Nash.

I turned to Nash. "I guess I shouldn't be surprised, Gus. Sprague got you in some of his photos, huh?"

He shook his head. "Don't be ridiculous."

"Who are you covering for, then?"

He smiled.

I nodded. "Okay, I get it now," I said. "You're blackmailing your friends, right?"

He shrugged. "I don't look at it that way, Brady."

"There's some other way to look at it?"

"I prefer to think of it as insurance."

Stone's eyes were darting back and forth from Nash to me, as if things were moving too fast for him. But his gun never wavered from my chest. "Mr. Nash," he said, "I was thinking—"

"Don't," said Nash. "You shouldn't think, Lieutenant. It's not your strong suit. Just shoot him. Let's get this over with."

Stone frowned at him. "But how're we going to explain it?"

"It's pretty obvious," said Nash. He looked at me and grinned. "And brilliant, too, if you appreciate improvisation. Mr. Squeaky Clean Attorney here is a closet pedophile, as we'll discover when we get into that safe in his office. You gotta watch out for those middle-aged bachelors who live alone, you know?" He shook his head with mock sadness.

"Yeah," said Stone. "That's pretty good, Mr. Nash. But how're we gonna explain shooting him?"

"Come on," said Nash. "Think about it. The man was armed and dangerous." He smiled. "You and I, Lieutenant, we had our suspicions, brilliant lawmen that we are. Coyne might've fooled some people, pretending to discover the professor's body in the barn that his own hired killer had left there. Didn't fool us, though. We kept our eye on him. Followed him here, and . . ." He shook his head. "Imagine! The honorable Brady Coyne collected disgusting photos of his own client's son. And he seemed like such a nice man, too."

"Horowitz knows all about it," I said. "First thing he'll do is dig out all those other photographs. You're sunk, Gus."

"Oh," he said, "you mean Sprague's computer? Well, see, Brady, the reason you came here was to destroy that evidence."

Sprague half turned, peered into Sprague's office, lifted my gun, squinted, and fired twice. It sounded like two bombs exploding inside the house.

Sparks flew from the big CPU on Sprague's desk, and then a wisp of smoke wafted up. It had two big holes in it.

"What about the boy?" I said.

"You killed him, Brady." Nash grinned. "With your own gun. You're a very bad man."

"So you and Stone are going to be heroes, huh?"

Nash shrugged modestly. "Oh, we're just doing our jobs. Though I'd expect the media might find our quick action rather heroic once the whole story comes out."

I turned to Stone. "What's in it for you, Chris?"

"I'm a cop," he said. "I'm doing my job." He glanced at Nash.

"That's right, Lieutenant. And you'll be rewarded. I've got big plans for you. Now do it."

Stone leveled his gun at my chest. "Do you understand now, Mr. Coyne?"

I nodded. "I understand everything."

"I'm not that stupid, you know."

"I never said you were stupid, Chris. You're just ambitious and misguided."

"Not as much as you think."

Then, strangely, he winked at me.

I watched the muzzle of his automatic as it moved away from my chest and pointed at Nash. "I used to admire you, Mr. Nash," he said. "But Horowitz was right. You were playing me for a sucker."

"Chris—"

"Drop the fucking gun," said Stone.

"Wait a minute—"

Stone pushed his gun toward Nash's face. "Do it!"

Nash let my revolver slip out of his hand onto the floor. "You're making a very stupid mistake, Lieutenant."

"I'm pretty sick of being called stupid," said Stone. "Just shut up for a minute, and you listen to me for a change." He smiled. "Ready? Okay. You're under arrest, August Nash. You have the right to remain silent. Anything you say can be used against you in court. You have the right to talk to a lawyer for advice before we ask you any questions and to have him with you during questioning. If you cannot afford a lawyer, one will be appointed for you before any questioning, if you wish. If you decide to answer questions now without a lawyer present, you will still have the right to stop answering at any time until you talk to a lawyer. Do you understand?"

Nash laughed. "I understand that your career is over."

"I'll take my chances," said Stone. He turned to me. "Mr. Coyne," he said, "why don't you go get that cell phone and call Lieutenant Horowitz. I think he deserves to be involved in this."

An hour later Stone had taken his prisoner away in handcuffs, and Brian Gold and I were sitting in Ed Sprague's living room with Roger Horowitz and Marcia Benetti.

I told Horowitz what had happened. "My guess is," I concluded, "after Stone killed me, Nash was going to kill both him and Brian, here, with my gun. His story would be that Brian had come to me for protection, and I brought him here and killed him and plugged Sprague's computer to destroy the evidence. Nash and Stone interrupted me, and I shot Stone, and Stone got off a shot at me before he died. Something like that."

"Any questions would be answered when they found those photographs in your safe," said Horowitz. "They'd explain your motive for killing Sprague and . . ." He glanced at Brian.

"I know what happened," said Brian quietly.

Horowitz nodded. "You'd be dead," he said to me, "and your good name would've been thoroughly trashed and Gus Nash would be a hero. If Stone hadn't thought clearly for once in his life, it could've happened that way."

"It took him a while," I said. "But he is a good cop."

Horowitz shrugged. "You know, Coyne," he said, "you're as pigheaded as Stone. What the hell did you think you were gonna accomplish, coming here?"

"I wanted to get those photos," I said, "see whose faces were on them."

"Yeah? Then what?"

"Then I was going to dump it on your lap."

He was shaking his head. "This case is fucked, I hope you realize that."

I nodded. "That's what I've been thinking."

"If I know Gus Nash," said Horowitz, "we'll never be able to link him to Bobby Klemm. Maybe if we had those photographs . . ."

"They were all on Sprague's computer."

"Yeah," said Horowitz. "And now that computer is deader 'n a doornail."

Brian had been sitting beside me on the sofa while we talked. He had said nothing. He'd kept his head bowed, and I knew he was thinking about Sharon, what he would say to her, how he'd explain it.

Now he lifted his head and touched my arm. "Uncle Brady, can I say something?"

I nodded. "Of course you can."

He looked from Horowitz to Marcia Benetti, then turned to me. "All that time I was just wishing I was dead," he said softly. "It didn't seem fair that Jenny died and I didn't, and I couldn't stand the idea of my mother ever knowing . . . what I'd done. Then when you came to talk to me at Jason's, said you'd seen those photographs, I thought about killing myself, I was so ashamed. But I started thinking about my dad. Somebody killed him because of me. And I was thinking about Chief Sprague, and the more I thought about him, what he'd done to us, the more I hated him. And I knew there had to be somebody else involved. That was whoever hired the guy who killed my dad and Sprague. And when I thought about all that, I didn't want to die anymore. I wanted to find out who it was, and I wanted to kill him. It was that Nash guy, right?"

I nodded.

"Well," said Brian, "I remember seeing him a couple times."

"Here?" I said. "When—?"

Brian nodded. "He was here with other people when we . . ."

"Did he—?

"No. He's not on any of those pictures Sprague took."

"How do you know?"

He reached into his hip pocket, pulled out something, and handed it to me.

It looked like a slightly oversized computer disk.

"Is that what I think it is?" I said.

"It's a Zip disk," said Brian. "You can store dozens of photographs on one of these things."

"And you got them from Sprague's computer?"

He nodded. "It's all there," he said. "I'm pretty good with computers. What do you think I came here for?" He handed the disk to Horowitz.

"Brian," I said, "do you understand what you're doing?"

"Yes," he said. "He's a policeman. I've just given him evidence."

Horowitz slipped the disk into his jacket pocket. "Lawyers," he said to Brian, "they can lock evidence up in their safe, refuse to let anybody see it. Us cops, we can't do that, you know."

"I know that," said Brian.

"You're a brave kid," said Horowitz.

"That was easy," said Brian, "compared to what I've got to do now." He looked at me. "I've got to call my mother."

I handed him Sharon's cell phone. "Do you want me to talk to her?" I said.

"You've done enough, Uncle Brady. I've got to do this myself." He stood up. "I'm going in the other room, okay?"

I waved my hand at him, and he headed for the kitchen.

He came back about five minutes later. His cheeks were wet, but he was smiling. "I want to go home now," he said. "Can somebody give me a ride?"

THIRTY

⇥ ———————————————————— ⇤

I was moving papers around on my desk the following Tuesday afternoon when Julie scratched on my door. I called, "Enter," and she opened it and held it for Horowitz.

I got up from my desk and went around to shake hands with
him. "You want some coffee?" I said.

He shook his head. "Only got a minute. Wanted to fill you
in."

I smiled at Julie, and she nodded and pulled the door closed
behind her.

Horowitz and I went over to my sitting area. He slumped
on the sofa, and I took the chair across from him.

"I'm working with Stone," he said. "His idea."

I nodded.

"Suddenly I'm not such a hardass," he said. "Suddenly I'm
full of good advice."

"You?"

He smiled. "Anyways, our geeks got those pictures off that
disk, did their magic, blew 'em up, enhanced 'em, and presto.
There's maybe half a dozen faces on 'em—besides the kids, I
mean."

"Who?"

He waved his hand. "Let's just say you've seen these faces more than once, pictures in the *Globe*, making important pronouncements on the TV news."

"And you've got them having sex with children."

He nodded. "No shots of Gus Nash, though."

"Doesn't surprise me."

"So far, we got nothing on him," he said. "Poor Stone. He squeezed the bastard as hard as he could. But Nash is cool. He covered his tracks."

"He's a murderer, Roger. He's the one."

"Sure, I know. But we gotta link him with Klemm. Which we're trying to do. So far, nada."

"What about those pictures?" I said. "What's going to happen to them?"

"They're all the evidence we got."

"Roger," I said, "Nash threatened me with a court order to open my safe. I would've refused. I would've gone to prison before I'd let those photos out of my hands."

"They're out of your hands now, Coyne."

"And they could be used as evidence in court?"

"If it comes to that, sure."

"What about those kids?"

"They're our only witnesses."

I shook my head. "Do you realize—?"

Horowitz gave me his evil Nicholson grin. "You think I like the idea of parading a bunch of sweet teenagers on the witness stand, making them tell the world how they fucked strangers for gas money?"

"It's not like they were posing for those photos," I said. "They didn't know Sprague was hiding in the bathroom with his camera. You make them testify, let the tabloids get ahold of those photos, it would wreck their lives, and their parents', too."

He shrugged. "Let's hope it doesn't come to that."

"So now what happens?"

"Stone and me, we're shaking some trees, having conversations with all the sick bastards whose faces—and other body parts—appear in those photos. Dropping Nash's name, letting the implications sink in. We'll see what happens."

After Horowitz left, I opened my safe and took out the manila envelope Jake had given me. I removed the photographs, put my wastebasket between my knees, and tore each of them into pieces the size of postage stamps.

There were copies of those photos on the disk Brian had taken off Sprague's computer, I knew. But still, ripping them up felt good.

Sharon called me a couple of days later. "I haven't thanked you," she said.

"You don't need to, Sharon. How's it going?"

She hesitated. "It's hard. Brian—he's very ashamed of what he did. He's having a rough time. And I know I'm not helping any. I keep finding myself being angry with him. What he put me through. And about Jake, of course. It's the wrong way to feel, but I can't help it."

"I suspect it's a pretty natural way to feel," I said.

"He won't leave the house or talk to anybody. He refuses to go back to school."

"Understandable."

"He's got to get on with his life," she said. "We both do."

"It's going to take time. You both need to talk to somebody." I hesitated. "Has Brian told you—?"

"He told me everything, Brady. It was the first thing he did when you and those two officers brought him home the other night. He came in, and we looked at each other, and then we hugged each other and cried, and then he said he had to talk to me, and he had to do it right then before he lost his courage. I know it was harder for him to tell me than it was for me to

269

hear it. I was just so—so happy to see him, to know he was alive."

"So what are you going to do?"

"They've finally released Jake's body," she said. "Brian and I, we've decided not to have any kind of service or anything. Jake wouldn't have wanted it, and we can't put ourselves through it anyway. We're going to spend some time with my mother in Wisconsin. We're leaving on Sunday."

"How does Brian feel about that?" I said.

"He thinks it's a good idea, putting distance between himself and Reddington. Anyway, Brian and my mother have always gotten along great." She laughed quickly. "I don't know how long I'll be able to stand it, though. Mother will wear me out."

"While you're there," I said, "you should both find somebody to talk to. Besides your mother, I mean. You shouldn't put it off."

"Yes," she said. "That's important, I know." She hesitated. "Anyway, Brady Coyne, I just wanted to say thank you. You've been a good friend. It's very awkward talking to you now. You know all our secrets. So if you don't hear from us for a while, please remember that we love you."

"I know," I said. "Me, too."

She cleared her throat. "Well, good-bye."

"Good-bye, Sharon," I said.

Benny Goodman was tootling on the stereo and a vat of corn chowder was simmering on the stove. It was Saturday night, and Evie and I were sitting on the floor in my living room. She was leaning back against the sofa, and I was sitting cross-legged in front of her. Her bare foot was in my lap. I'd wedged cotton balls between each of her toes, and I was painting her toenails. I'd picked a glittery purplish-blue color, which she okayed on the grounds that it was still winter and she wouldn't be wearing sandals in public anytime soon.

It was delicate work, and I was focused on the task, holding her foot steady with my left hand while I painted with my right.

She was humming along with Benny's clarinet and sipping from a glass of wine.

"I thought I'd lost you," I said. I bent close to her foot and blew on the wet polish. "You were acting . . ."

"Distant," she said. "Bitchy."

"Yes."

"I had a great time with Mary at the museum and down at Foxwoods," she said after a minute. "And all the time, I was thinking, Brady would never do this. He'd hate it. All we do is lay around the house, eat, make love, watch old movies. We don't do anything. We don't go anywhere. We don't have any fun. That's what I was thinking."

"I always thought we had fun," I said.

"Of course we do," she said. "We have plenty of fun. But it's always the same kind of fun. What happens when eating and making love stops being so much fun? Anyway, that's how I was thinking when I was with Mary. Brady and I, we're in a rut, I was thinking. This is all it's ever going to be. Eating and drinking and screwing every weekend until we can't taste our food and we get too old to screw."

"You should've said something," I said.

"I did," she said. "And you confirmed what I was thinking. You said you hated casinos."

"Well, I do."

"And shopping and concerts and the beach . . . and everything I like to do."

I slid my hand up her leg. "Not everything."

She picked up my hand and gave it back to me. "Be serious," she said.

"Must I?"

"For a minute. Let me finish." She paused to take a sip of her wine. "When I heard on the TV that you'd shot that man in your office, and then I kept trying to call you and got no

271

answer, I realized that I was stuck with you. With all your faults, with all your—your *guy* shit—I loved you. And it pissed me off. Do you understand?"

"No," I said.

She sighed. "I was wondering why I couldn't've fallen in love with a man who'd take me to casinos and concerts, who'd go shopping with me. I was thinking there had to be such a man out there, and if you and I split, I'd eventually find him."

"There probably is. Maybe you'd be happier—"

"Oh, shush," she said. "Are they dry yet?"

I touched one of her freshly painted toenails with the tip of my finger. "Yes. And they look great."

"Then come here." She patted the floor beside her.

I moved around so that I was leaning against the sofa next to her.

She grabbed my hand with both of hers, squeezed it tight in her lap, and laid her head on my shoulder. "I finally figured it out," she said softly. "The things I don't like about you are also the things I love about you. I couldn't stand a man who'd follow me around while I shopped. Men who need casinos and concerts to be stimulated and entertained aren't my kind of men. I like a man who's happy just being with me, who finds me all by myself sufficiently stimulating and entertaining."

"You," I said, "are an endless source of entertainment and stimulation."

"Well," she said, "I happen to like casinos and concerts and museums, but I can enjoy them without you, and I'd enjoy them less with you if I didn't think you were having as much fun as I was. And I like you, and I don't need other forms of entertainment to be happy with you."

"I don't mind museums that much," I said. "I like art. Watercolors, especially. I wouldn't mind—"

She jabbed her elbow into my ribs. "Oh, shut up. Listen. Do you want me to take up fly-fishing, join you everytime you go?"

"Well, if you want to . . ."

"Tell the truth."

"I like fishing with Charlie and Doc and J. W.," I said. "But if you want to try it sometime, maybe we could . . ."

"I don't," she said. "Maybe I'd do it if I thought it would make you happy. But it wouldn't. Not really. Not if you knew that's why I was doing it. You'd rather go off with your guy friends and do guy things, and that's okay with me. It really is."

"What you really mean is, you want to go off with your girl friends and do girl things, and you don't want me tagging along, being miserable."

"Or being jealous, or worrying about me."

"Jealous? Me?"

She laughed. "So now do you understand?"

I shook my head. "Of course not. I couldn't begin to understand you. You are puzzling and fascinating and thoroughly mysterious."

"Thank God," she said.

The vernal equinox—the first day of spring—came on a Wednesday, along with a driving rain that utterly failed to dampen my spirits. I celebrated the turning of the seasons by telling Julie to hold my calls for the afternoon. I had important business to attend to.

I called Charlie McDevitt and Doc Adams and J. W. Jackson and made fishing plans with each of them. Doc and I were going to spend a week hiking in to some mountain trout streams in the Pisgah National Forest in western Carolina at the end of April. I convinced Charlie that it was time we revisited the Beaverkill and Willowemoc in the Catskills, and we made reservations for five days at the Roscoe Motel for the middle of June. J. W. and I decided to enter the Martha's Vineyard Striped Bass and Bluefish Derby in September. He and

273

Zee insisted on putting me up for the week in the guest room of their new house on the dirt road overlooking the salt ponds by State Beach.

It looked like a good year.

I flipped through some new fly-fishing catalogs and old *American Angler* magazines for a while, and then I laced my fingers behind my neck and put my head back and closed my eyes and daydreamed.

A little later, when I looked out the window, I saw that the rain had stopped and the clouds were breaking up and the sun was peeking through the cracks.

Spring!

It was around four o'clock. If I left now, I could get to Stoddard's before they closed. I needed a couple of new fly lines and some spools of tippet material and—

Just then my phone buzzed.

I picked it up. "This better be good," I said to Julie. "I told you to hold my calls."

"Lieutenant Stone is here," she said. "He says it's important."

I sighed. "Okay."

Julie brought Chris Stone in. When she started to ask if we wanted coffee, I quickly shook my head. She shrugged and closed the door behind her.

I shook hands with Stone. "What's up, Chris?"

"I only got a minute, Mr. Coyne, but I wanted to be sure you heard it from me first."

"Heard what?"

"It's one of those good-news bad-news things," he said. "Gus Nash's lawyer wants to make a deal."

"A plea bargain?"

He nodded. "Me and Roger, we've been puttin' the screws to those people in those photographs. Made it clear we want Nash, suggested we might give 'em immunity in return for their depositions."

"And they turned over on Nash."

He nodded. "On the photos and the blackmail. Can't touch him on the murders, though."

"So what's going to happen?"

"We make the deal, avoid a public trial," he said. "Keep those photos, those kids out of it. That's Nash's leverage."

"What happens to him?"

"It'll probably shake down to three or four years, maximum security, no special considerations."

"That's not a lot," I said. "Hell, he hired a guy to kill two people, and he was prepared to kill several others, including you and me."

"Yeah, but we can't make the case." Stone shrugged. "Law enforcement officer, big DA involved in kiddie porn? His colleagues in Cedar Junction will make that an extremely unpleasant few years." Stone blew out a long breath. "Anyway, that's what's happening. Figured you had a right to know." He hesitated. "That's only part of the reason I wanted to see you."

"What else?"

"To thank you. You were right. You and Horowitz. You both always told me my head was up my ass, and I guess it was, because if it hadn't of been, maybe I would've listened to you. Gus Nash used people. He was using me. I should've stuck with Horowitz, listened to him. He's the best. I could've been a good cop."

"You are a good cop, Chris," I said. "When it came down to it at Sprague's house that night, you did the right thing. And Roger tells me you've been working your ass off on this case."

"Yeah," he said, "but for me it's personal, see? I just want to nail Nash. Horowitz says a cop should never let it get personal."

"It's not supposed to be personal for lawyers, either," I said. "But sometimes you can't help it."

Sharon Gold's letter came to my office on the second Thursday in April. It was postmarked Madison, Wisconsin, and written on pale blue notepaper with a dark green fountain pen.

"Dear Brady," it began.

I wanted you to know that Brian and I are doing all right. We stayed with my mother for a week or so, and then we agreed that it would be better if Brian and I found a place of our own. We weren't ready to go home. So we're now renting a little house on a lake. It's very pretty and peaceful here, and the neighbors are friendly and don't ask questions about us.

Brian has enrolled in the local high school. He's made some new friends, and he didn't have much of a problem catching up on his schoolwork. He's a very good student, you know.

We're both seeing psychiatrists. I still have dreams, and I know it's going to take a while, but I can see the improvement. It's going to take a long time for both of us. But we're getting there.

I'm temping at an advertising agency in Madison. I go to work every day, and it looks like they want to hire me. It's not a lot of money, but it could turn into a career, and I think I'm going to accept it.

Brian and I have decided we're not going back to Reddington. I know you can understand that.

I'll be calling you one of these days to arrange things for us. I'm going to put the house up for sale and have all our stuff shipped out here. This feels like the right thing to do, and Dr. Benning and Brian's doctor both agree with us.

We want to thank you for everything. You are a dear friend and a sweet man and we will never forget you.

She signed it, *"Love, Sharon and Brian."*